Don't Take a Lo

PAUL LUDFORD is now retired, having spent time as an apprentice cutter in a corset factory, waited at table in an ocean-going mail/passenger ship, operated printing presses, and worked his way up to management level in an international insurance company. Not content with taking life easy in his retirement from his management role, he spent two seasons caring for two charter cruisers operating on The Solent in the South of England before becoming a bus driver. During his time on the buses, he spent several happy years meeting people and listening to their stories as he drove between Portsmouth and Brighton, probably his most enjoyable paid occupation.

Now in his second retirement, he has discovered his love of writing. There is no limit to his imagination as his keyboard takes him to places and situations, he would otherwise never have experienced. It is his hope that his readers will be able to take themselves off to another place as they sink into a comfortable armchair, pick up this book, and leave their busy lives behind for a while.

Don't Take a Look

Paul Ludford

First published 2021

ISBN 978-1-914408-97-7

Printed in Great Britain by

Biddles Books Limited, King's Lynn, Norfolk

This book is dedicated to my lovely wife, Margaret
and also, to the memory of Gill who stood by me
for forty-four amazing years.

~~~~

My thanks should be given to Margaret for her encouragement and for her time spent in assisting and advising me throughout the process of writing this story.

My thanks also to Peter with whom a pleasant and interesting day was spent on board his narrowboat *Grey Hare* as he regaled us with many facts and stories about The Basingstoke Canal.
~~~~

Other books written by Paul Ludford

Missy – *A novel*

Imagination – *A book of 40 Short Stories*

Prologue

Odiham, October 1916

The figure emerged from shadows which were now transforming into total darkness. All was still, apart from the gentle sway of branches in the trees and the slow movement of the canal water which could no longer be discerned as the daylight finally succumbed to the gathering night. Silently the figure paused to listen. Apart from the gentle rustling of leaves and the sound of distant music the quietness, which had encouraged venturing out from the comparative safety of the log pile, enveloped the wharf. Satisfied there was no immediate danger of being observed, the silent figure cautiously took a few steps toward the quay before pausing to listen and peer into the blackness of the wharf. All seemed clear. A few more steps, then without warning a loud plop broke the silence. The figure stopped moving, madly beating heart seeming to fill the night with its rapid pulse. *It's okay, just a fish. Calm down and breath. A few more steps, that's all. Committed now.* Before those steps were taken however, the concealing darkness evaporated as the near-full silvery moon suddenly appeared from behind scudding clouds which had hidden the sky for the last few hours. The hump of the bridge spanning the canal, just a hundred yards upstream, could now be clearly seen against the sky. To the horror of the furtive figure, a soldier's outline was revealed on the parapet. *Has he seen me?* The soldier hoisted his rifle onto his shoulder as he turned. It became clear that his back had been toward the wharf, but now his moonlit face was coming into view. *He'll see me for sure if I don't do something. The water, it's the only option.*

Crouching down, the figure silently slipped into the freezing water and sank down until only the head was exposed. Stretching one hand down, the shivering figure managed to fill a clenched fist with clay, sufficient to cover a white frightened face. *Dear God, he's coming down to the quay, he'll see me!* Slowly, the young soldier walked down the slope from the bridge, rifle resting on his right shoulder. *Please let a cloud cover the moon.* He had reached the empty broad-beamed barge which was lying alongside the quay. Carefully, the soldier examined the hold which was open to the sky, having unloaded its cargo of coal before the daylight had faded. He checked the mooring lines before moving forward to the loaded narrowboat the furtive figure had been silently making for. With the soldier being momentarily out of sight from the surface of the slowly moving water the figure slipped behind the thick wooden rudder, thankful that the depth of water was only chest high.

Suddenly the quietness was disturbed by the thud of something heavy being placed against the side of the boat. This was followed by the rattle of a matchbox, then the rasp of a match being struck. *Not here! Why here of all places? Must stay quiet and calm until he moves on.* Suddenly the red glow of the cigarette came into sight as the soldier, having retrieved his rifle from the side of the boat, came into view. Having checked the mooring rope he took one step, which placed him immediately above the cowering figure. Casually drawing on the cigarette before tossing the stub into the water the young man looked both ways along the bank before placing his rifle on the ground, unbuttoning his uniform trousers, and aiming a steady stream into the water. It was at that point that the quietness was shattered, *'What the hell?'*

Chapter 1

Smoke curled up from the weather-stained chimney pot high above the yellow thatch of the large farmhouse. This had been a crisp sunny autumn day, but now dusk was creeping in, leaving just sufficient light to see details of the cobbled yard. Immediately opposite the house stood a wooden barn which was showing signs of neglect, its large door, although closed, still leaving a gap where it should have been firmly fastened to the wooden frame. To the left, spanning the gap between cottage and barn, was the old stable in which two large working-horses were slowly munching their bran. On the other side of the yard and to the right of the cottage was a small milking shed which sat alongside a covered storage area in which heavy farming equipment was kept. In the distance, an owl could be heard as it proclaimed its territory prior to starting its evening hunt. Closer to the house, a fox barked as it slinked through a nearby coppice of trees. In the reedy shallow of the pond at the back of the house, two frogs croaked their presence, whilst nearby crickets chirruped their endless evening chorus.

After the busy activity of everyday farm life, calmness settled over and around the yard and surrounding buildings, the only movement to be seen was the slowly curling smoke lifting from the chimney. Beneath that chimney however, was the kitchen where one wall boasted a large blackened range upon which the content of a pot was bubbling. A large oak table, which had endured many years of scrubbing, sat in the centre of the room, its squat legs resting firmly on flagstones, also scrubbed to a near shine. A freshly baked loaf occupied the centre of the table alongside a butter crock. Washing was draped over a rack, which was hoisted to the ceiling opposite the range, the most noticeable garment being a pair of patched long-johns no longer as white as they may have been long ago. A mangle and dolly-tub occupied a corner near the butler sink.

A slender girl, dressed in a pinafore, was preparing the evening meal. Places had been set for three, although only two chairs, one with curved armrests, were drawn up to the table. As the girl added a little salt to the pot, she hummed a song under her breath about keeping the home fires burning. She smiled at the sentiment of the song which had become popular among the troops. However, thoughts of the battle going on in France didn’t occupy Johanna’s mind for long as she added a little more salt and stirred the rabbit stew. She had enough battles of her own to occupy her mind, running the arable farm with a sullen labourer and also with a crippled father who did his best under the circumstances. It was just as well that half the land was underutilised and mainly lying fallow. Why her brother, and Norman, their previous long serving and competent farm hand, had to go and sign up was beyond her. She was just thankful that her father was no longer fit enough for such nonsense, otherwise she was sure he would have been talking about going with her brother to join the smiling recruits the previous year. She remembered their final embrace before John had given a cheery wave and called out, *“I’ll be home by Christmas, Sis, when it’s all over.”* Together, the young men, some of them boys, had swanked and sang their way through the village with its pavements filled with cheering admirers as well as tearful wives and mothers. *Why do men always want to go off and fight? Why did you have to volunteer, John? You loved working on the farm and you knew how much dad relied on you.* Johanna frowned as she thought about her father, now in his late thirties but crippled by an accident with a panicked horse four years ago on her thirteenth birthday. He still missed his wife Ethel, Johanna's mother, who had lost her battle with pneumonia ten years before the accident. He spoke about her every day. Johanna was no longer sure if her memories of her mother were her own, or simply the stories her father told her over and over again. Apart from an old sepia photograph encased in a silver frame and standing on the oak dresser in the parlour she could not visualise her mother or remember her voice.

'Dad, the stew's ready, can you put those boots down now and come to the table?' Johanna's father was sitting in his usual low armchair alongside a blazing fire. An old newspaper was spread across his lap as he worked. He was wearing his old sweat-stained flat cap, a striped shirt, devoid of collar and with sleeves rolled up. The braces of his baggy trousers were at that moment hanging below his waist.

'Okay lass, just finished as it happens, smells good, my juices are fair running.'

'You and your old boots, why would I ever need a looking glass when I can peer into the dubbin on those boots of yours?'

Holding them up and peering fondly at the objects under discussion Phil replied, 'You c'n mock all you like, but these boots have lasted me years and have many more in 'em, you'll see. I'll start on yours after supper.'

'Thanks Dad,' said Jo softy and with a fond smile, 'Do you want a slice of bread with your stew? I'll do it while you wash your hands, and kindly remove that dirty old cap before you come to my table.'

'You're as bad as your mother with your mithering, although you're a good lass and no mistake. Yes please, bread n butter will go well with that stew, I reckon. I notice the milk yield has been down these last few weeks, but that's normal this time of year. How's the lower meadow coming on, lass?'

'Well, Pat's been doing the tit pulling for the last two weeks, I don't think the girls have taken to him somehow. He's a bit impatient and rough with them. He forgot to put the kicking strap on Bluebell yesterday, or just didn't bother, and she managed to kick over a full bucket, before we got it to the cooler. I was furious with him when he took his stick to the old girl. I had to remind him that accidents like that are always the farmer's fault, never the beast. Ploughing will be finished tomorrow, although our John would have got it done in half the time. I don't know what that useless Pat gets up to half the time, and I don't like the way he looks at me. Why did we have to take him on? We don't know anything about him, or where he came from. Oh, another thing, his furrows aren't straight, not the way you like them.'

'I know lass,' replied Phil with a frown, 'But nobody else was free to take the job after Norman, so he's all we've got for the duration. Don't you fret, Jo. I want to go down and take a look at the lower pastures tomorrow. I may have to consider renting them out, or even selling. We don't need that land and it's under used. I'll look in at the meadow at the same time and have a word with Pat. And as for looking at you, well, he's a man and you're becoming a very attractive young lady with that dark complexion and those beautiful brown eyes of yours, you'll get used to men admiring your looks given time.'

With a frown, Jo dished up the stew and buttered the bread as her father put his boots away and sealed the tin of dubbin. He then lit another gas-mantle before limping over to the butler sink to rinse his hands under the hand pump. After drying them he took his place at the table where he glanced at the empty place setting with a sigh. 'I miss that lad so much, but there's always hope. Let's hold on to that.'

'Cap!'

'Oh yea, forgot, sorry,' said Phil as he whipped off the offending article, tucking it beneath his knees. 'Evenings drawing in, won't be long before we start seeing frost on the ground I reckon. Better make sure Blacky and Champ have a good bed of straw in their stalls tonight, I'll pop out after supper.'

'It's okay Dad, I'll do it, why don't you pop down to *The Feathers* after you've finished your stew and have a game of dominoes or something? You haven't been out for a couple of weeks now; it'll do you good.'

'Sounds a tempting idea to me, lass. What would I do without my favourite daughter, eh?'

'Just as well I'm your only daughter, otherwise it could be a problem having a favourite.'

'Naa, if she were like you, you would both be my favourites.'

'Get on with you, you daft apeth, eat your stew, then be on your way before I change my mind.'

An hour later, with the washing-up done and her father on his slow way to the village pub, Jo turned down the gas lamps, slipped her coat and boots on, lit a hurricane lamp, and let herself out of the side door into the darkness, to bed the horses down for the night. Silence had descended upon the farm, apart from the constant noise of crickets. Several bats silently skimmed the buildings on their blind quest for flying insects. Jo didn't mind the bats and scorned the myth that they could land in her hair and not be able to be freed without having to cut her hair off, something she might have cause to think about in the not-too-distant future.

Silently, Jo stepped across the cobbled yard, the moon casting her shadow firstly on the ground before her and then onto the wall of the stable as she approached the open door. *Strange, I could have sworn I closed that door. Perhaps Dad went in there on his way out.* As Jo stepped through the open door, enabling the feeble light of the hurricane lamp to filter into the darkness, there came a loud curse followed by a scuffling noise.

'Who's there?' called Jo in alarm.

Silence.

'I know you're there. I'm going to fetch my father.'

'I don't think so, little lady.' A silky voice, full of menace which came from somewhere in the flickering shadows.

'Pat, is that you?'

Without warning, a hand suddenly shot out of the darkness behind a bale of straw and grabbed Jo's wrist. Before she had a chance to scream, another hand covered her mouth and, at that moment, the hurricane lamp dropped from her hand. Immediately flames began to lick the straw at her feet. Still holding Jo's wrist, her assailant frantically stamped on the burning straw, but it was immediately clear that alone he was unable to contain the spread of flames. With the hand no longer covering her mouth, Jo shouted, *'Let me go! Quick, stamp on the flames. There's water in buckets near the door, I'll fetch it.'* Having said this, she was able to wrench her arm from the weakened grip before stepping to the side of the door frame where she immediately located the two buckets. With no other thought than to save the stable and the horses, Jo grabbed one of the buckets and threw the content over the flames before repeating her action with the other. Together they were able to stamp on the few remaining flames. Although it seemed longer, all of this happened in a less than two minutes.

No longer thinking of any danger to herself, Jo became aware of Blacky stamping in her stall as smoke drifted around the confined space. In the sudden darkness she could hear Pat coughing while continuing to stamp on the blackened straw. There was no longer any doubt as to who he was.

'Pat, I don't know what you thought you were doing in here, but you had better go. I'll tell my dad about this in the morning and you will most likely be sacked.' She turned away to attend to the horses. In a soothing voice she said, 'Okay Blacky, it's all right now, nothing to be frightened of, calm down, there's a good, good girl.' Jo had stepped across to the stall and was gently stroking the head and neck of the fractious horse. She was pleased to see that Champ was quietly nodding his head, otherwise he was relatively calm. Turning to face the door, she saw Patrick's retreating silhouette framed in the opening as he walked out into the yard. 'Good girl, Blacky, it's all over now, who's a beautiful and clever girl then? Nothing to be afraid of. Well done.' As she continued calming the horse, Jo became aware of her own heartbeat and the fact that she was trembling, she knew the horse would be aware of her emotional state and did her best to calm her own nerves as she continued talking quietly to the mare who was still tossing her head. *What on earth was Pat doing in here? I thought he had gone home hours ago. Was he up to no good? Had he left something here and returned to fetch it? Why did he manhandle me the way he did? What was it he called me? "Little lady!" That was it, "Little lady", how dare he treat me in such a way? I've never liked the man with his shifty ways, I will insist that dad gets rid of him in the morning.*

Over half an hour passed before Jo felt she could leave the horses, having ensured that both were well fed, watered, and had sufficient straw scattered in their stalls. Yawning she stepped outside and turned to close the door. Pulling her coat tighter around her she took several steps towards the cottage when she became aware of the figure stepping from the shadows.

'Pat, I told you to get out of here, if you don't ... *Ouch! Let go of ...'* Patrick had stepped quickly forward and had twisted one of her arms behind her back. He muffled Jo's voice, placing his hand over her mouth. Struggling to get away she managed to kick one of Patrick's shins before he forced her arm even further up her back.

'So, you want to play it rough do you, little lady?' That same silky voice. 'That suits me, I like a bit of rough. let's go and play in the barn, shall we? You'll like that, won't you?' With that, Jo found herself being frog-marched to the barn entrance where the man was able to slip them through the gap in the doorway. 'Okay, here we are, I've made it nice and cosy for us up in the loft, you climb the steps first, and don't even think about screaming. If you do, I'll have to hurt you and you don't want me to do that, do you?'

In the musty darkness, Jo was manhandled up the steep wooden steps leading to the loft. Stepping off the top rung she immediately swung around and kicked at the head of the emerging man, causing him to lose both grip and balance. He disappeared. With a wildly beating heart, and holding her breath, Jo peered into the darkness below. She could hear no sound and see no movement. What should she do? There was only one way down. The steps. With all her senses heightened, Jo turned around and as quietly as possible fumbled for the first step, then the second ... no sound ... then the third and the fourth. Suddenly, an iron grip took her ankle, causing Jo to scream while kicking against the grip. Her leg was momentarily freed as her boot came off, but too late, the other leg was seized and she found herself being pulled down into the strong arms of the lust filled man. For the first time, she tasted raw fear.

'Let me go!'

'I don't think so, we 'aven't 'ad our play time yet 'ave we? You 'urt me when you kicked me, but that's okay, a bit of 'urt always comes with pleasure, don't you think? If you keep struggling you might 'ave to 'ave a little bit of 'urting before things begin to get a little more pleasurable, it's your choice, little lady. Why don't you just relax in my arms while I slip this coat off, we don't want anything coming between us now, do we?'

'Pat, please don't do this, you're *frightening* me.'

'No need to be scared, you know you want it. I've seen you looking at me with your dewy brown eyes. Now, I'm just going to hold your wrist while I undo this blouse.'

'No!'

As Patrick fumbled with the top button, causing him to ease his grip, Jo ducked away from him and turned to run for the door. Unfortunately, her bootless foot became entangled in the discarded coat, causing her to fall forward onto her hands and knees. In panic she tried to crawl away from the enraged man but he managed to grasp her leg before she made any ground. Trying to scramble forward against the tug on her leg Jo's hand brushed against something, grabbing onto it she realised it was a pitchfork which had been leaning against one of the loft supports. Suddenly, feeling herself being lifted from the floor, Jo swung the pitchfork with all the strength she could muster. She felt it make contact before it was wrenched from her hands and tossed to the ground.

'Oh yes, little lady, it's much more fun when you struggle, now where were we? Oh yes, the blouse. Now you undo those buttons so that I can see what delights you're hiding there, do as I say 'cos I 'ave a knife in my belt and I wouldn't want to have to prick your pretty little face, now would I?'

Trying to ignore her hammering heart and shaking fingers, Jo quietly said, 'No need for the knife, Pat.' Looking directly into his lust-filled eyes Jo slowly undid the top button, then the next.

Starting on the third button, she said seductively, 'Do you like what you're seeing, Pat?' Licking his lips in anticipation, Patrick was taken totally unaware as she said more loudly, 'Well, see how you like this!' and at the same moment, kicked him as hard as she could between his open legs. He was doubled up in excruciating pain, unable to resist when Jo, using every ounce of strength she possessed, gave him a violent shove, causing him to stagger and fall hard onto his back. It was unfortunate for them both that the discarded pitchfork had been lying, twines uppermost in that spot. Patrick didn't move. He remained on his back with eyes closed. As Jo peered down at the still body of her assailant the small amount of moonlight entering from the open door revealed a greater darkness on the straw around the still figure.

'Oh my God! Blood! I've killed him, oh my God, Pat? *Pat! Wake up! Can you hear me?' He's dead! What should I do? They'll say I murdered him. They'll hang me. Oh my God, help me.*

Chapter 2

Dad,

I am so sorry to be leaving you in this way. I Have no choice. He tried to rape me. I was so frightened. First, he nearly burned the stable down, then he dragged me into the barn. I didn't mean to kill him, I tried to push him away and he landed on the pitchfork. I didn't know what to do. I will be alright, you mustn't worry. You have to find someone else to help with the farm, don't try to do it on your own, you can't. Remember we talked about getting a Land Army Girl. Ask Farmer Gill, they've got two working on their large farm, haven't they?

Please check on my lovely Blacky and make sure she's okay. Don't forget the harrier is coming to re-shoe her on Monday. Keep an eye on Marigold's tits, they're still looking sore. I have been pulling them myself cos I'm more gentle. May have to get Mr Adams in if she doesn't improve. See if you can get Farmer Gill to lend you a hand with the milking till you find someone, he may even lend you one of the land girls till it's sorted.

It will be harvest before you know it, I expect the rector will be round to see what we can offer.

I love you so much. Maybe I will be able to see you again one day. But now I have to go.

Hopefully it won't be too long before John comes home for good. I have borrowed some of his clothes, I know he won't mind.

Your favourite and loving daughter

Johanna x

P.S. The carter will haul the milk churns onto his cart in the morning if you leave a note. Just say I've had to visit a sick aunt or something.

Chapter 3

In a state of shock and confusion, Jo had stumbled through the gap in the doorway of the barn before remembering her discarded coat and boot. Without any conscious thought she had tip-toed back to where the body was lying and quickly grabbed the garments without looking at the prone figure. Not stopping to put the garments on, she had hobbled over the yard, tears streaming down her cheeks. She had not even been aware of the cold air on her partly exposed breasts as she headed for the sanctuary of the kitchen door. Once inside, she had slammed and bolted the door before kicking off the remaining boot and running along the hall to the staircase. With trembling fingers, she had unlatched her bedroom door, slammed it shut behind her and flung herself onto the narrow bed where she clutched the patchwork quilt around her and sobbed into her feather pillow. *Oh my God! Oh my God! What have I done? What can I do? I wish it were a real nightmare. It is a nightmare! Must go and tell Sergeant Edwards. No, I can't do that, he'll have to arrest me. Oh my God! Dad, I need you to tell me what to do! No, I mustn't involve him, he won't be able to take any more pressure.*

As her heart and breathing had taken on a steadier pace, rational thought had taken over the practical girl. *Must get away from here. Dad will have to tell the police but that won't be for a few hours. What do I need? Clothing, yes that's it, and some food.* Unravelling herself from the quilt, Jo had dried her eyes on the hem of her partly open blouse and, after lighting an oil lamp, had looked behind the curtain which stretched across the corner of her room where her frocks, skirts and cardigans were hung from a cord. *No these won't do. I know! I'll borrow some of John's clothes, much more practical. I can even pretend to be a boy. They'll be looking for a girl, won't they? Hair! Must cut it off and wear a cap. Yes, that's it. I'll pack some scissors with the food and do it later, no time to waste now.*

Once in her brother's room, with a feeling of intrusion Jo had searched for what she considered to be sensible clothing, ensuring that they would be warm enough for the autumn and winter. After all, she had no idea where she would be, over the coming weeks and months. She was pleased to discover that everything fitted her slender frame. For the first time, she was thankful that her breasts were small enough not to have to wear a brassier. She had shuddered again at the thought of those evil eyes on her chest. Over a thick woollen jumper which had ragged holes in the elbows, she tried on a navy-blue jacket and cap and finished the effect with the thick red scarf which she herself had knitted and presented to John the Christmas before last. Inspecting herself in the full-length mirror in her own bedroom Jo was somewhat startled by her transformed appearance. It felt so strange to be wearing trousers and braces and, in spite of her desperate situation, she could not supress a surprised grin. Satisfied that she had done all that she needed to here, Jo had taken a final glance into her neat bedroom before descending the stairs. In the kitchen she sliced some bread and cheese, filled a flask with water and packed it all into her brother's knapsack which had been hanging behind the door since he had last used it. *Now for the letter.* Jo had entered the parlour and from an oak bureau she extracted writing paper, pen, and a bottle of ink before sitting down to compose the letter to her father. It had not been easy to find the right words and she was not helped by her falling tears, some of which landed on the words, causing them to blur as the wet ink spread out.

Jo made several attempts with the letter before she was vaguely satisfied, acknowledging to herself that nothing she committed to writing could ever express her sorrow to be leaving her father in such circumstances. Having returned the writing material to the bureau she walked over to the dresser, lifted the framed photograph and with a small trembling voice said, ‘Look after him, Mum. I love you both.’ It was all she could do. Jo glanced around the kitchen for the last time. As she did so, she remembered the scissors. *Nearly forgot those, I’ll be needing them soon.* She turned off the gas mantles and, grasping the knapsack, slipped out of the side-door into the night.

With a heavy lump in her throat Jo walked to the stable, having avoided looking at the dark gap in the barn doorway. Had she gone into the barn, for whatever reason, she would have been shocked to see that there was no body. Had it not been for the blood staining the floor it would have been as though nothing untoward had ever happened there. Totally unaware of this however, Jo stepped into the stable where Blacky let out a snicker as she became instantly aware of the girl’s presence.

‘It’s okay Blacky, only me.’ The horse turned her head, anticipating the possibility of an apple being offered. Jo reached up to hug the mare's neck and kiss her velvety lips. 'I will miss you, old girl. Now you behave yourself and look after the farm for me, and make sure Champ pulls his weight.' With a final pat on the horse's neck and with tears in her eyes Jo slipped out of the stall to give Champ a stroke before leaving the stable. Having adjusted the knapsack on her shoulders she took a final glance at the house before leaving the yard and walking down the lane in the direction of Warningford Village. Half an hour later, the sound of an accordion, accompanied by a male voice, came to her ears from the direction of *The Feathers.* Having quietly approached the pub she cautiously leaned on the window sill of the public bar and, standing on tip-toe peered into the brightly lit interior. It didn't take her long to spot her father who was leaning an elbow on the bar while holding a pot of ale, chatting, laughing and singing with friends from neighbouring farms. She recognised June who worked in the local post office. It was she who was providing the music on a highly lacquered accordion. Jo reflected on the fact that; on more than one occasion she had noticed the way John had looked at the girl who was a few years older than herself.

'What are you up to lad?'

'Wha....?'

'Are you looking for someone, your dad maybe? If you point him out to me, I'll let him know you're here.' It was a late middle-aged man, dressed in a tweed jacket long passed its best and wearing the inevitable flat cap of a farmer. Contrary to what his voice suggested, his ruddy face displayed a warm smile beneath a bushy moustache.

'Err ... no, it's okay. I was, um ... listening to the music.'

'Well, best be off with you then. Lads shouldn't hang around here in the dark. Go on ... off you go. P'raps yer mum will give you a cup of cocoa. Good night.'

He mistook me for a young boy. It works, even before I cut my hair! Taking a last look through the window, Jo saw the stranger join her father and his group of friends. There was more laughter and light punching of shoulders between old friends. Her father seemed so happy at that moment, causing tears to stream down her cheeks as she thought about the letter awaiting his return to the cottage later that evening.

Quietly, she said, 'Good bye, Dad. I love you. I hope you will be able to forgive me some day.'

Chapter 4

A mile from Meadow Farm and in the opposite direction from that taken by Jo, the weakened man had left the lane, pushing through familiar bushes that led to a small coppice. Stopping for a moment to clear the dizziness that threatened to overcome him, Patrick peered at the encampment. All was as he expected it to be. A light, glimmering through a chink in the carelessly drawn curtain, the embers of a fire glowing in a shallow pit to one side of the horse-drawn caravan. The horse with its head low to the ground, tethered to a post which had been driven into the earth. Bales of hay, smuggled away from the farm during the previous week stacked nearby. Miscellaneous shapes in the gloom behind the caravan, some covered by sheets of canvas. Tenderly touching the bump on the back of his head Patrick allowed the bout of dizziness to ease before limping forward. Although he was not immediately troubled by it, for he had more pressing things on his mind at the time, he had hurt his ankle when falling from the loft steps. *Bitch! She could have killed me,* he thought bitterly. As Patrick staggered toward the caravan steps, he became even more aware of the uncomfortable feeling of his shirt sticking to his back. He knew the wound was bad but had no way of telling just how bad. He also knew that he had lost a fair amount of blood. *Mav will have to sort that out with her rags and potions. Nothing that a bottle of whisky won't sort out once the woman has cast her stupid spells over me.*

He slowly eased himself up the steep wooden steps to reach the curtained door. It was bolted on the inside. Suddenly overcome by the unfairness of it all, Patrick rattled the door handle and shouted, *'Mav! It's me. Open up!'* There being no response, anger boiled up inside him. *'Mav! Get your fat arse off that bed and open this door! I'm bleeding to death out here?'* Aware of a shuffling sound inside, followed by the drawing of the bolt, Patrick stepped back to allow space for the narrow door to open outwards.

The woman, dressed in a flowing orange skirt below a bright yellow blouse, stood in the doorway glaring at her husband. 'Where the hell have you been? I fed your dinner to the horse long ago. What's all this about bleeding? You been fighting again? Or did y floozy's husband catch you at it, just like last time? And the time before. No doubt ya got what was comin' to ya.'

'Out the way, woman. Can't ya see I'm 'urt? Get ya stuff out while I take these things off.' Patrick had pushed his way passed his wife and was gingerly easing himself out of his shirt.

Mavis leaned out and glanced around the clearing before pulling the door closed and drawing the bolt. Turning to her husband she shouted, *'Don't you go getting ya bad temper with me, get over to the lantern so's I can see.'* Pushing his long lanky hair to one side, she peered at Patrick's exposed back. Mavis realised there were two fairly deep wounds, one of which was slowly oozing fresh blood which was mixing with the blackened congealed mess on her husband's back. 'You'll live. Now hold still while I do some swabbing. It'll hurt a bit. *Serves the sex-mad fool right. If I'm not very much mistaken, this was done by a pitchfork. Shame he didn't get it right up his arse, that would have cooled his appetite.* 'Pitchfork then, was it?'

'Yea. I went back to the barn after they had settled indoors, to do a bit of honest thieving. Before I knew it that mad daughter had crept up behind me and stabbed me in the back with the biggest pitchfork you've ever seen in your life. I thought she was going to kill me.'

'Oh, is this the one you said was so ugly even the cows wouldn't look at her? The one with a double chin and hair under her nose?'

'Yea, that's right, it were her that done it. I tell you, that girl ought to be locked up. I ain't never goin' back there again. It's time we moved on anyhow. There's too much army around 'ere. Could lose the 'orse to them if we're not careful. Think we'll go Guildford way, plenty of farming down there. Should find a job easy like.'

'Yea, I thought you would say that. Funny that whenever we take to the road there's always been a woman involved somehow. Hold still. Anyhow, I wouldn't mind seeing our Lil again, last I heard she was down Woking way. I'll start stowing come morning.'

'Ouch! that 'urt! Mind what you're doing woman!'

'Oh, did it? So sorry.'

'Ouch! you did it again, you've got no idea of the pain you're inflicting on me, Mav.'

'Yes, I have, Patrick, but I think it's nothing compared with the pain I've put up with all these years. Nearly done. Oh, and by the way, the whisky bottle's empty, I finished it after dinner when you didn't come back.'

~~~

The music slowly faded as Jo walked into the darkness. Passing the glimmering lights of the last cottage, she continued walking as she peered into the shadows of high hedgerows on either side of the lane. The unfamiliar boots made a clumping and scraping noise as she tried to avoid the many potholes which had not been filled since the outbreak of war. She knew that at some point she would have to leave the lane. The question was which way should she go? North or south? She was familiar with the town of Alton as that was where they would often go to market. But would anyone recognise her in that area, and would the police start putting up WANTED posters there? She doubted it, but she preferred not
~~~

to take the chance. She had also visited the small town of Petersfield when the church had organised a charabanc visit to the fayre by the lake before the war started. *No, it's best to stay away from any familiar territory. It's north then. Avoid Basingstoke and get further up country.* As she tramped on, tears streaming down her cheeks, her mind was working overtime. How far could she get in the darkness? The near full moon helped, but once she left the lane there would be all kinds of obstacles and dangers lurking, waiting for that careless moment. One thing was for sure, she had to put as much distance as possible between her and the farm before daylight.

Thoughts of the farm brought a lump back into her throat. As farms went in this part of Hampshire, it was large, in fact too large for her and her father to manage, particularly now that John had gone. Also, the large house had seemed so empty with only the two of them. How would it feel to her father now, she wondered. The fields mostly in use produced crops such as wheat, oats, turnips and potatoes, all of which were in great demand now that the submarines were cutting off food supplies from America. They also had twelve cows which produced sufficient milk to add to their income. It wasn't a lot, but she loved it. The milking, collecting eggs from the hens, working the fields, even mending gates and fences. *I never did get around to mending that barn door. John was supposed to do that. Oh, why did he have to go? What was it June said about men down at the post office? "Men can only think with their knobs and fists cos there's nothing in their heads apart from the beer that passes through to their fat paunches." A bit unkind perhaps.* Jo could not think of John and her father in that way, for both were hard working and thoughtful. Thoughts of the barn made Jo shudder as she increased her pace along the narrow lane which was so familiar in daylight. In the light of the moon however, everything looked so different. Shadows loomed out of the hedgerow, trees became houses until she reached them and realised what they were. As Jo peered ahead, she saw what could be a gap in the hedge on the side she would need to leave if she were to start going north. Approaching the gap, she could see a broken stile set in a wooden fence among the overgrown bushes. It was then that she knew where she was. On their way to market on the wagon they would pass this stile which had a signpost she had never had time to read. This seemed to be the best option. Reluctantly leaving the lane with its comparative safety and firm footing, Jo gingerly stepped over the stile before hoisting the knapsack on her shoulders to a more comfortable position. She took a deep breath before setting out across the recently ploughed field following the direction pointed by the signpost. She was relieved to discover that the furrows were conveniently in line with the direction she was taking.

As she plodded on, Jo's thoughts naturally returned to the moment her life had changed for ever. One moment, a happy girl doing what she loved to do, the next a fugitive on the run. How could such a thing happen, and so quickly? Even now, her father would be happily chatting to his friends, possibly thinking of the nightcap he would share with his daughter before retiring to bed, all the while oblivious to the shock that awaited him. Her thoughts turned to the attack. For sure Pat intended to steal her virginity from her in a mad moment of lust. *Why did he think he could do that and get away with it? Did he think I would go along with it? Why would he think that? "Dewy eyes", that's what he said, "Dewy eyes". Why would he say that? I've never led him to think I was interested in him, apart from his work, have I?* The more Jo thought about the frightening encounter and the feel of Pat's eyes on her partly exposed breasts with their engorged nipples the more confused and doubtful she became.

Reaching another stile on the far side of the field, Jo paused to sip some water from her flask. She could hear the distant sound of a goods train chugging its way slowly through the night across the countryside. Where was it going? London perhaps? In a strange way, the sound of that distant train gave her a sad but comforting feeling. Things were still going on as they normally did. In not too many hours, before first light, the carter would drive into the yard, turn his team in the narrow-confined space and come to rest by the churns. His combined load would then be taken to Four Marks station in time for the milk train. All very normal, but it won't be, will it? Not this time. Tears continued to fill Jo's eyes and run onto her cheeks. Impatiently she swiped them away with the back of her hand, gave a loud sniff, and climbed the stile which would lead her into a wooded area.

As she stepped down, she was startled by a loud voice coming from behind her, 'I wouldn't go in there, lad. The gamekeeper has set some man-traps. Last incomer that did that stepped in one of them. Had to have his foot taken off after they found him. Not only that, this is my patch so hop it!'

Jo swung around with a hand over her rapidly beating heart, to be confronted by a roughly dressed man wearing a black eye-patch over his left eye. As he moved, a clanking noise could be heard coming from the direction of a canvas bag which hung from his shoulder. Pretending to be at ease and with her deepest voice, she said ‘Thank you for the warning mister. I’m not poaching, I’m passing through and not sure where I am.’

‘Oh? Passing through, is it? Where are you headed, son?’

Nodding in the direction of the woods Jo replied with a confidence she didn’t feel, ‘Nowhere in particular, just north I suppose.’

‘Running away, are you? Well, it’s not my business. If you want north you want to skirt along this boundary till you come to a lane. There you turn left. I would stick to that if I were you. It’s dangerous going cross-country at night. You don’t know what sort of dodgy characters you’ll bump into … like me for instance. After about a mile or so you’ll come to a village called Binstead. You’ll know it because the first thing you’ll see is Holy Cross Church, right in front of you. At the crossroads, go straight ahead and you’ll come to Isington. Then you’ll cross the Alton to

Farnham road and after that you'll reach a place called Well. If you haven't decided to do the sensible thing and return home by then, the next big place will be Odiham. You want north, that's it.'

Impressed by the man's educated voice and the detail in which he had directed her, Jo said, 'Thank you, I think I can remember all that. Are you really a poacher? I always took them to be nasty individuals, but you seem to be kind and helpful.'

'I'm not a poacher by trade or choice, son. I lost my job months ago after the boss's wife made an inappropriate suggestion to me and I told her to leave me alone. She told her husband some tale about me and that was it.' With a broad grin, he continued, 'If you'll take my advice, lad, stay away from girls, they're nowt but trouble. Although, I suspect that could be difficult in your case, if not impossible. Mind how you go now, um… lad, and think seriously about what you're doing. Things at home may not be as bad as you think.'

Oh my God, he knows I'm a girl! With as gruff a voice as she could manage, Jo asked, 'When you're not poaching what sort of work do you do?'

With a chuckle the man replied, ‘Oh, this and that, whatever comes along.’

‘Have you ever worked on a farm?’

‘Amongst other things, yes. Why do you ask?’

‘If you know about farming, and if you’re interested, I know there’s a farm on the far side of Warningford, *Meadow Farm* I think it was called.’ Jo pointed back the way she had come. ‘When I passed it, they seemed a bit short-handed.’

‘Did they now?’ The man raised an eyebrow. ‘And how would you know that?’

‘Oh, I just guessed, I didn’t see anyone around, that’s all.’

‘I see … You just guessed, and why would you be telling me this?’

That’s a good question, thought Jo. *Because I like him, I suppose. Strangely, I feel safe with him.* ‘Seems you need a job, and that farm might be happy to take you on if my guess is right, that’s all.’

'I seeee .... You just want to be helpful.' The man grinned. 'Who is it you're trying to help I wonder? And why are you telling me, a stranger and a poacher?'

'You seem to be a man who could be trusted, I could be wrong, but I don't think so. Call it wo ... intuition.'

'Well, a regular job would be good, certainly better than this. Although I'm thinking it's nigh on time I did my bit and signed up to Kitchener's Contemptibles. Tell you what, lad, why don't you come with me and point this farm of yours out to me. If you're right, there could be work for two for a while?'

'No,' interjected Jo in alarm. 'As I said, I'm going north.'

'Shame. What's your name by the way?'

'Jo ... that's all, just Jo.'

'Well, Jo. If I do see this farm of yours, and I'm not saying I will, I'll let them know someone called "Jo" passed by.'

Alarmed with how much she had revealed to the stranger, Jo replied, 'No, no point, they wouldn't know me.'

'I see,' replied the man. 'In that case I'll leave you to it then. Such a shame, we might have made a good team, I think we understand each other. My name's Graham by the way.'

Having said their goodbyes, Graham quietly slipped into the night. Within seconds there was no sight or sound of him. Taking his advice, Jo took the direction he had indicated and soon came across the lane. Feeling there was little chance of being spotted this far from home, and seeing the sense of staying out of fields and woods Jo set out for Binstead at a lively pace assisted by the silvery glow of the moon. The route she took was exactly as the stranger described and, well before dawn, Jo had reached the small hamlet of Well. She had seen no other person. After passing through Well she started thinking about where she could hide and rest during the coming day. As it turned out, the answer came within half a mile when the gathering daylight revealed a hay rick alongside a hedgerow which separated two fields. Being familiar with the construction it didn't take Jo long to burrow into the rick and slightly conceal the entrance she had made. By the time she was satisfied with her work, Jo was feeling very hungry and foot-sore. She eased off her brother's boots with a sigh of relief before delving into the knapsack to find her cheese and bread. She also found one of the apples she had managed to pick from a garden tree as she passed through Isington during the night. While eating the food, Jo's thoughts inevitably turned to her father and the farm. She hoped that he would be able to get the help he needed and also wondered what was happening now that Sergeant Edwards would have seen the body, and how long it would take to get the search started. With these troubled thoughts going through her mind, sleep caught up with the exhausted girl as the first hint of dawn appeared in the eastern sky.

Chapter 5

'We've had coppers out all night, scouring the neighbourhood, Mr Simons, no sign of the girl … or a body for that matter.' Sergeant Edwards was in his late fifties, and surprisingly rotund for someone who cycled anywhere his duty took him. Peering at Phil through his bushy eyebrows he continued in his ponderous manor, 'From what I've seen in the barn it would appear that whoever it was, although injured by the fall onto the pitchfork, was able to leave the scene before you went in to investigate.' He paused for a moment, caressing his right earlobe between thumb and forefinger. 'Are you sure you saw nobody in the yard, or on your way back from *The Feathers*, or hear anything unusual?'

'I've already told you Sergeant,' retorted Phil in frustration. 'I saw and heard nothing apart from an owl hooting away.'

'Aye, you did. Tell me, did you have a lot to drink last night?'

'I don't like what you are inferring, Sergeant. No more than four pints and if there was anybody lurking, I was sober enough to know about it.'

'Yes … well … I have to establish my facts. Now tell me, who works here apart from yourself and your daughter?'

'Since my son, John, went over there to do his bit, we have a man named Patrick who does the heavy work.'

'And you say this man hasn't come in today, is that right?'

'That's right, do you think he could be the man who attacked my Jo?'

'Too early to say, Mr Simons. Can you describe this man?' Taking out his notebook and pencil from a top tunic pocket, Sergeant Edwards licked the pencil point and raised his bushy eyebrows as he studied the worried face of the farmer.

Phil scratched his unshaven chin as he sat at the kitchen table thinking. 'Let me see now, height about five-seven or eight, slight in build, long black hair, looks a bit greasy, sometimes kept in a ponytail, a tattoo on his right arm if I remember, some sort of bird, perhaps an eagle or hawk, I'm not sure.' As he finished scribbling in the notebook, Sergeant Edwards enquired if there was anything further to add. 'All I can say is that he has the appearance of a traveller, we get a few of them around at harvest time.'

Phil watched impatiently as the police sergeant carefully wrote in his book while constantly licking the point of his pencil. *"Appearance of a traveller,"* he repeated slowly as he wrote. 'I see, do you have an address for this man, Mr Simons?' he asked, pencil poised over the notebook.

'No, I'm afraid not. He said he's between addresses at the moment and would let me know.'

'So, you wouldn't know how to contact him and you don't have a surname?'

'Afraid not, replied Phil, shaking his head with a frown. 'You take who you can get with all the able men away. Now what about Jo? What are you going to do about finding her? She must be at her wit's end and scared to death while we're sitting around here talking. It's been a whole night and day now, and heaven knows where she's going to spend this night. It's cold and dangerous out there.'

'Believe me, sir, I understand your concern,' said the sergeant while flipping the notebook closed and returning it to his pocket. 'I have a daughter of my own around Johannah's age. The note she left you, says she's borrowed some of her brother's clothes but you were unable to describe them, that would have helped. We've checked with the local army recruiting office and also the railway station, nothing there I'm afraid. We've considered posters but, if she sees one anywhere, that will drive her further underground, given the circumstances. Tomorrow we intend broadening the search and involving other forces. Meanwhile, try not to worry. I'm convinced our man is very much alive and keeping his head down. It's not a murderer we're looking for, just a frightened kid who will show up sooner or later. Based on what you've told me this evening we will also be checking up on any gypsy communities we come across, although generally speaking, they are, in the main, decent folk, some even serving in the trenches.' Slowly, the policeman eased himself from the chair, fastened the bottom of his trouser legs with his cycle-clips and placed his helmet onto his head. 'Thank you for the coffee, I'll see you tomorrow with an update and, God willing, your daughter.'

Don't Take a Look

~~~

Smoke curled from the brightly painted chimney which protruded from the stern cabin of the narrowboat. The family of four had just enjoyed a breakfast of thick bacon sandwiches, a luxury confined to loading days, as mornings would never allow time for such a meal while the boat was swimming along the cut. At such times "Bait", as breakfast was known by boaters, would consist of a hunk of bread and lard which would be eaten on the move.

The head of the family, also captain of the boat, was dressed in thick woollen trousers, striped shirt and buttoned-up waistcoat. The one touch of colour in his dress was a bright red kerchief tied loosely around his neck. On his head was the cap which seldom parted company with the unruly hair beneath. Ed allowed himself a few more minutes enjoying the pipe which protruded from below his thick moustache, before sliding the hatch open and calling down to his eighteen-year-old son, 'Okay Ben, let's have you. Time to get started with the sheets, the ganger's turned up with his men to shift the timber. Should get it loaded by the end of the afternoon.'
~~~

The captain, known as a ‘Number One’ by virtue of the fact that he was one of the few who owned his own boat, moved forward to start removing the flats, planks and stands before unhitching the canvas covers on the shore side of the boat. As he did so, Ben, while picking with his finger nail at a piece of bacon wedged between two of his back teeth, emerged from the cockpit and took the other side. Together they worked in harmony to prepare for the first of the logs to be shipped. There was no need for words as they both knew the job from years of experience.

Trade on the Basingstoke Canal had been diminishing prior to the outbreak of war, mainly due to competition with the railway which carried goods in a fraction of the time taken by a canal boat with its average speed of around two miles per hour. Also, this particular canal, apart from being in danger of having insufficient water for navigation, had changed hands several times due to financial difficulties. However, in the year 1914, within a few weeks of the outbreak of war with Germany, an ample supply of water had been obtained by the partial diversion of water from a stream at Odiham.

It was having seen a notice stating that the canal had re-opened, that encouraged Ed to try his luck with trade on the newly opened cut. He had previously plied his trade between London and Banbury, on the Oxford Canal, but having heard that the Basingstoke Canal was back in business he had decided to run between London and Basingstoke for a while to assess the possibility of setting up a lucrative trade on the more southerly cut. He was unaware at that time that the canal was soon to be taken over by the Inland Waterways & Docks Department of the War Office and was to be managed by the Royal Engineers.

The cargo of timber being loaded into *Red Rose* would take five days to reach London, possibly four if most of the locks were in their favour. Without let-up in the work of loading and levelling the cargo Ed reflected on the changes he had seen over the previous two years on this canal. Broad beamed barges capable of carrying sixty tons had been introduced to the cut. The waterway was used mainly to carry government stores and munitions from London to a large army base in Aldershot. Ed was content to be used for the conveyance of goods such as chalk, timber, cereals, and coal. He had studiously avoided taking on dangerous goods such as munitions from London, and unpleasant cargos of horse manure from the camp at Eelmore. *Best left to the army,* he thought.

Another development during those two years was the introduction of a German Prisoner-of-War camp near the cut at Frimley. Ed reflected on the fact that the POWs were happily engaged in the work of loading cargos, and even doing maintenance work along the cut. He was always greeted by friendly waves from these men who were most likely content to be away from the horrors of the front and allowed to work in the relative peace of the countryside of England. He had even heard that some of the prisoners had been allowed to marry local girls. *A step too far, perhaps? If our Ruby were still alive, I'd never let her anywhere near one of those enemy soldiers, regardless of their apparent friendliness.* The thought of his fifteen-year-old daughter brought back the painful memory of that fateful day, some eighteen months ago, when she had slipped on a wet lock gate, having opened one of the paddles, and while crossing over to open the other. She had been swept beneath the boat and there was little to be done for her by the time she was hauled out. It was a fact of life on the canals that children were vulnerable to accidents and sickness such as tuberculosis. Large families were favoured on the canals as children were regarded as essential crew members at a very early age, and expected to earn their living, often being loaned out to other boats. *Red Rose* now had to make do with four crew members. Apart from Ed who mostly led the mule when under way, there was his wife Marge who was normally on the helm, Ben, a quiet thoughtful lad who's responsibility was to run on ahead to set the locks, and six-year-old Beth who helped with cleaning, cooking and sewing, also on occasions, steering *Red Rose.* Apart from their specific responsibilities, all of them were expected to be involved when mooring and handling the various sorts of cargo, as well as cleaning out the hold once empty.

Life was anything but easy for the Fraser family who were typical of so many boat families who plied the canal system around the country. Most of the narrowboats were company owned and manned by employed families who had the right to live on the boats, but who were constantly under the orders of the wharfingers who organised their cargos and journeys. They were expected to be constantly on the move when not loading or unloading. Schooling for the children was difficult due to the constant movement of their homes. It was expected that they attend local schools on the bank whenever they were in one place for more than a day or so. Days for the families most often started before daylight and ended late into the evenings. Although Ed and his family had to work hard, as a Number One, Ed at least had the ability to decide where they would trade.

As the sun climbed to its highest point, the autumn warmth that penetrated into the half-filled hold did little to cheer Ben as he worked. He loved this life, although it was all that he knew. At the same time, for the last few months his thoughts were turning to the possibility of exchanging the rough and dirty clothing of a boater to that of a soldier's uniform, and "Doing his bit over there" as the expression went. As a canal man, he was exempt, as was the all-important mule, but that didn't prevent the accusing looks pointed in his direction by women and servicemen on leave, particularly when entering a pub with his dad when the day's work was done. On their last time in the docks of London a young lady had broken away from her friends and held out an envelope which, although surprised, he took from her outstretched hand. Noticing the look of contempt the woman displayed on her face, he curiously opened the envelope and found that it contained nothing other than a white feather which slipped out and floated to the wet cobbled ground. He had, of course, heard of such gestures but had never imagined he would be the recipient of such an emblem of shame.

Apart from anything else, Ben couldn't escape the thought that he had a duty to fight alongside the hundreds of thousands of other young men who were "Over there". But then again, how would his father ever manage without him? This was the dilemma which occupied most of his thinking these days.

'Come on lad,' called Ed, 'You're slacking, what you thinking about then?'

'Oh, nothing much, Dad. Sorry,'

Ed, the nephew of a farmer, had left his parents and the waterways at the age of fourteen to help his uncle on the farm for a few years. "Good experience for you," his father had said at the time. "You can learn a lot there, then decide what you want to do. You can always come back to us, if you want." Two years later, he was back on the boat. He had enjoyed life on the farm, but had missed the canal life too much. Since his parents had passed on, he had become the owner and skipper of *Red Rose* and never regrated his decision to return from the farm.

The hard, manual work progressed into the afternoon as the sun slipped down and the water level crept up the sides of the narrow-boat, giving evidence, if required, that the boat was becoming well laden with several tonnes of timber. While the work of loading went on, Marge had not been idle. She had spent a good part of the day cleaning the main and fore cabins, assisted by Beth. It was a sad fact that shore people regarded the boaters as gypsies, thinking of them as illiterate, dirty and smelly. It was not uncommon to be at the receiving end of missiles such as stones, bits of metal and even such items as old broken prams as they passed under bridges in the towns. In reality, although it was clear to see that their working clothing was stained and dirty due to the work they did, and most were indeed illiterate due to lack of schooling, their cabins, bedding and clothing were mainly spotless. The womenfolk took great pride in their confined floating homes. When not cooking on the small range, or attending to children, the wives would usually spend their free time, such as it was, knitting socks for the family or beavering away with a hook, crocheting such items as belts, shelf edgings, box covers and even horse ear caps which were designed to prevent flies entering their ears. Often these items would be sold along the cut to add to the family's income or to purchase small luxuries such as fruit, or even sweets for the children.

'Look mummy, I've nearly finished this one. Do you like it?' asked Beth while proudly holding up the paper shelf-edging she had been carefully cutting-out with a pair of stiletto scissors.

Putting down her knitting with its four needles and placing it on the side-bed where they had both been sitting, Marge made a great show of minutely examining her daughter's work 'Well, you 'ave made a good job of this, luvvy. Daddy will be very pleased to see this on his pipe shelf when he's finished with the loading. Now, hold up your 'ands so I can see them.' Beth did so, as she let out a giggle, for she knew what was to follow. Lightly touching each finger, Marge started counting, 'One .. two .. three .. four ..five .. now let me see, what comes after five?'

'Six, you old silly, it's six,' laughed Beth while placing her thumb on her mother's nose.

'Oh, silly me, course it is. Seven ..'

'Six!' the child shouted. She never tired of the old joke.

'Oh yes, six .. seven ..' With Beth loudly joining in, the last three numbers were called out amongst much laughter. 'Clever girl, you didn't cut any fingers orff with them scissors. Now that I know you have all your fingers, you can 'elp me prepare the dinner for those weary men when they come down, can't you? Now, let's get those tilly-lamps goin' so's we can see what's what.' With that, Marge carefully got to her feet while holding on to the small shelf which served as a table, a necessary precaution, as the boat was constantly rocking as the loading continued.

Marge was a large woman with a big heart. Well organised, she always ensured that the cabin was spotlessly clean and tidy and that her husband and children were well fed. She was content with her life on the cut, steering the narrowboat, in addition to her work as a devoted wife and mother. She was a jolly person, always ready for a good knees-up, as well as a loving comforter when the need arose.

Just as Marge prepared to light the stove, Ed poked his head down the hatch and, with a grin, said, 'Another hour luv, then we'll be sheeting up. Don't bother about cooking, we can go to *The Swan* for a pint and a pie while we've got the chance. Maybe we can have a bit of a sing-song while we're there.'

'Sounds good to me, Ed. We ain't had a good old yarn with nobody for a while now. In that case, Beth and me can pop along to the stable and see Skippy's nice n snug, I fancy getting out to stretch me old legs and it'll do Beth good to get out.'

Two hours later, with the cargo of timber securely sheeted up, the two men stood in the aft cockpit and washed their upper bodies using a bucket of canal water. As smart clothing was normally reserved for weddings, funerals and fayres the two of them slipped back into their working clothes before climbing down into the lamp-lit cabin.

'I see you two have been busy with the brasses today, our Marge. They look right good and shiny,' said Ed appreciatively while looking around the small space.

'I helped too, Daddy,' piped in Beth who was bouncing on the side bed. 'And I cutted out some shelf-edges for your smelly old pipes, and I still have all my fingers, look.' As she boasted her achievement, she was holding out both hands to her father for approval.

'Well so you do, little one, and the shelf looks just the ticket, you clever girl. Thank you. Now, if we're all ready, let's go an' eat. My tummy's been growling at me ever since I talked about having a pie for me supper.'

'Oh, is that what it was,' piped in Marge, 'I thought it was thunder.' A remark which set Beth off in a fit of giggles.

Soon the four of them were walking the short stretch along the towpath, heading for the humpy bridge which would take then across the canal to the pub with its inviting warm glow in its windows. They were totally unaware of the pair of eyes watching them from the deep shadows formed by the piles of timber.

Chapter 6

'What the hell!' What you bleedin' playing at, Private? Put your little fiddle stick away and pick up that bleedin rifle. Next time I want to see it lying on the ground will be next to your dead body, and don't tempt me! Get on with your patrol and don't come back till midnight. *Understood?'*

'Sorry Sarge. Yes Sarge'

'Well don't just stand there, Get going, and get those bleedin' trouser buttons done up before I 'ave you on a charge for being improperly dressed while on duty!'

'Yes Sarge, sorry Sarge.'

'You'll be sorry if you cross me again, boy.' Sergeant Blaker stood with hands on hips, head shaking on his thick neck, as he watched the retreating figure who was still trying to button his fly while holding his rifle. 'Bleedin' hamatures, what's the harmy coming to I hasks?' he muttered under his breath as he watched the boy's retreating figure. 'Not a day over sixteen and he finks we don't know 'is proper age. Poor kid, what chance 'as he got over there?'

With bated breath, and having slipped behind the boat's rudder, Jo had fearfully listened to the dialogue. She was shivering so much she was afraid the sergeant would hear her. She listened to his mutterings and then, to her relief, heard his boots crunching on gravel as he marched away. Turning her head, she watched the parapet of the bridge for a moment, wanting to be sure that the coast was clear before she moved. Although she saw no movement, she forced herself to remain up to her shoulders in the freezing water for a further five minutes or so. She could hear the sound of singing coming from the pub on the other side of the bridge. Without a sound, Jo crept from behind the rudder and reached her hand up to the edge of the quay. Checking there was no movement in the yard she attempted to haul herself out of the water. To her horror, she found that her long emersion in the water had taken what remained of her strength. After making several fruitless attempts to hook her arms over the edge and haul herself up she unstrapped her soggy haversack and lifted it up on to dry ground. Jo was alarmed at how weak she had become, even without the dead weight of the haversack she was still unable to haul herself out of the deadly freezing water. *Dear God,* she thought in despair, *I don't want to die like this.* It was then that she heard a child's voice coming closer.

'Come on you slow coaches, I'm here first, I said you couldn't beat me,' called out the child as she came into view at the boat's stern. It was at that moment that the little girl noticed the wet haversack and the hand holding onto the quay. The quietness was shattered by a piercing scream followed by her panicked voice. *'There's a wet monster in the water trying to get me!'* By the time she had uttered the last word the child had retreated the way she had come, and the imagined monster had quietly slipped beneath the surface.

~~~

Jo became aware of being manhandled down some steps in an extremely confined space, the combined smell of polish and paraffin invaded her senses. She also detected the smell of beer on
~~~

the breath of the man who was reaching up to take her from the hands of a younger man who was clumsily lowering her.

'Okay, Ben, I've got him, let go. Right, Marge, you get him out of that wet clobber while we hang around out here. Don't be too long about it, it's getting cold out here.'

As Marge led the semi-conscious stranger into the warmth of the tiny cabin she answered, 'Okay, this won't take long. Now then, young man, let's get those wet things off ya and get you towelled down, then a nice 'ot drink of cocoa will 'elp to get the blood circulating again. I reckon our Ben'll have some gear that's about your size. Go on, get them trousers and that shirt orff, I dare say you ain't got nothin' I 'ain't seen afore. don't mind me, and 'urry up, so's the others can come down.' As Marge was saying this, she fumbled about under the side-bed to find a spare blanket to wrap around the boy until Ben could fetch something suitable from his fore-cabin. Looking up, she noticed that the boy had stripped down to his strange underwear but was standing with his back to her, still shivering and with his arms wrapped around himself in an attempt to get warm. 'I see, so you're a bit shy are ya? Don't mind me luvvy, I'll turn me back while you get the rest of them things off and get this here blanket wrapped around you. It's a good job our Beth saw you in the cut and we got you out sharp-ish, otherwise you would have been a gonna for sure. Now then luvvy, what's ya name then?' With there being no answer, the kindly woman turned to Jo with an inquisitive look. With the blanket held protectively around her naked body Jo stood in the centre of the cabin and although she had managed to cut most of her hair off during the day, she was convinced that her deception would be realised the moment she opened her mouth to answer the question. It was at that moment, that she hit upon the idea to play it dumb. Releasing her hold on the blanket with one hand she pointed to her mouth and shook her head as she looked pleadingly at the woman. 'What's this you're tryin' to tell me, luvvy. Are you telling me that you ain't able to talk, that you're dumb?'

Yes, that's it! I have to be dumb from now on. With that thought, Jo nodded her head in agreement.

'Oh, you poor thing', uttered Marge as a sympathetic look crossed her weather-beaten face. *'Are you deaf as well?'* she shouted, forgetting that the boy had clearly heard everything she had said up to this point. Jo shook her head indicating that she was not deaf.

'Are you finished down there?' What's with all that shouting? came the irritated voice of Ed from the hatch. 'Were getting ruddy cold up 'ere, an' it's well passed Beth's bedtime. We're coming' down.' With the clumping of boots on the wooden steps, Ed ducked his head beneath the hatch cover and stepped into the dim light of the cabin. He glanced at the figure of the blanket wrapped boy who had turned his back on the apparently angry man, who said, 'I've sent Ben to fetch some of his clobber from his cabin. I think it best that Beth beds down with us in the cross-bed tonight so as this young man can get a good night's sleep in the side-bed. Addressing himself to the blanket wrapped figure he said sharply, 'Least you can do is to show your face to the captain whose boat you're in, turn round boy, let me see your face. There's something fishy going' on here and I don't mean this fish we've just dragged out the cut. What's your name then?'

Clutching the blanket more firmly around her shivering body, Jo slowly turned to look at the man before looking appealingly at his wife who immediately jumped to Jo's rescue, saying, 'The boy is dumb, my luvvy, he can't speak.'

The moment of silence that followed was broken by Ben's voice above the hatch, 'Here, Beth, take these old things, I'm off to me bed.’ A hand appeared through the opening, clutching a bundle of clothing which Beth, who had followed her father through the hatch and was still poised on the steps, took from her brother. Having jumped down from the bottom step the child placed the clothes on her side-bed before stepping over to Jo and saying, ‘I like you. I know you’re a boy but I think you’re pretty. You’re allowed to use my bed, I don’t mind, I like sleeping with my mummy an’ daddy. Good night.’ With that embarrassing observation Beth climbed up onto the cross-bed and pulled the thick curtain across so that she could remove her outer clothing in privacy.

Throughout this time Marge had been boiling water on the stove for the boy’s cocoa and had sliced a thick crust of bread which she had layered with lard. ‘Get this down you, boy, it’ll warm you up.’ Turning to her husband, she said, ‘Ed, I think the questions can wait for the morning, we’re all tired and the lad needs to get some sleep, ‘e looks about done in.’ Turning to Jo she gently said, ‘Whatever’s ‘appened, you’re safe in ‘ere for tonight. We’re off to bed, when you’ve finished that bread and cocoa, turn that lamp off and get snug an’ warm in our Beth’s bed.

Can you do that?' A nod from Jo. 'Good, get some rest and we'll sort all this out in the mornin'. Come on, Ed, leave the lad alone for now, eh?'

'But I ....'

'In the morning, leave it till then'.

As the curtain closed behind the couple, Jo finished the cocoa and half of the crust which, in spite of her hunger, made her stomach turn, then making sure that the curtain was firmly closed, she removed the blanket and slipped into the underwear provided by Ben, before turning out the oil lamp. She found that the bed was narrow but comfortable enough after spending the daylight hours in a hay rick.

The bed was indeed adequate, but sleep was defeated by thoughts that invaded the girl's over stretched emotions. *How did I get into this mess? How is dad coping? Could he ever forgive me for leaving him so abruptly when he clearly needs me in both home and farm? Has he managed to find some help? Are the police out hunting for me? Course they are! What's going to happen in the morning? Will the man turn me in to the police? Where can I go? I need to feel dad's arms around me telling me it was all a bad dream and it's now gone away. Why is this happening to me? I don't deserve it.* All of these thoughts, and more, constantly tumbled around the girl's head, a girl who yearned to be the same age as Beth, who's bed she was in, and without a care in the world beyond when she could next play with the new clutch of kittens in front of the kitchen range.

Ben - In the fore-cabin - *Where did he come from and who is he? Why do I have to give up my clothes? Well, he can't stay, there's no room for passengers. Anyway, why isn't he in the army, like I should be?*

Marge - In the cross-bed - *The poor, poor lad, So young and, somehow fragile. How did he Take a Look in the cut? Like a drowned rat when Ed hauled him out. Why can't he speak if he ain't deaf? There's more to this than meets the eye or me name ain't Margaret Charlotte Bennet. I'll see what the lad's got to say for 'imself come mornin'. 'E can use our Beth's slate, if 'e can read and write that is.*

PC Edwards in Warningford - *Time must be running out for that girl, must be near on thirty hours now. Where did she spend last night, I wonder? If she thinks she's wanted for murder she probably walked through the night, but in which direction? Where did she hole up during the day and where is she now? How can I be tucked up in this warm bed when she's out there somewhere? Tomorrow we'll alert the lads in Alton, Basingstoke, Farnham and Farnborough, spread the net around a fifty-mile radius, must check the farms as well. Might even come across a gypsy camp, in the main they are decent folk and wouldn't protect a rapist.*

Phillip – in Meadow Farm - *Oh my lovely Jo, where are you? Come back luv, you didn't kill him, it's all right, they only want to find you to bring you back safely. Please my darling girl, go into a police station and tell them who you are. Where are you? Please get a message back to me, I'm so worried and afraid....*

Young soldier - at Broad Oak Bridge - *My feet are killing me, and this ruddy rifle's getting heavier by the minute. When I signed up, I thought I was going to see something of France straight away, not be stuck here on this stupid canal. Eight weeks now, learning to operate locks, building bridges and taking them down again, what a waste of time. Even those POWs further up the canal have it better than us. And as for that Sergeant Blaker, too old to do real fighting so they let him loose on us. All bull and piss. Heartless sod, he doesn't give a damn about any of us, and he's definitely got it in for me. Another hour and I'm off for a kip whatever he says. At least my training's near finished and I'll soon be over there.*

Jo's brother, John – at the River Somme in the Region of Picardy, France - *Will this bombardment ever end? So many dead. Life is cheap and has ceased to have any meaning. Another day gone and I'm still alive, at least in body. But my brain is dead! I can't think anymore, I don't want to think! Poor Ted, he was right alongside me, then poof ... Gone ... Nothing ... Just like that! Betty back in Warningford is going to be heart broken when she hears that her fiancé is dead. Warningford, dear, quiet, peaceful, Warningford. Market stalls all colourful and brimming with food, children playing, farmers yarning, wives gossiping, all so normal. Not like this stinking mud, rats and shell holes. How are things at Meadow Farm I wonder? Coming up to harvest now. Unbelievable that it's all still going on and so close to this living hell. Must write to Dad and Jo when I get the chance, stop them worrying too much. Have to do it soon though, if the rumours are true, we'll be going over the top again before the week's out. I'll try to do it tomorrow. Can't believe I saw a bird yesterday, might have been a sparrow, too far away and too quick. How on earth is it surviving in this hell hole? I miss the dawn chorus and the sound of trees rustling in the breeze. I even miss that bossy little sister of mine, and Dad. Still, only another month if I make it that far. Then leave in dear old Blighty. I can impress them with my new stripes, "Corporal" Simons. Yea, that sounds good.*

Chapter 7

As the early morning light penetrated his half open eyes, Graham slowly gazed around the small bedroom which had become his home since being dismissed from his previous job on a farm just a few miles north of Winchester. Laying on his small but comfortable bed, not for the first time he reflected on his life which had brought him to this point. At the age of two, following the death of his parents during a flu epidemic, he had lived and grown up in an orphanage until, at the age of thirteen, he had been fortunate enough to have been taken on by a nearby large estate shortly after his birthday. He had worked hard and was quick to learn. During his time there he had studied hard and had risen to the position of Gamekeeper, then Head Gamekeeper, which, apart from allowing a good salary, had included a small woodland cottage in which to live. He had become well-liked and respected within the local community, particularly when he took up the role of church warden in his local parish church. His manner, as well as his handsome features inevitably made him popular with the spinsters and young ladies in the surrounding neighbourhood, so much so, that more than one member of the fair sex had let it be known to him that an approach would not be spurned. However, Graham had resisted making such advances as he was certain that when the right one came along, he would have no doubts in the matter.

Just before the outbreak of war with Germany things had taken a turn in Graham's life. He had tasked himself to replace some broken tiles on the church roof, but it had all gone horribly wrong when he had slipped down the steeply sloping roof and plunged over the edge, falling some thirty feet onto the corner of a tomb-stone. The surgeon, who subsequently operated on him, managed to save his shattered left leg, but was unable to do the same for his left eye, and had doubts about the right one. Many months of recovery had taken its toll, resulting in the loss of his job on the estate, along with his home. Determined not to become an unem-ployed cripple, Graham worked through the inevitable pain that resulted through extensive exercise, much to the concern of the nurses who attended him. With sheer stubbornness, he managed to start walking again, but a limp became a permanent feature, along with an eyepatch.

Much sooner than would otherwise have been expected, having accepted the kind offer of his vicar to live in the rectory until he was able to put his life back together, Graham had said his farewells to more than one tearful nurse. It was the vicar who had paid for Graham's medical bills. As it turned out, his stay with that kindly clerical gentleman was not to be for long, as one of the church members, a local farmer, willingly took Graham on with a fair wage and accommodation in one of his outhouses. Meals were to be taken with the farmer, his wife and two children. An ideal arrangement, or so Graham thought. It wasn't to be long however before it became clear that the wife had more than a passing interest in this good-looking young man with that rather fetching eyepatch who had come into their lives. She had been one of those secret admirers who had set their eyes on him before his accident, and now, here he was, sitting at her table, so strong and so handsome, so close, so available, or so she thought.

Stupid woman. She had everything. A good husband, lovely children, a comfortable home, why did she think she could have me? Graham thought bitterly as he allowed himself time to shake off the lethargy that sought to hold him in its grip. For a minute or two longer, still fully dressed after his failed nightly hunt, he remained on the bed, allowing the weak daylight to infiltrate his sleep deprived brain. Hunger gnawed at his stomach and he remembered that he had not eaten since the previous morning. He reflected on the fact that he had had no luck with his snares for three nights now. His thoughts turned to the girl who was, for whatever reason, pretending to be a boy. *What was she running away from, I wonder? Pregnant maybe? Although I didn't see any sign of that possibility. She clearly had no idea where she was headed, so, makes me think she was fresh on the road, maybe just a few hours. She spoke of a farm, what was it now? .... Meadow, that's it, Meadow Farm. She seemed keen on sending me in that direction. Why was that I wonder? Damn her eye, why can't I get her out of my mind?*

In frustration, Graham eased himself off the bed and retrieved the chamber pot from beneath. Buttoning-up, he glanced through the condensation on the window pane noticing that this was a bright morning with a hint of frost on the grass beneath the window. A movement beyond the lawn caught his eye and, for a moment, he watched his landlady pegging out some washing. Guilt filled his mind as he recalled that he had been unable to pay any rent for the last two weeks, and yet she had made no demands, even offering him food, which he felt unable to accept. Her husband had been away with his regiment for over a year and life for her had been hard, being forced to take in washing and ironing when she wasn't spending hours cleaning wherever she was needed. She didn't talk much about her husband who, from the few comments she had made, it seemed, was not overly kind to her.

Having rinsed his face and shaved with cold water, Graham brushed his fingers through his hair, slipped his jacket on and let himself out of the small room. Descending the narrow staircase, being careful not to disturb any of the crumbling plaster on the walls, he entered the steamy kitchen where Polly was now standing over a tub, pounding more washing with a dolly punch.

'You're up then, Graham, I was about to bring you up a cup of tea. Pot's on the range, help yourself.' Polly continued punching the clothing amongst the suds, not looking up as Graham stepped around her and over to the range.

'Thank you, Polly, shall I pour you one?'

'That would be nice, sit yourself down, once I've got this lot through the mangle, I'll cook you some breakfast, and don't argue this time, I insist. Tonight will be better and I'm sure you'll catch something to sell at the butcher's shop, you'll see.

'I've made up my mind, Polly. Today, I'm going down to the recruitment office to sign up. I can't keep sponging off you.'

Stopping her pounding, Polly looked up and wiped her wet brow with the back of her hand and said sharply, 'Graham, you can't, they won't take you. You know it's impossible with that leg of yours, not to mention your eye, or should I say, lack of an eye? They'll laugh you out the door before you can say anything. Stick to what you know you can do.'

'Poaching! Is that all I'm good for? They're getting desperate, so I've heard. They'll take me this time, I know it.'

'No, they won't, luv.' As she said this, Polly left the punch standing in the tub and walked over to her lodger, a man she was becoming very fond of. Placing her hand on his stooped shoulder she gently repeated, 'They won't.'

'Maybe you're right, still, it's worth a try. You've been so good to me Pol, this can't go on, you know that, don't you?'

~~~

'Boy!' Startled, Jo quickly lifted her head from the pillow and looked around the small cabin as she tried to orientate her fuddled mind. *'Come on! Rouse yourself, let's have you out of there! Can't hang around all day, got to get to Frimley before dark.'* It was the man, Ed. He was standing at the open hatch at the top of the steps, cap on his head, red kerchief around his neck, shouting down to her. *'Come on, shift yourself!'*

'Ed, give the boy a chance, he's only just woke up,' called Marge while looking up at her husband. She was standing by the side-bed with an enamel cup in her hand. 'Ere you go, luvvy, don't mind 'im, 'is bark's worse th'n his bite. he has to remind himself who the captain is every so often. Get this down ya, it'll do ya good. Hot lemon an' 'oney. When ya good n ready come on up and bring that bread and lard what I made ya. You can eat it as we're swimmin' along. Unless ya wanna go bankside now, that is?' Saying this, Marge gave Jo a warm smile and raised her eye brows as though expecting an instant decision. With no reply coming from the dazed lad, she shrugged her shoulders and said,
~~~

'The others are ready t' go and the mule's 'itched. I can tell Ed's castin' off so if you decide to go on the bank, you're free to go and you can step off whenever you likes. If you 'appen to be still wiv us, come lunchtime though, I'll 'spect a few answers mind.' With that warning, Marge shifted her weight and ascended the steps, a lot faster than might be expected with a woman of her rounded shape.

As Marge disappeared through the opening, Jo became aware of a change in the movement of the boat which had now ceased its rocking. Clutching the mug in her fist she eased herself into a more comfortable sitting position that enabled her to peer out of the kitchen window. She was mesmerised by the sight of tall grasses and bulrushes gliding slowly passed, as though it were those that were moving and not the silent boat. Jo had had a restless night, some of which was caused by the fact that she had slept for much of the previous day, but mostly because her troubled thoughts played the scene in the stable and barn over and over in her head. Then, of course, it was the constant nagging worry of her father trying to come to terms with this new loss, as well as running the farm, work which could never stop, not even for a moment. On top of all of that, there was the thought of what the coming day would bring. How would she explain herself? How could she? An exhausted sleep had eventually banished further thoughts, a deep sleep that held the troubled girl in its grip for the remainder of the night, until the rude awakening just a few minutes ago.

Having finished the hot drink, which she enjoyed, Jo tackled the hunk of bread with its thick coating of lard. She managed half of it again before her stomach violently objected. Placing what was left of the bread on the plate, she wished she had kept back some of the lemon and honey drink to clear her taste buds. Jo glanced at the open hatch to be sure nobody was watching, then inspected the old clothing provided by Ben, before lifting the bed covers off and quickly slipping into the unfamiliar garments. As she did so, she wondered what had happened to her own, or rather to John's wet clothes. Warmly dressed, Jo peered around the small cabin, noticing how clean and tidy it was. For such a compact space everything appeared to have its own allotted place and, no doubt there were many cupboards and lockers hidden in concealed spaces. The curtains surrounding the windows on both sides of the room were brightly coloured, as indeed were such things as shelving, bedding, buckets and bowls. It was as she was looking around that Jo noticed the brightly decorated chamber pot under her bed and realised that she should use it before going outside. A few minutes later, Jo crept up the steps and stood in the opening, head above the hatch, shading her prickly eyes as the low sun momentarily blinded her.

'Ah, so you've finally managed to show yourself, lad,' greeted Marge with a smile and looking down at her. 'You were dead to the world, so we left you as long as we could. 'Ow you feelin?'

Jo gave the woman a thin smile and nodded her head indicating that she was okay, then she pointed to the used chamber pot clutched in her hand.

'Give it 'ere.'

Reluctantly Jo reached up and handed the offending article to the grinning lady and watched with embarrassment as the content was tipped into the canal before being placed on the counter floor just in front of her. Tearing her eyes away from the pot, Jo became aware that Marge was holding the highly decorated handle that clearly steered the silently moving boat. Gingerly she stepped up onto the counter and turned around to see that the boat was being pulled along by a mule up on a path some distance ahead of the boat. Surprisingly the rope, or *'snubber'* as she was later to learn, between mule and boat appeared to be quite slack. Jo had no way of knowing that most of the mule's effort was in getting the boat moving and that, once it was swimming, its own weight carried it forward with little effort on the mule's part, particularly when swimming with the flow of the stream. Walking alongside the mule were the two men. Father and son, both the same height and build, even wearing near identical clothing, as they had been the previous evening, except the younger man's kerchief was yellow with blue spots. Riding on the bare back of the mule was the little girl, Beth. She was wearing a dark blue pinafore and a grey bonnet.

'Ain't any locks along this reach to be dealing with for a few hours, except for a swing bridge at Crookham. Plenty of locks after Deep Cut, later though. It's an easy morning, what with the flow 'elping us and only one lock. Be diff'rent tomorrer, you'll see, if you still reckon to be with us by then, that is.'

In spite of her immediate concerns, Jo was fascinated with everything around her. They had left the town of Odiham behind and were gliding sedately between tall trees which dominated both banks. Up ahead, on the towpath, the mule plodded on without effort, the child riding high on its back, the father walking alongside. Every so often ducks would suddenly appear, quacking as they fussily swam away from the sides of the boat and into the swaying reeds along the bank. A pair of gracefully flying swans overtook them while making their peculiar honking noise before rising above the trees up ahead. Occasionally, there was a loud plop alongside the boat as it slipped quietly through the water. Jo was left to guess what had caused the expanding rings on the surface following those plops, she assumed fish of some sort. After a while, she noticed they were approaching a seemingly low bridge spanning the brown water just ahead of the boat and, at that moment, she saw Beth duck down on the mules back and hold on to its neck as the bridge arch narrowly missed the girl's head. The mule didn't pause as it negotiated the protruding path which skirted around the bridge support. Marge gave a small grunt as she pushed the steering handle toward Jo to enable the boat to avoid the protrusion and enter the bridge opening in the middle of the canal.

'Ere, take the tiller for a mo', while I dip the po. Keep it as it is, you'll soon get the feel.'

'I can't do that!' yelled Jo in alarm.

'Yes, you can, I can tell you're a bright lad. Focus on the bow, the front that is, and try to keep the same distance from the bank.' There was a moment of silence as Jo took the tiller and, biting her lower lip in concentration, peered ahead. Nothing changed for a moment, then she noticed the bow was beginning to point toward the opposite bank. To try to correct the swing Jo eased the tiller over, but in the wrong direction. Quickly she eased it over the other way, but too far. Panic took over and Jo lost all sense of direction. Everything seemed all back to front.

'Move over lad. I've got it. So then, you ain't no more dumb than I am. You said you couldn't steer. 'Spect you didn't realise you spoke aloud in yer panic did ya? You and me need to 'ave a little talk, don't we? P'raps we'll find out if you got any other little secrets you want to get off that chest of yourn. Speaking of your chest, if you be a boy then that there mule ain't no more a mule than a flying pig. What's going on, lass? Are you in the family way, or somat?'

~~~

'Sorry, you must have known we couldn't take you. You seem keen enough but you would be a liability with your condition,' The recruiting sergeant was shaking his head and tapping his pencil on his front teeth. 'Do yourself a favour and stick to whatever it is you do to earn a crust. Thank you for coming in anyway. Mind how you go and kindly shut the door behind you. Good day to you.'

That had been an hour ago, an hour in which Graham had wandered the busy streets of Farnham waiting for the return petrol-driven omnibus to Odiham. He was considering his situation and the fact that it was not fair on Polly to expect her to go on supporting him. After all, she should be able to let out that room to someone who could pay a regular rent. Not for the first time, he cursed the stupidity that allowed him to climb that church roof, a mistake which had changed his life for ever. *Perhaps I could get back into farm labouring even though I'm a half-blind cripple. I'm good at that and at least I can win back some self-respect.*
~~~

Farms must be crying out for labourers these days. Like the one that girl, come boy, was on about. Meadow Farm. She said it wasn't far from where I saw her, I think I know it. If it's the one I think it is, it's close enough to stay on with Polly and pay a regular rent. The thought of Polly made him smile, regardless of his depressed mood. She had become a good friend and he had become fond of her. Limping across the street and realising he had twenty minutes to spare before the arrival of the omnibus, Graham headed for a small café where he would kill time over a coffee.

~~~

Some five miles had passed before Ben voiced the thoughts that had been running through his head for the last hour. 'I don't like it, Dad. What do we know about him? Nothing! He could be a thief on the run, might even be a German spy, have you thought about that? People don't just suddenly appear out of nowhere, specially them that don't speak. I reckon he ain't speaking 'cos
~~~

he's a German. You have to get him off the boat Dad, he could even murder us in our sleep.'

'Hold on, son. Now you're letting your imagination run away with you. He ain't no spy, he's too young and he don't even look like a German. They all has fair hair, and they're all big n beefy according to the papers. I've seen the pictures. He's just a frightened kid. Anyway, Germans wear them funny helmets with a spike sticking out the top.'

'You can joke all you like, Dad, but I'm telling you, something ain't right and I'm going to find out.' As he finished speaking, Ben glanced over his shoulder to see his mother talking to the boy who was, at that moment, leaning on the cockpit coaming with his back to them.

'Barley Mow bridge coming' up, Ben. You jog on ahead and check the bend. Don't want to meet an army barge head-on in that silted up corner. They won't give a damn about us, likely make our Skippy take a look if it suits them.' The expression *"Take a look"* was a term used by canal-folk, meaning to fall into the water, or *"cut"* as they called the canal. With Ben having run on ahead, Ed reflected on how calm and peaceful it was along this reach. Just the steady sound of his clod-hoppers, Skippy's feet treading the towpath, accompanied by the jangling of the harness, the distant chuckling of disturbed water as the boat's bow cut through the calm surface behind him, the rustling of the leaves in the trees, the twittering of a skylark somewhere overhead, clearly heard but hard to spot against the deep blue of the sky. It was so difficult to think that little more than one hundred and fifty miles away young men were dying in their thousand's day by day, all over the assassination of some foreign duke somewhere a couple of years back. Once again, he gave thanks for the fact that Ben was in an excluded occupation. It would break his mother's heart if he were to be called up, only to die over there.

An hour and a half later, Ash Lock came into view shortly after they had followed a right-hand bend in the cut. Ben had nimbly run forward in the hope of setting the lock in their favour. That was not to be, however. Ben had to keep his distance as he watched a gang of soldiers, under the instructions of a frustrated sergeant, emptying the lock in readiness for a barge to enter from downstream. Their efforts were accompanied by much shouting and swearing from the mouth of the sergeant. It took all of Ben's willpower not to be seen smirking at the inept uniformed men. A fifteen-minute job took all of thirty-five due to the barge having straddled the entrance to the empty lock as they lost control at the last minute. No doubt, the sergeant would be having strong words with the unfortunate men back at barracks later.

At last, Ben was able to signal to his waiting father, a safe distance further back, to bring *Red Rose* through the top gate. Keeping well clear of the oncoming loaded barge with its crew of novices, Marge skilfully steered their much smaller narrowboat into the vacated lock. Having done so, she passed the monkey fist, a knot on the end of a rope, to Ben who looped it around an iron bollard before passing it back to his mother. Meanwhile, Ed had started closing the heavy gates behind *Red Rose*. Jo found that she was fascinated, as she watched the family working like a well-oiled machine. Very quickly, Ben had opened the paddles on the downstream end of the lock, using his windlass which, Jo had noticed, the two men kept looped on their leather belts when not in use. She was mesmerised as the narrowboat started sinking lower within the enclosed lock with its streaming wet and weed infested walls. Looking up at Ben, she was startled by the glowering look she received from the boy who was waiting to swing the lock gate open once the water level was the same as that on the downstream side of the lock. *Why does he hate me so much?* she asked herself.

Following the painfully drawn-out explanation to Marge, of what had happened to her back at the farm and how she had spent her last two days, Jo had kept herself apart, in as much as she was able within the confined space of the boat. At mid-day as they were approaching Mytchett, Marge called out for Beth to come on board to take over the tiller. The six-year-old nimbly climbed down from the mule's back, then waited on the tow path for her mother to bring the boat close into the bank so that she could hop across the gap between bank and counter. With a grin she slipped past the boy and, having stepped up onto a small stool, which was clearly made for the purpose, she took over the tiller and peered over the cabin top as her mother stepped aside. This was the job she loved the most, apart that is, from grooming Skippy in a stable along the bank at the end of each day. Young and small as she was, Beth was as competent with the steering as her mother. She always puffed up with pride whenever she noticed the looks of shock and amazement on the faces of bank-side folk upon seeing such a large vessel in the hands of a child.

'Okay, luvvy, it's all yourn,' said Marge with a smile. 'A few bridge 'oles ahead so be careful. I'm goin' down to prepare the grub for lunch, and the nosebag for Skippy.' To Jo, who was staring at the grinning girl in amazement, she said, 'You can come down and 'elp me.' As she busied herself lowering the table on its hinges, thus revealing the compact food cupboard behind, Marge thought about all that the girl had told her. *By 'eck, that's a rum affair. Poor kid, she must be out of her mind with worry. Surely, they don't 'ang innocent young girls who try to defend themselves, do they? I can understand 'er not wanting me to tell anyone but I'll have to tell Ed when we moors up tonight, we don't keep secrets from each uvver, least ways not for long. That'll give the girl another full day.*

'Okay, here we are, you can slice the loaf with this 'ere knife while I cut the cheese. So, you've been runnin' a farm then, and lookin' after your dad. 'Ow's 'e gonna cope without you?'

Blinking to dispel the tears which threatened to fill her eyes, Jo replied, 'In the note I left him I suggested he gets some Land Army Girls in. Mr Gill on the neighbouring farm will help, I'm sure.'

Pausing in her slicing of the cheese Marge sighed before softly saying, 'Luvvy, why don't you go back? I'm sure things will get sorted out. Ow do you know that man's dead anyow? Did you feel 'is pulse or check 'e was breavin?'

Not looking up from her task with the bread knife Jo replied, 'No, but there was lots of blood and he didn't move when I called his name. I can't go back and end up in prison, or even hanged.' Suddenly Jo dropped the bread knife on the table and put her hands up to cover her face as the dam burst, allowing tears to stream down Jo's cheeks.

'There-there, you poor thing, let it all out, child. You need to release all that there stress and worry.' Saying this, Marge pulled the distressed girl into her ample bosom and held her tight while Jo sobbed into the comforting warmth she had never known from a mother.

~~~

'Corporal ……. Over here lad, a word.'
~~~

'Sarge.'

The young man summoned by the platoon sergeant was tall with broad shoulders and a deep chest. His thick black hair had become considerably longer than he would normally prefer and his dark complexion, the result of a life spent in the open air on the farm, was still evident beneath the stubble and mud smears which had almost become a permanent feature of his handsome face with its soft brown eyes. From the moment he had stepped into the trenches he had stood out amongst his comrades. A hard worker who exuded self-confidence in the face of danger and uncertainty. He had quickly gained the attention of his commanding officer which had resulted in a rapid promotion to the rank of Corporal.

Carefully folding a half-completed letter and a pencil stub into his battledress pocket, John eased himself off the ammunition box, which had been serving as a chair, before following his sergeant along the trench whilst taking care not to slip on the muddy duck boards. *What now? What's he found to moan about this time?* thought John as they left the exhausted mud-caked men sitting wherever they could find the least wet ledge, or box. As he followed the older man, John studied the bearing of this regular soldier who seemed always to be smart and alert. For sure, he was a tough taskmaster but he was fair in his dealings with the men under his charge. He was well respected by them, as much as by the officers in their platoon. Having navigated a number of trench intersections they eventually arrived at the sergeant's mess which was no more than a shallow tunnel with crude planking serving as walls and ceiling. A sheet of canvas served as a door, although at that moment it was tied back to allow light into the dank space.

'Sit down, John.' A small wooden table stood in the centre of the room upon which an unlit candle stub was wedged into a whisky bottle. Spaced around the table was an assortment of folding canvas chairs. There were three two-tier bunks with neatly folded blankets, and a number of small cupboards. John became aware that he and the sergeant were the only occupants at that moment.

Before John had managed to select one of the lowest chairs, leaving a higher one for his superior, the sergeant asked, 'Would you like a glass of ..' the question was immediately overtaken by the familiar and deadly sound of a high explosive shell shrieking toward the British lines close by. Instinctively the two men ducked their heads as the loud *Crump* was followed by earth cascading through the overhead timbers into the room, accompanied by a cloud of dust which hung in the still air. 'Sweep that muck off the table, lad, here use this old towel, I'll get the bottle and glasses. Best brandy, good for clearing the dust from the old tubes.' After pouring two generous tots of the golden liquid, Sergeant Langley returned to the table and placed one of the glasses in front of John before dropping into his chair with a heavy sigh.

'Down the hatch. I'll come straight to the point, lad. Today is Sunday in case you've lost track amidst this shamble. On Tuesday, at 05.00 hours, we're going over the top, a big push. There will be the usual barrage starting at 02.30 hours. If the Hun didn't already know it, and I expect they do, the barrage will tell them all they need to know. They'll be expecting us. You can be certain they will throw everything at us the moment they see the first helmet rise above ground. It won't be pretty, John. Captain Goodacre will lead our platoon, he's a good man. Your job will be to make sure every soldier climbs over the top, the moment the whistle blows at 05.00. Any sign of holding back will be dealt with on the spot, if you take my meaning? It will be an instant death penalty. You can be certain that Captain Goodacre will be first over, you are to see that the rest follow. I will be close by the captain at all times. Once in the first Hun trench, we will round up surviving prisoners and keep them safely under guard, your job. Medics will be under the command of Lieutenant Ash and you are to liaise with him regarding injured enemy. Take my word, corporal, it will all seem like the world's gone mad and everything's a total shamble. Just stay with it and use that common sense of yours. All clear so far?'

'Yes, Sarge,' replied John before taking a much needed sip of the brandy. 'What do we do till then?'

'See that your men strip, clean, and oil their rifles, then make them do it again. Also make sure they get their bayonets sharpened. It's likely they'll be used as much as bullets, if not more. Also see that they get as much rest as possible. Remember, not a word for the moment, the men will get their briefing at the appropriate time.'

As John stumbled away from the Sergeant's Mess, partly under the effect of unaccustomed alcohol, and partly reeling with the dread of what was soon to take place, he tripped over several pairs of muddy gaiter-clad legs and slipped off the edge of a duck-board into a foot of stinking mud, before finding his friend, Norman.

‘Hey up, John. What’s the hurry, you look as though you’ve seen a ghost. What’s brewing?’

‘Oh, Hello Norm. Can’t say at the moment, sorry.’

‘So, the rumours are true then, were going over.’

‘I didn’t say that!’

‘Didn’t have to, mate. When?’

‘Can’t say, you’ll hear soon enough. Meanwhile, let’s get some grub. Then I’ve got a letter to finish. You might like to think about writing home as well.’

‘Yea, I’ll do that … Is that brandy I can smell on your breath?’

~~~
~~~

Dear Dad,

Hope this letter is finding you well and that things are okay on the farm. I hope harvest went well, I can imagine Jo working her fingers to the bone. She's a good little worker, knows what she doing, but don't tell her I said so. Hope your leg isn't playing you up too much. I should be coming home next month for a spot of leave. I can't wait to see you both and to eat one of Jo's apple pies. I'm looking forward to seeing trees and walking through the fields. I miss the sound of skylarks, we don't see many birds here. Things are not so good over here but you mustn't worry, me and Norman are keeping our heads down like you told me to. Would you believe, they've made me up to corporal. Doesn't mean much really, just more work, if the sergeant wants anything done it's me he details· Still, it keeps me busy and stops me thinking too much· I expect you've heard by now that Ted has copped it· He wouldn't have suffered, so that's a good thing· He will be missed in the village cricket team·

Dad, I know I have never said it before, but I want you to know, I love you, and tell Jo I love her too, even if she is a bossy snotty-nosed kid·

I have to stop now, as it's getting busy and I have things to be doing· I will be seeing you soon so keep the kettle on·

Lots of love to you both

(Corporal) John xxx

Chapter 8

Lunch had been eaten by the crew of *Red Rose* whilst still on the move. Having wolfed down her bread and cheese as though she hadn't eaten for a week Beth had given up the tiller to her mother in favour of sitting astride the mule. Up ahead, Jo could see a bend in the canal and was puzzled by the appearance of a group of men working along the bank. Noticing the frown on Jo's face, Marge gave a smile and said, 'German prisoners of war, been 'ere for a while now, working the banks and 'elpin' with the loadin' of the large barges. They're okay. Quite friendly really. Strange to fink that over there,' she pointed in a vague southerly direction, 'our boys are killing their lot on site while we waves to this lot wiv a smile.' Shaking her head, she sighed, 'I dunno, it just don't make any sense to me. Why don't folk just leave each uvver alone and just get on wiv their lives?'

Sure enough, as the boat approached, many of the overall-clad figures stopped what they were doing and greeted the family with waves and smiles. Somewhat surprised, Jo instinctively found herself blushing before remembering that she was supposed to be a boy. Allowing herself to give a curt acknowledgement with a slight lift of her arm, she turned her back to them for fear that her secret would somehow be more obvious to an enemy soldier.

'Won't be long before we ties up at the end of Deep Cut and before the first in a long stretch of locks,' Marge informed Jo. 'We could 'ave got furver before the end of the day but Ed likes to 'ave a clear run through.' Taking her eyes off the canal ahead, Marge turned to Jo before saying, 'What do you want to do, luvvy? I 'ate the thought of you bankside on your own, but if you decide to go and take your chances it would be best to do that as we pass Mytchett. Someone might 'elp ya'. But, if you takes my advice, it would be best for you to stay put wiv us, while we sort things out. It's up to you.'

Thinking about the hateful looks she had been getting from Ben, Jo replied, 'You've been so kind to me, but I know I'm in the way. All I ask, is to be allowed to stay with you until we reach London, then I can disappear. I can work for my keep till then, I could help you clean and cook, or help with the mule, I'm good with horses, we've got two heavy horses back at the farm.'

'London! Do you know what ya sayin', girl? Why, you wouldn't last a week there without some bloke takin' you for a pro.' I ain't gonna let that 'appen. If you're still wiv us by the time we reach that god-forsaken city, you stay wiv us, no argument. And let's get it clear, you ain't in the way.' Marge surprised herself by her reaction to what Jo had said. She was a nice kid, for sure, but why was she feeling so protective toward her? Was it because she would be a similar age to her Ruby, she wondered? Or was it simply because the girl was in trouble and desperately in need of help? For the first time in many months, Marge became aware of tears welling up as she thought of Ruby. She had been such a blessing to her and Ed. Always happy. Always dreaming of the man, she would one day meet. Such a romantic. Now she was gone, just like that, there one minute, gone the next. How she had missed her laughter these last eighteen months. Suddenly she was pulled back from those painful memories as Jo reached across the tiller and gave her a quick hug.

'Thank you, Marge. You must let me work to earn my keep while I'm with you.'

An hour later, with *Red Rose* tied safely to the quay at Frimley, Ed stepped from the quay onto the counter, followed by Ben who scowled at Jo before making for the fore-cabin. Ed shook his head as he watched his son go forward then addressed himself to Jo, saying, 'You're still with us, I see. Well, if you intend staying for the night you can make yourself useful.' Pointing to Beth who was standing alongside the mule, he continued, 'You can go with her to settle Skippy for the night. She knows what she's doing. And, tomorrow you can help with the locks.' With a brief nod, Jo stepped down onto the quay and followed Beth and the mule in the direction of the stables.

'I'm ever so glad you're still with us,' said Beth as they walked along together, 'and I'm really sorry you can't speak. It must be so hard having thoughts buzzing round and round your head and not be able to let them out like butterflies in the wind. Daddy says I talk too much, but I know he doesn't mean it. And mummy likes having a good chat when we swim along together. I bet something really dreadful happened to you to make you stop talking, like seeing a murder or something. Ben doesn't like you, I heard him saying things about you to daddy, but you mustn't mind him, he doesn't like anybody.'

Back on the boat, Ed carefully placed his windlass in the monkey hole, where it was safe and secure, before coiling the snubber, the thick rope used for towing, and was now checking the lashings which held the canvas sheets. Satisfied that all was secure, he stepped down into the warm snug cabin and gratefully took the enamel mug of tea Marge was holding out to him. Removing his cap and settling on the side-bed, he said, 'We need to talk about that lad, Marge. We don't know the first thing about him, where he's from, what he's been up to, who he's running away from. He might even be wanted by the cops for all we know.'

'Yea, well I can answer some of them questions, Ed. Just relax with ya tea for a minute and 'ave a listen.'

Ten minutes later, with a half mug of lukewarm tea in his hand, Ed stared at his wife before emptying the mug with a grimace and saying, 'You mean to tell me the lad's a girl?'

'Yea.'

'That he .. she can talk?'

'That's right.'

'That she's on the run from the cops, like I thought?'

'Yea, but no. She's on the run, but not in the way you might 'ave thought.' Marge then recounted to Ed all that Jo had told her during the day.

Scratching the back of his neck, the confused skipper said, 'Blimey, what should we do, Marge?'

'We let her stay with us 'till we get back to Odiham. Then we can see what's what.'

'Marge, you're talking nonsense. We should hand her over to the police, if she's wanted for murder.'

'But she didn't murder that man, I doubt that he's even dead. She never checked, she just panicked and ran. Anyhow, I promised 'er we wouldn't do that, and we won't.'

'Who's murdered who, ma?' It was Ben. Neither of them had noticed him standing at the top of the steps.

Over the meal of kedgeree that evening, with the five of them cramped in the small but cosy cabin, conversation was stilted, apart that is, from Beth. 'I *thought* you were a girl, Jo. I even told you that you're pretty, remember? And you can talk, even though you aren't saying much. I'm so excited to have a girl I can talk to about stuff, like I used to talk to our Ruby. We can talk about make-up, and frocks, and how to kiss boys, and …'

'That's enough, Beth,' said her father abruptly. 'Let Jo have a chance.' Placing his fork down onto his cleared plate, Ed looked at Jo for a moment before gently saying, 'Tell us about the farm, Jo. And your dad.'

~~~

It hadn't taken long for Graham to find Meadow Farm nestled amongst the trees in the lane beyond Warningford. It had been a bitter blow to him that he was considered unfit to serve in the army. He had always taken pride in whatever job he did, and even though, deep down, he knew that he would not be accepted, it didn't make it any easier to swallow. His frustration was exacerbated by the fact that his leg was causing a fair amount of pain due to the miles he had walked that day.

As he entered the farmyard, he was just in time to see a middle-aged man limping into a barn. Aware of his own limp Graham
~~~

headed for the open barn door and, upon reaching it, called into the dusty darkness, *'Hello?'*

A moment later, the man, now holding a pitchfork, limped warily out of the gloom and, peering at Graham suspiciously, said, 'What can I do for you, mister?'

'Good afternoon, sir,' replied Graham with a smile. 'A fine farm you have here. Would you, by any chance, be the owner?'

'And what if I am?' replied Phil who had not come any closer to the stranger who looked somewhat threatening with his black eyepatch.

'My name is Graham Stephens and I'm looking for work. I can turn my hand to most things connected to the land. I'm willing, strong and honest. The army turned me down, otherwise I would be over there.'

'All very interesting,' replied Phil. 'But I've no need of extra hands at the moment, least of all a cripple like me. Good day to you.' Thus saying, Phil turned and started walking back into the gloom of the barn interior.

Graham watched as the man turned away, then called out, 'Did you have a lass named Jo working here, by any chance?'

The man stopped walking and swung around to face the stranger. *‘What do you know about Jo, mister? If you’ve ...’*

‘I met her, two nights ago. Dressed as a boy, trying to *be* a boy. She said she was headed north. Mentioned that this farm looked short-handed and might have work going.’

Stepping closer to Graham, Phil asked, ‘How did she seem? Was she hurt in any way?’

‘Nothing physical I could see, but she looked like she was hurting inside. So, I was right, she did work here. Why was she so intent on getting away so late in the day? Did you sack her, or even ..?’

‘No!’ Phil’s shoulders sagged as he continued quietly, ‘She’s my daughter. We’ve been looking for her these past two days. The police have been searching and intend widening the search tomorrow.’

‘The police!’ said Graham. ‘I didn’t realise it was that serious, what’s she done?’

‘She’s done nothing!’ exclaimed Phil abruptly. Continuing more softly, he said, ‘It’s what’s been done to her that concerns

me, I'm sorry, forgive me. Come into the house, what's your name again?'

'Graham.'

Placing his hand on his visitor's shoulder, Phil said, 'Well, come in for some refreshments, Graham. You look as though you need it. I'll tell you about it if you tell me all you know about my Jo. For the first time since Friday, you've given me hope.'

Listening to Phil's account of the events (as far as he knew them) that had led to Jo's sudden departure from the farm, her home, Graham became more uncomfortable with the fact that he had done nothing about the runaway at the time. Could he have stopped her? Not with words, and certainly not physically. She was so intent on going north. But he could have come here, to Meadow Farm, sooner, he supposed. 'I'm sorry, I should have come sooner. Had I realised …'

'Don't blame yourself, Graham,' said Phil as he poured the tea. If anyone is to blame, it's me. I should have listened to her. So, you think she was heading for Odiham then?'

‘I would think so, that’s the direction I pointed out to her to keep her out of the woods. She just said that she wanted to go north, so who knows where she is by now?’

‘It’s a start,’ replied Phil. ‘Do you mind telling the police what you’ve just told me? It might narrow down their search.’

‘It’s the least I can do,’ replied Graham while sipping his tea.

‘Best I can do is four pence an hour, unless you want to board, in which case it’ll be two pence.’

‘Do you mean, you’ll take me on?’

‘Well, between us, we’ll have at least one pair of good legs. We’ll give it a week, starting tomorrow, see how you get on. If you do alright, the job’s yours. Now, I need to go down to the village and have a chat with Sergeant Edwards. Likely as not, he’ll want to talk to you in the morning. Start at six-thirty with the milking, does that suit you?’

Chapter 9

'There's a flask of tea on the bottom,' said Polly as she buttoned up the knapsack and handed it to Graham. 'There's also a piece of left-over rabbit pie for your lunch. I've put an apple in as well. I'll cook you a nice meal for this evening, to celebrate. I'm so happy for you, Graham. I'm sure it will all work out, and I hope they soon find that girl.'

'Thanks Polly. You've been so good to me,' said Graham as he slipped the knapsack over his shoulders. 'I can't stop thinking about Jo. If only I had been able to stop her when I had the chance.'

'Oh yes? What, you think you should have grabbed her and put her over your shoulder? Don't blame yourself, luv. At least you can put the police on the right track. Now, you'd best be off. You don't want to be late on your first morning.'

'Okay Polly, you best get back to bed and get a few more hours sleep before you have to get up. You had no need to wake up special, just for me.'

'No, but I wanted to,' replied Polly quietly. Before Graham had time to realise what she was doing, still in her dressing gown, Polly reached up and kissed his cheek. 'There, be off with you.'

So many thoughts were running through Graham's mind as he carefully limped along the lane in the pre-dawn darkness. A new job, doing what he most liked, working the land, his conversation with Phil the previous afternoon, the girl and her whereabouts at that moment, the pending interview with the police sergeant, but most of all .. that kiss. It was the first time such a thing had happened since he had been lodging with Polly. He imagined that he could still feel the warmth of her lips on his cheek. The more he thought about it, the more he realised how fond he had become of Polly, the wife of a man serving his country overseas. *Perhaps I should board at the farm after all? But then, would that be fair on Polly? To leave just as I've started earning? No, I'll just have to control my feelings.* Controlling his feelings was one thing, but controlling his thoughts as he limped along the lane in the brittle air which steamed his breath, was another thing entirely. He remembered the day Polly had taken him in as a lodger. How she had put him at ease in her gentle and quiet manor. How she had listened to his story with sincere interest during their first meal together. That moment when she had leaned across the table, tenderly removed the eye patch and unflinchingly stared into his face, saying, “It’s okay, Graham, you don’t need to wear this while at home.” He might have been embarrassed, shocked even, but instead, felt accepted and comfortable as he looked into her warm violet eyes. She was not beautiful, attractive would be a better description. High cheek bones with dimples, particularly when smiling, which she seemed always to be doing. Short curly hair, with a touch of grey showing through the black, maybe? A soft but matter-of-fact way of speaking. No nonsense, straight to the point. A couple of inches shorter than himself, slim. Shaking his head with a smile, Graham tried to put the picture of his landlady out of his mind as he began to focus on the farm ahead, and what might be expected of him by the owner who was clearly in distress.

It was not difficult for Graham to pick up on the familiar skills of farming. Although the milking parlour was less than ideal, he was soon in the routine of tit-pulling with the small herd of cows, although he noticed Phil looking in on him a few times during the process. His next job was to tend to the two shire horses, first checking their feet to ensure there was no foreign matter to be hooked out. As he entered the barn to sort out the feed, he noticed the large gap in the door-frame and made a mental note to attend to it as and when time allowed. Whilst in the barn, his mind went back to the girl who had had to fight off her attacker in this place. Where was she now, he wondered.

Shortly after nine-o-clock, whilst working in the stable, cleaning and polishing the tack, Phil walked in, accompanied by the police sergeant. Following introductions, Sergeant Edwards asked Graham to recount all the details of his encounter with Jo; the time of night; what she was wearing; what was said; her state of mind; the direction in which she was walking as they parted. Somewhat to Graham's concern, he was also asked how he happened to be in the vicinity of the woods at that time of night. It was fortunate that Graham had always been interested in owls, and was able to impress the policeman with his knowledge, as he described his hobby of owl-watching. Impressed, the sergeant may well have been, but Graham noticed the sceptical look on his face as he was writing in his notebook.

'I see, sir,' said the officer while raising his bushy eyebrows. Did you see any, what with only having one eye?'

'Any what?'

'Owls, of course, Mr Stephens. I suggest you stick to that .. erm .. story, should you be asked by anyone else to describe your night-time activities. Better still, give the ..erm, hobby up, now that you're honestly employed. Understood?'

Unable to stop a sheepish grin appearing on his face, Graham replied, 'Understood, officer. Thank you for the advice.'

Turning to the grinning farmer, the sergeant slipped his note-book into his breast pocket, carefully fastened the gleaming button, then said, 'You'll be interested to know that we found your ex-employee, north of Guildford. A Mr Patrick Stibbs. Travelling with his wife in a caravan. When questioned, he claimed that your daughter attacked him with a pitchfork for no other reason than that he had returned to the barn that evening to recover a coat he had left there during the day.'

'That's preposterous!' expostulated Phil. 'My Jo would never do such a thing.'

Fingering his earlobe with a frown, the officer continued, 'When asked why she would do such a thing, he told our man that the girl had always hated him and had threatened to kill him on more than one occasion.'

'You can't believe *that,* surely!' demanded Phil, who's face had turned purple with rage.

'I don't,' Sergeant Edwards slowly replied. 'However, Mister Stibbs wasn't inclined to return, to press charges. So, as we can't hold him without a key witness there's nothing we can do, I'm afraid. The important thing now is to find Johanna. We've got a number of forces in North Hampshire on the lookout, I'm sure it's just a matter of time.' The officer paused for a brief moment, glanced at Graham, then said, 'I'll bid you both, good day, and will return as soon as we have more information. Meanwhile, should the young lady happen to return of her own accord, be so kind as to let me know immediately.'

~~~
~~~

Jo had surprised herself with how quickly she had taken to working on the canal. She had slept soundly the previous night, partly due to the weight of secrecy being lifted from her shoulders. The main reason however, was how easily and warmly the family had accepted her in their midst. In the warmth and subdued light of the cabin, the previous evening, they had given their full attention to Jo as she had recounted her horrific experience. For a moment, she had become concerned as a look of fury had crossed Ben's face. She remembered worrying, *He thinks I've allowed myself to be ruined, that I somehow encouraged Pat to do what he did to me.*

As that thought had entered her mind, Ben had suddenly struck the table with his clenched fist and said, 'If I could get my hands on him, I'd *kill* him.'

'There's to be no killing, son!' Ed had said sharply. 'What's done is done. The important thing is that this lass bravely fought him off and came to no harm. Now we have to think about getting her home to her father, where she belongs.'

As feelings had calmed down, Jo had talked about her father and her life on the farm. She had been puzzled by the look of discomfort on Ben's face when she had got around to talking about her brother, now fighting in the trenches.

Laying in her small side-bed when the family had finally retired for the night, Jo had thought about Ed's words. For the first time, she had allowed herself some hope that things might get sorted out. It all seemed so much more positive now that she had people to confide in and with whom she could share her concerns. She also thought about Ben's reactions throughout the evening. For sure, his attitude had softened toward her, he had even smiled at something she had said. This morning, it had been Ben's suggestion that Jo should help him with the many locks they would be encountering throughout the day. Meanwhile, Beth was competently handling Skippy while Ed and Marge, left alone, were able to spent much of the morning on the counter, talking, something they rarely had the opportunity to do.

The lock procedure had been an education for Jo. The day started with the two of them walking along the towpath together through Deep Cut, a section of the canal which was overlooked by high tree-filled banks on both sides. During that time, Ben had explained the principle of how the canal system worked. How it had been necessary for the builders to skirt around the hills keeping mainly to the contours of the land, how a constant source of water, often from natural springs, was necessary, how steps, known as locks, were created where it was impossible to avoid a climb or fall as the canal crossed the country. He also spoke of the hard life of the *water gypsies,* as the boat people were known. The long days; the illnesses suffered by the children; the lack of regular schooling. It had appalled Jo when Ben told her that it was not unknown for children from large families to be lent, or even given away, to other boat owners who needed extra crew.

'Food has always been a problem for us,' Ben had told Jo at one point. 'The food shops don't like serving us, and now we're at war, with food shortages, they prefer selling, whatever they've got, to the locals rather than to us. It's not even as though we can grow our own vegetables.'

This was a different side to Ben that Jo had not seen earlier. He had previously come across as a sullen individual who had seemed to resent her being there, but now, he gave the appearance that he was actually enjoying her company. As the first lock appeared at the end of Deep Cut, Ben carefully explained the sequence of action which would enable the boat to safely fall to the next level whilst avoiding the danger of inadvertently draining the upper pound due to raising a paddle in the wrong order. On this first lock, he told Jo to work alongside him as he used his windlass to raise and lower the paddles and also heave the lock gates open or shut as the boat passed through. It was heavy work but, fortunately, Jo was used to hard manual labour, so she was quickly in her element. She was particularly pleased when she noticed the look of approval on Ben’s face as she worked more and more unassisted as they passed through various locks throughout the day. It was therefore with some surprise, later in the afternoon, when she realised that she had barely thought about her troubles as she absorbed herself into this way of life.

It was after the evening meal with the family gathered in the snug lamplit cabin, that Ed broached the subject of Jo’s predicament. After glancing at Marge, he addressed Jo and asked, ‘Have you thought anymore about what you should do, luv? We’ll be in London the day after tomorrow likely as not, and we’re not happy with the thought of you wondering those streets. The wife and me have been talking it over and we think you should stay with us for the return to Odiham. We’ll be back there by this time next week.

I've had a chat with Ben and, if you're happy to do so, he's agreed to go to your farm with you, so you can talk to your dad. He'll be able to tell you whether or not you're a wanted person and I don't suppose he'll hand you over to the cops even if you are. What do you say, girl? You can always come back to us if you can't stay at the farm, we can plead ignorance if they catch you. 'Cos of what we are, they'll believe us, seeing as how most bank-side folk think we're illiterate. What do you think?'

Looking firstly at Marge's worried face, then back at Ed, Jo replied, 'I don't want to put any of you in danger. You've been so kind to me. Whatever happens to me, I'll never forget you. Do you mind if I sleep on it and tell you what I think in the morning?'

'No, of course not, dear,' chipped in Marge. 'It's a big decision. P'raps a good night's rest will make things clearer by mornin'. Why, you're crying, dear,' she said as she noticed tears appearing in Jo's eyes. With that, she raised herself from the bench and stepped around the table to give Jo a hug. 'There-there, you 'ave a good cry, get it orff ya chest. You've been through a lot these passed days.' Turning to Beth, who had been sitting, open mouthed, listening to the conversation, she said, 'Come on you, bed. The same as last night, and none of ya fidgeting this time.'

Regardless of her physical exhaustion, Jo was to experience a night of restlessness as she pondered the alternatives. If she were being honest with herself, she knew that travelling further north, or even making her own way in London, was a frightening thought. She had no money and little experience other than farming. The autumn days would soon be turning into winter. How could she survive? She had left home in a panic, not having given any thought as to what she could do, apart from run away. It was clear that she would be unable to stay on the boat. She was not prepared to place their lives at risk, regardless of what Ed had said, and, in any event, there was no room for her. She turned to the idea of Ben accompanying her to the farm, and could see the sense of it. *At least dad will know I'm okay if nothing else.*

Once again, she felt tears filling her eyes as she thought about her father, and it was not helped when John's face came into her mind. He had been so proud as he marched away to war. *Where are you, John? What would you advise me to do? None of this would have happened if you hadn't gone off and left us. Stay safe, dear brother, Dad needs you so badly now. What are you doing at this moment?*

~~~

An unusual quietness had descended upon the battlefield during the afternoon and early evening. There had been some excitement when a Fokker, bearing the black German crosses on its wings, flew low over the British lines during the afternoon. The helmeted pilot could clearly be seen peering through his goggles over the cockpit rim as he passed overhead. Amidst the jeering, one or two soldiers took pot-shots at the aircraft, more in frustration and excitement than the hope of actually hitting it. There had also been a moment when a black and white dog had suddenly appeared in *no-man's land* between the opposing trenches. It was scampering around the bomb craters, no doubt looking for anything that would satisfy its hunger. Several soldiers from both sides had started whistling encouragement for the dog to come to their side before it eventually trotted further down the line without a shot being fired at it.
~~~

John had been one of those who had watched the dog, with bated breath. *Please, don't let it be shot. Let it live.* Long after the dog had disappeared from view, John was still thinking of the animals back on the farm, the horses, cows and chickens. *Perhaps we should get another dog after this lot's over, regardless of what dad says about it.* His father had been reluctant to replace the faithful collie who had been his constant companion for fifteen years. Glen had died in his arms following a short illness before the war. Both he and Jo had encouraged their father to get another dog, but Phil was adamant that nothing could ever take Glen's place in his home, or heart.

'Hello, mate, you looked as though you were miles away, what are you thinking about?' Norman had suddenly appeared out of the darkness and had propped his Lee-Enfield rifle against the fire-step and sat down alongside John. 'Let me guess, you're thinking about home, right?'

'Hello, Norm. Do you want a fag? Yea, I was thinking of the farm amongst other things. Ploughing should be done by now. Hope they've managed to get that done. Did you write that letter?'

Taking one of the cigarettes from John's proffered tin, Norman replied with a grin, 'Matter of fact, I've written two. One to me mam and the other to your Jo. Hope you don't mind?'

'Why should I mind? I thought you were getting sweet on her,' replied John as he gave his friend a gentle punch on his upper arm. 'Has she given you any reason to hope?'

'Not yet, but I'm working on it. How can she resist the return of a conquering hero, eh?'

'Well, that's me sorted,' laughed John, 'but what about you?'

'Very funny, you wait and see, by the time this lot's over, I'll have so many medals on my blinking chest they'll have to carry me home.'

'Well, if you want to take on our Jo, you're already a hero in my way of thinking. Mind you, she can cook as well as she can nag.' For a moment, John's face became more serious. 'Norm, you do realise she's only sixteen, don't you? I mean, you wouldn't ... *you* know.'

'Course not, mate, her virtue is safe with me, I can wait and hope though, can't I?'

'Yea, course you can, Norm, and the best of luck to you.' For a while, the two friends sat quietly finishing their cigarettes. Both were thinking in their own way, about an attractive sixteen-year-old girl who was mature beyond her years.

Will she ever look at me as a potential lover and husband, and not just as a farmhand, I wonder? thought Norman.

Stay safe, little-one. Look after dad and don't let him do too much around the farm. I love you both, so much. If I don't make it, remember me with pride, not pity. You're strong, you'll be okay. With a loud sniff, John reached a hand out to grasp Norman's shoulder, 'Well, my friend, tomorrow's the big one. We'll get through it together, then back to dear old Blighty for a beer or three, or four. We've done it before and we'll do it again, you'll see. Now, I think I'll move along and check the boys are bedding down. See you in the morning, mate.'

~~~
~~~

An owl hooted in the distance as Graham, laying on his bed, peered at the open window, the curtains lifting occasionally as a gentle breeze rustled the leaves on a nearby silver birch. Apart from the encounter with Sergeant Edwards, he had enjoyed his first day at Meadow Farm. He had immediately impressed Phil as his quickly reviving knowledge enabled him to work unsupervised and without having to be told what to do. He had enjoyed that moment when, at mid-day in the relative comfort of the barn, he had opened his knapsack to remove the food Polly had prepared for him. He had been touched to find that she had even placed a carefully folded table cloth over the various wrapped items. Even more so, when he realised it was the one, she had been so carefully embroidering by candlelight over the last few months.

Polly had warmly welcomed him home at the end of a satisfying day, firstly enquiring about his leg. For a moment, Graham had imagined what it would have been like had she been his wife fussing over him. She had even taken the trouble of warming his slippers in front of the fire. The rabbit pie, served with a few vegetables and thick gravy, had been shared in candlelight as Graham had answered Polly's questions about the farm and his first day there. *Such a domestic scene should not be shared between a landlady and her lodger,* he now thought, as he watched the twitching of the curtains, worrying about his growing feelings for Polly. *It isn't right to have these sorts of feelings for another man's wife.* he admonished himself. He was aware that Polly's marriage was less than perfect and that her husband preferred the company of his friends at the local pub rather than hers, but even so ..

Sleep escaped Graham as he lay there listening to the night noises. The owl continuing its call for a while, then the bark of a fox, quite close, by the sound of it. Below the rustling of leaves in the breeze he thought he could hear the chirruping of crickets. There was also an occasional creak as the old cottage settled in the cooling air. *No, that's not the timbers settling, it's coming from Polly's bedroom,* he realised. Graham continued listening, his senses now alert. Yes, it was Polly. He could imagine her walking back and forth across her uneven floor. At one point, he heard her bedroom door latch being carefully raised, then a creak on the stairs. *Should I go and see what's wrong? No, I mustn't. If it's something serious I'm sure she would knock on the door, or call out. Who knows what might happen if I go to her?* Eventually, his tiredness took over as he gave himself up to sleep, a sleep with dreams he would prefer not to think about in the morning.

Chapter 10

With a violent start, John awoke to the sudden crash of the expected barrage, which was timed to start at three o-clock on this Tuesday morning. He was aware of soil cascading down from the timbered roof of the dugout as the ground trembled beneath him. He, and several of the men with whom he was sharing the space, started coughing as dust filled the air around them. The smell of vomit invaded his nostrils as one of the men heaved in the darkness. The noise of the barrage was far greater than John had expected, and far louder than anything he had ever heard before. The solid wall of sound filled his head so that, for the moment, he was incapable of rational thought. The trembling beneath his bunk seemed to increase as the minutes slowly passed, or was this because his own body had started its own trembling? Yes, he was afraid. Afraid of failing to climb over the top, afraid of succeeding in climbing over the top. Out there, in the open, what chance was there? Contrary to belief, it was not going into the trenches that soldiers feared, rather, it was leaving the trenches that carried the dread. The trench was their temporary home, a place of relative safety as long as you didn't show a head above the lip. In just under two hours, they were going to raise not only their heads but their bodies, arms and legs above that lip. To what? The big question on all of their numb minds; *what will happen to me?*

As John covered his face to try to protect his lungs from dust, as well as trying to blot out some of the crashing sound, his biggest fear was the possibility of letting his men down if his feet turned to jelly and refused to carry him forward. The unspoken word was that to fail to go forward was to be instantly shot, no plea, no trial. He wasn't sure that it was true, but he shuddered at the thought of that happening to him.

The thunder of guns continued, without pause. The sound was terrifying to him, but what would it be like at the receiving end? He had been told by Sergeant Langley that there would be a very small number of the enemy left alive in the German trenches after the barrage. That their mission would be to go forward and wipe out any resistance. A mopping up exercise. That all sounded too good to be true. He knew that the last big push five months ago had resulted in thousands of deaths with nothing gained on either side. As his brain became more immune to the noise, rational thought was returning. He had to rouse himself and his men to take up position on the firing step. It was always possible for a sudden Hun attack under the confusion of noise and the flashing of explosions around the battlefield.

Shoulder to shoulder, the mud caked men leaned forward just below the rim of the parapet. Rifles held in readiness, bayonets gleaming in the constant flashes of light, cigarettes shared. Nobody speaking. No point. Just wait. Try not to think. This time tomorrow, it will all be over, but in what way? Suddenly with a momentary shock …deafening silence! … A cough, the clinking of equipment, someone retching, the scraping of a match, the squelch of someone walking along the floor of the trench.

'Steady, men. It'll be a breeze, nothing to worry about.' It was Captain Goodacre moving along the line, pistol hanging from a lanyard, Sergeant Langley in tow. 'Won't be too much resistance, I suspect.' His voice was soon lost in the ringing of John's ears. *Please let it be soon, let it be over, let that whistle blow.*

John's prayer was answered less than two minutes later. Whistles sounded along the line. No more time to think, this was it, the moment he had dreaded. Almost without realising it, he was on his feet and over the top along with hundreds, thousands of men up and down the line. He was unaware of his own voice as he continually screamed the only word he could, at that moment, *'Chaaarge!!!'*

Foot in a muddy puddle; jump over some wire; bullets zinging passed his ear; step on a body, soft unmoving; a scream to the right; skirt round a bomb crater; more bodies half submerged in oozing liquid; an explosion ahead through the smoke; more bullets zinging and thudding, into what? A man ahead falling. They are no longer running, more of a stooping jog, always going forward. A man is sitting in the mud looking at the place where his foot should be. Another man walking in circles looking for something, it seems. There are fallen men at every clinging step he takes forward, some lying still, others twitching or crawling. A machine gun is chattering up ahead, another to the right. He is half way there. *Keep going, keep going, forget the noise and the smoke ignore the flashes. Must keep going.* An officer, pistol in hand, lays face down in the mud. *Captain Goodacre, perhaps?* Men are yelling now, rifles held low down at their sides, with bayonets pointing forward. John is beyond fear now. His one purpose is to use the bayonet as soon as possible, nothing else matters …. He doesn’t feel the bullets that smack into his body.

Chapter 11

Jo had never been to London before. The largest city she had ever visited was Portsmouth which they had passed through on their way to Southsea when the village had organised a charabanc trip to the seaside one summer, several years before. She could recall standing on the pebbled beach, with her skirts lifted above her knees, being delightfully splashed by each incoming wave. How she would have loved to be fully emersed in that clear water on that hot July day, if only she had owned a costume that allowed such a thing. Now, peering down into the fast-running flow of the River Thames, being emersed in such murky and smelly water was the last thing she wanted.

She had not known what to expect as they had entered London with its buildings all along both banks. The river was wider than she had expected, the buildings taller and more grand. The roads along the banks and on the bridges were so busy with a mixture of horse-drawn and petrol driven vehicles of all sorts. She had particularly liked the bright red omnibuses. In her frustration with having had to stay hidden for several days she yearned to be free, and maybe enjoy a ride on one of those omnibuses, preferably on the open top deck which was reached by curved steps on the back of the vehicle. That ride must wait for another time however, as once they had moored at the busy wharf, Ed had advised Jo to stay out of site for the duration. Although disappointed and frustrated, she could see the sense of Ed's advice, for police officers were nearly always to be seen walking slowly along the wharfs. There had even been a frightening moment when one of them had stopped to watch the loading of coal into *Red Rose's* hold before stooping down to peer through the cabin window. 'Nosey bugger, stay here, Jo,' uttered Marge before shifting her weight speedily up the steps onto the counter. 'Whacha lookin' for officer? This 'ere cabin is private, go an' poke yer nose in somewhere else. Me daughter's 'avin a wash and don't take kindly to men sneakin' a look. So, clear orff.' Needless to say, the embarrassed young man had made a rapid and undignified exit from the scene, much to the amusement of some nearby coal-blackened men leaning on their shovels.

It was with relief when, two days later on a dry and bright Sunday, *Red Rose* left the Thames and entered the relatively short stretch of the River Wey that would soon lead to the lower reach of the Basingstoke Canal. By the end of the first day back on the canal, Ben and Jo were working more effectively as a team and, as such, were becoming more relaxed in each other's company. Jo's thoughts were no longer confined to her troubles and the plight of her crippled father, although those thoughts continued to invade her sleep deprived nights. During the daytime however, there were so many distractions, apart from the work in which the young couple were engaged. Jo was enjoying the discovery of wildlife she had never previously encountered. She was excited to see creatures such as herons standing like silver/grey statues along the bank, and water-voles swimming into the shelter of the bank as the boat approached. She was delighted when Ben pointed out an otter just before it effortlessly dipped beneath the surface. Jo's keen eyes had been the first to spot a dormouse amongst the reeds with its golden coat and thick furry tail. Her favourite however, were the kingfishers with their magnificent deep blue colouring as they illusively flashed into the trees ahead. It had become a competition between the young couple throughout the long days to see who could catch most glimpses of these magnificent little birds.

During those days, Jo often thought about her older brother. She reflected on the fact that John would love to experience what she was seeing and doing. How she wished he could be with her here in this delightfully peaceful countryside with its sedate pace of life amongst these friendly, hard-working folk. She didn’t like to think of him over there fighting for a cause she didn’t understand. Putting his life in danger, for what? How would it affect him? Would the whole experience of killing other men change him in some way? Would it make her gentle, caring brother a hardened man? Could their close relationship ever be the same again? She had heard of men being sent home with missing limbs, or blind, or deaf, or shaking with fear, some even brain-dead. That any of this might happen to John didn’t bare thinking about. It couldn’t, it mustn’t.

Well into the second day of their return journey on the canal, while the young couple rested on the beam of a lock gate as the lock slowly emptied in preparation for *Red Rose* to enter, Jo asked, ‘Ben, you wouldn’t ever want to go and sign up, would you?’

Startled by the question, Ben replied, ‘Why do you ask?’

‘I noticed the look on your face back in London whenever you saw a soldier. Like you were embarrassed, or ashamed, or feeling guilty, or something. You won’t ever go and do anything silly like signing up will you? I mean to say, you’re in a reserved occupation, aren’t you?’

‘What’s it to you, if I did sign up?’

‘So, you *are* thinking about it then?’

‘I never said that! Anyhow, it’s none of your business what I do. After I’ve taken you back to your farm, I might think about it, if you must know.’

‘Please don’t, Ben. Your family needs you, and I …’

‘You what?’

‘I would miss you, and be afraid for you.’

Ben remained silent for a moment before quietly saying, ‘You’ll be going back to your farm, I suppose.’

‘I don’t know, Ben. It all depends on what we find there. Why?’

'You said you would miss me, but you won't, because you'll be gone.' To Jo's surprise, Ben suddenly slipped off the beam and walked away. For a moment, she watched him, thinking that his purpose was to step across the closed upstream gates to prepare to open the downstream gate opposite where she was seated. However, that was not the case. Ben continued walking passed the gate and, with hands in pockets and hunched shoulders, took to the towpath as though heading for the next set of locks. Jo was confused by this sudden turn of events as she recounted their recent conversation. *Something I said must have upset him, but what was it? Surely not the thought of me leaving?*

'What's up, lass? Where's Ben?' It was Ed, who had previously been standing alongside Skippy, with Beth, on the bank just short of the lock. They were waiting to move *Red Rose* into the drained lock once the gates were opened by the youngsters.

Jumping down from her seated position on the beam and, for the first time noticing that the water level was ready for the gates to be pushed open, Jo replied, 'He's walked on to the next lock.'

'Okay, lass. You follow him. Help him set the next one. I'll finish off here. Don't want to waste any more time, do we?' he said pointedly. Without waiting for an answer, Ed turned and waved *Red Rose* forward. By the time Skippy will have taken up the strain and got the boat moving he will have opened both gates and lowered the paddles. With an embarrassed apology for the wasted time, Jo set out to catch up with Ben, thankful for John's clothing she was again wearing, which enabled her to run faster than would otherwise be possible in a skirt.

Meanwhile, in the distance, Ben was angrily kicking any loose stone he came across as he allowed his thoughts to provoke him. *Why did she have to come? We were alright till she decided to push her way in. Why should I care if she leaves as fast as she arrived? Why does she care if I go in the army? Why can't she mind her own business? Why am I feeling so angry, and sad at the same time? Do I even like her now? I do! I like her, like I liked our Ruby, but in a different way. What's wrong with me? It'll be best when she's gone.*

'Ben! Wait for me!' He heard Jo shouting, but tried to ignore the call. *'Ben, wait!'* His pace slowed, although he continued looking straight ahead. Soon, he became aware of her panting breath approaching from behind. Still not turning, he asked, 'Did Dad send you on?'

‘Yes, he wants the next lock set up before they get there. Are you all right, Ben?’

‘Why wouldn’t I be?’

‘No reason, I just wondered why you took off like that.’

‘You can wonder all you like; we’ve got work to do.’

Feeling hurt and confused by this change in her new friend’s attitude toward her Jo remained silent for the remainder of the walk. At the same time, Ben was only too aware of her hurt and cursed himself for being the cause, although he was unable to find a way of lightening the mood that had spoiled what had so far been a pleasant day. He was able to admit to himself that he couldn’t remember a day in his life when he had enjoyed the canal so much. Something inside him wanted to admit that to Jo, but he found no way in which he could make himself so vulnerable to this girl whom he still barely knew.

Chapter 12

The telegraph boy doesn't wait to find out if there is to be an answer. There never is, with this kind of telegram. The front door closes quietly behind him as, with relief, he walks back to his red bicycle and places his left foot on the peddle and scoots off before cocking his right leg over the saddle.

The message is abrupt and without emotion: *"It is my painful duty to inform you that a report has been received from the War Office notifying the death of …….Message of sympathy from There Gracious Majesties the King and Queen ………I am to add that any information that may be received ……… I am, Your obedient Servant, Officer in charge of Records*

With shaking hands, the telegram is placed on the kitchen table, amidst the remains of a frugal lunch. So sudden, so painful, so final. On the range, the blackened kettle comes to the boil, but is ignored. The telegram, just a piece of paper really, tells of the destruction of a person's life and, in itself, could be the destroyer of other lives.

~~~

Graham wondered where Phil had got to. They had been working together during the morning repairing fences. Since his return, half an hour ago, from the barn where he had benefitted from another of Polly's packed lunches, he had not seen his boss.

Something must have held him up, I'll see if I can manage on my own for a bit, although this job is much easier with two. As it turned out, Graham didn't have to struggle on his own for too long before he noticed Phil limping up the field toward him.

'Sorry to keep you waiting,' muttered Phil as he approached. 'Now, let's get this job done before dark, shall we? I'll hold the post; you use the sledge.' The afternoon wore on, one post after another firmly planted into the ground. There was little in the way of conversation as Phil seemed content to work in silence. Graham guessed that his boss was thinking about his two children, one missing, the other fighting in the trenches. He wondered about the son who, God willing, would one day return to the farm.
~~~

He was aware that his job here might come to an end when that happened, particularly if the other farm hand also returned. It was the story of his life, just get settled then everything changes. And what about the girl? Will she ever come back, he wondered? *No wonder, Phil is so quiet,* he thought to himself. *What must be going through his head at this moment?*

As though Phil had read his thoughts, he suddenly broke his silence and said, 'I can't stop thinking of my Jo. Worrying where she is. What she's doing? Is she safe? While I'm up here building fences, she could be in all sorts of danger. Please God, bring her home to me.' For the first time, Graham noticed tears in the tough man's eyes as he held onto the next post to be planted in the soil.

'Let's call it a day, Graham,' said Phil at last. 'My heart isn't in it. Dark soon anyway. Take the tools back to the barn and be off with you, I'm going for a walk.'

As Graham walked home to his lodgings, he was very much aware of the burst blister on his right hand. Not for the first time that day, he thought about the encounter with Jo in the darkness that night a week ago. Now that he knew the girl's father, it seemed inconceivable to him that he had not only let the girl go, but had even told her the direction in which she should walk. He remembered that he had directed her as far as Odiham. *Where would she have gone from there? Alton seems the logical answer. Although she might have turned toward the Basingstoke canal. If I were on the run and needed a hiding place and shelter and, at the same time, needed to keep going, what would I do? The canal! Why didn't I think of that, before?*

At last, the welcome sight of Polly's cottage came into view. As he rounded the corner of the cottage, he was a little surprised to see the washing still on the line in the fading light. Polly would normally have taken it in before the evening dampness settled in. He was about to unpeg the sheets when he remembered the blood on his hand and decided it was more than his life was worth.

Letting himself in, through the unlocked kitchen door, he immediately noticed the uncleared table and that there was no sign of any preparation for the evening meal. In fact, the cottage had that empty feel. Removing his knapsack he walked through to the parlour, quickly glanced around the neat empty room, then walked to the foot of the narrow stairs where he called, 'Polly?' Not a sound. Louder, *'Polly?'* His voice seemed to echo back down the narrow stairwell. Now, he was really concerned. He quicky climbed the stairs and stepped across the landing to Polly's open bedroom door. He paused before peering into the room. There was still enough light to tell him the room was unoccupied. The bed was made and the room was tidy, apart from the wardrobe door having been left open. *Where is she? Something's happened.* He took a final glance around the room, which he had never previously seen, before descending the stairs and passing through the kitchen to the back door. He walked into the garden and around the outside of the cottage, peering through the gloom. The cottage backed onto some now darkened woods. There was no sign of his landlady. Not sure what he should do, Graham decided to take the washing in before it became even more damp, but then remembered his bloodied hand. He re-entered the kitchen to wash his hands under the pump, then drying them gingerly on the kitchen towel, stepped over to the dresser where he lit the oil lamp and turned up the wick. It was at that moment that he noticed the buff-coloured paper, half covering a plate on the table. He knew instantly what it was.

Lifting the telegram that could only be the bearer of bad news and, at the same time, possibly explain the mystery of Polly's absence, he read the formal words. *Oh, Polly. You poor, poor thing.*

Such a nasty shock. You must be so ... His heart went out to that sweet woman who deserved none of this. *Why do such bad things happen to the nicest people? It's all so unfair.* Replacing the telegram where he had found it, Graham slumped down onto one of the hard wooden chairs, wondering what he should do. *No point in running around like a headless chicken. Just have to wait till she returns from wherever she's gone. The washing! Best get that in, the least I can do.*

It was fully dark outside when the door latch lifted. Graham had just built up the stove and was about to peel some potatoes which were sitting on the scrubbed draining board. Turning, he watched as Polly quietly slipped through the door. Her swollen red-rimmed eyes moved slowly over the cleared table.

'Hello Graham. Sorry I haven't got your dinner done. I went for a walk. Sit down, I'll do us some sausage and mashed potatoes. Won't take long. Thank you for bringing the washing in. Do you want peas with it?'

'Polly .... I'm so sorry.'

'Don't say anything, Graham. I always knew it might happen. He was a good man really, although he never really loved me. I knew that. But he didn't deserve to die. He was so young, and popular with his friends. I don't know if I ever really loved him, to be fair. I could have loved him better, if I tried. It's so ..' She couldn't finish whatever she wanted to say.

As she faltered, Graham, stepped over to her and held out his arms. She briefly hesitated before stepping gratefully into his warm embrace. Together, they stood, wrapped in the comfort they both needed. With her head pressed against Graham's chest she allowed her emotions to overwhelm her as she cried tears of bitterness and sadness. She wanted this moment to continue as Graham held her tightly. She had never before felt such comfort and love from any man, including her father.

Graham, was also experiencing mixed emotions. He loved the feel of Polly in his arms with her head pressed to his chest. At the same time, he felt ashamed of feeling that way, for a woman who had just lost her husband. It was then that he admitted to himself that he was in love with her, and had been for some time, without realising it.

Neither of them wanted to release the other, Graham allowed his good hand to gently move up and down Polly's spine. Was it his imagination when he felt her press herself closer? He wasn't sure. Without thinking about it, he gently kissed the top of her head. The sobbing had stopped as Polly eventually lifted her wet face away from Graham's chest and looked up into his one blue eye. Gently, he pressed his lips to her forehead. She instinctively pulled his body closer and suddenly became aware of the hardness pressed against her belly. Releasing her arms, she stepped back in confusion, wiping her cheeks with the back of her hand.

'I'll get those potatoes peeled, then,' she said abruptly. 'Would you mind fetching more logs from the shelter?'

Dinner was eaten in silence. As Graham placed his knife and fork onto his cleared plate, more to break the silence than anything, he said, 'I've had an idea about that missing girl. Thinking about it, it's possible she might have come across the Basingstoke canal and hidden amongst the cargo of one of the boats.'

'Oh,' responded Polly and in her practical manner asked, 'Where could she go on a boat?'

'Well, it would be Basingstoke at one end and possibly London at the other. Or it's likely she'd be discovered and put ashore somewhere. If she got as far as London there's little hope of ever finding her. Sergeant Edwards said he might be calling at the farm in the morning, I'll mention it to him, although they've probably already thought of that, but you never know.'

'You're still feeling guilty about her, aren't you? It's not your fault, so don't take on about it so much.'

'I guess I can't help it, I like Phil and it worries me to see him looking so sad and lost. Polly, talking about feeling guilty, I'm sorry about earlier, you know .. I didn't mean to take advantage or anything.'

'Don't say anymore, Graham. What you did was good. I liked it. Perhaps I liked it too much.' Rising from the table, she said, 'Let's have a look at that hand of yours. You'll need a dressing on it to keep it clean tomorrow.'

A few minutes later, Polly carefully applied some sort of ointment to the blister before winding a bandage around the hand. Graham was very much aware of her gentle touch as she held his hand while working, although she seemed to be avoiding eye contact during the procedure. With tomorrow's lunch prepared and the dishes washed and dried, Graham checked the doors and windows while Polly made for the stairs. Having extinguish the oil lamp, he followed her up and passed Polly's closed door as he made for his own room.

It was in the early hours that Graham heard the squeak of his door hinges above the sound of rain now beating on his window pain. 'Graham? I can't sleep.'

'I'm not surprised, luv. Do you want me to bring you up a drink of Horlicks? That might help.'

For a moment, Graham waited for Polly's reply. He could make out the lighter shade of her outline in the darkness. 'No, I would like to come into your bed with you, is that okay? I don't want to have sex or anything, I'm not ready for that. I just need to feel your arms around me.'

Graham was momentarily stunned with the unashamed boldness, and innocence of Polly's request. With a catch in his voice he quietly said, 'If you're sure that's what you want. Polly, I have to tell you, I sleep naked, if you'll turn your back, I'll slip something on.'

'No, don't do that, Graham. Just move over a little while I get in. As he did so, Graham heard a rustling sound before she slipped in beside him. As their bodies came into contact, he swallowed hard, while feeling the softness of her naked body pressed against him. Without a word being spoken, she laid her head in the crook of his shoulder as he placed his arm around her. Not daring to move and very much aware of the stiffening in his groin, Graham laid awake until he heard Polly's breathing become heavier as she drifted into sleep. Graham was to have just three hours sleep before it was time for him to quietly slip out of his room before dawn, leaving Polly still soundly asleep in his bed.

Chapter 13

'How is he, nurse?'

'Still unconscious, doctor. Murmuring a bit every so often. Heartbeat steady at seventy-five, temperature high and rising.'

The Field Ambulance, or FA as it was known, was particularly busy following the failed "Push." The medical officer was having to prioritize the treatment of the injured soldiers, often simply prescribing pain killing drugs such as morphine, and waiting for the inevitable death. The FA staff of doctors, nurses, stretcher-bearers and orderlies were beyond exhaustion and were functioning more as robots than as human-beings. Within the last hour seventeen men had died under their care, and it was anticipated that John, the soldier who was subject to their conversation, would soon be joining them. He had been wounded during the push a week ago and had not been recovered from *no-man's land* until two days later. When first spotted, half submerged in a pool of stagnant water, during the second night, by a party of stretcher-bearers, it had been assumed that he was dead. However, after a dangerous and prolonged transfer back to the trenches and on to the Regimental Aid Post, some three hundred yards behind their front line, one of the bearers imagined that he saw one of John's eyes flicker. This had been sufficient for him to be immediately stretchered to a ruined farm building, four hundred yards further back, which was serving as an Advanced Dressing Station, or ADS. Here, the crumbling building was full and bustling with strained activity. John's stretcher was added to the many others which were lined up in the open, awaiting their turn. Eventually, following a three-hour wait, John was carried into the crowded and noisy building where his chest wound was quickly cleaned and bandaged. He was then placed in a horse-drawn ambulance which took him, with several others, to the FA where the surgeon had eventually found time to remove a bullet from the wound, along with remnants of his tunic and shirt. Since then, the VAD nurse had been keeping an eye on him.

'Punctured lung cases don't usually survive this long,' mused the exhausted surgeon. 'Most unusual. The infection alone, should have killed him. Must have been a strong fellow.'

At that moment, in spite of his delirium, John became partially aware of the conversation taking place above him. 'Punctured lungs ……… most unusual …….. unlikely to survive another …….. just keep him sedated …….. gone by the morn ….'

Before falling deeper into pain-racked blackness, John forcefully told himself, *Fight this! You can do it! You will not allow yourself to die!*

~~~

Later, that same Tuesday afternoon, ten days after leaving Odiham, *Red Rose* returned. It had been an uneventful journey and from Ed's point of view, although a profitable one. Jo, mostly with Ben's help, had become a proficient bank-side crew member, for it was mostly on the towpath that she had spent the time. The tension between her and Ben had eased and for the latter part of the journey they had worked efficiently together as a team. At days end, Jo had made herself useful in the cabin without getting too much in Marge's way, although in that confined space, it was
~~~

not easy. It had pleased Beth that her “new sister”, as she now referred to Jo, always accompanied her to the various stables along the way. In her natural elements, Jo had shown Beth how to properly groom and feed the mule, as well as ensuring her comfort in the designated stalls. Care of the mule was as important as any other job on the canal, for without the mule *Red Rose* would go nowhere. At this stage of the war, finding another mule, should it ever become necessary, would be difficult if not impossible, for horses, and particularly mules, were badly needed “over there”.

It was a pleasantly warm October evening. The day’s work was complete and the meal was over. Marge was busy tidying up the cabin and preparing the beds for the night. Ed was helping Beth with her arithmetic, something she enjoyed doing, particularly when assisted by her father. Ben had just returned from his fore-cabin and, seeing Jo standing on the counter alone in the darkness, asked, ‘Do you fancy a walk?’

They had been walking along the towpath together, all day, but Jo was both surprised and pleased with Ben’s invitation to join him. Having informed Marge of their intention, they stepped onto the quay and, skirting around some stacked timber, headed for the humpy bridge that would lead them into Odiham village.

'Are you still happy to go to your farm tomorrow?' asked Ben as they crossed the bridge.

Hunching her shoulders against the cold, Jo replied, 'Yes, I'm longing to see my father and find out what's happening.'

'Well, I hope things will be okay for you. That bloke was probably not dead. You said that you never checked, so anything could have happened. I suppose, if everything's all right, you'll be staying there.'

'Yes, but I will miss you all. I've loved being on the boat and seeing new places, and I've become quite fond of y.. all of you, you know? Like being a part of the family.'

'Yea,' Ben replied with a grin, 'well I suppose we've got used to having you around.'

'Having me around? Is that all?' asked Jo, playfully.

'Well, not *all,* returned Ben. I suppose you've had your uses, Mouse' he laughed.

'Ben Fraser! You are mean and horrible! And I *hate* you!' replied Jo, while trying not to laugh. 'Ben?' Jo stopped walking and

looked at him. 'You've become a good friend, I hope that whatever happens, we can still be friends, I …'

'Course we can, Mouse, you'll see.' With that, Ben continued walking so that Jo had to hurry to catch up.

It was with a shock, a few minutes later, as they stood together gazing into a clothing shop window, when a police constable silently stepped up behind them and said, 'What are you two up to then?'

Swinging round to see who had spoken in that way, Ben replied, 'Me and me kid brother are just looking, Mister. We're off the canal.'

'Oh, water gypsies, are you? What's the name of your boat?'

'Dancing Lady,' lied Ben without hesitation. 'We ain't been up this stretch before. We're leaving in the morning.'

'Just as well,' retorted the policeman. 'We don't want the likes of you lot hanging about here, especially in the dark. So, be off with you. Back to the ditch where you belong, and don't let me catch you thieving on the way.'

Jo, with her heart in her mouth, had tried as best she could, to hide her face behind Ben throughout the encounter. They quickly walked away from the constable who was standing watching the retreating couple. '*Wait!*' he suddenly called. Jo instinctively clutched at Ben's hand as they froze. Without turning, they stood still and waited for what was to come next. As he approached, the policeman asked, 'Did you happen to see anyone else lurking in the street?' Nodding toward Jo, 'Someone about your size? Male or female, could be either.'

'No, we ain't seen nobody 'cept you,' replied Ben.

'Okay then. Now, hop it before I change my mind and haul you in for loitering. And you, young man,' looking at Ben, 'should be in the army instead of swanning around on the canal enjoying yourself while our boys are fighting to save your miserable life.'

Quickly, the youngsters turned and continued walking in the direction of the bridge. In their agitation, neither noticing that they were still holding hands. 'They're still after me, Ben,' said a very worried Jo. 'I didn't like the way he was staring at my chest either.'

'Yea, I noticed that. I felt like clocking him. You need to be more careful, Mouse, if you get my meaning?'

Feeling her cheeks burning, and to cover her embarrassment, Jo said, 'I'm not so sure about going back to the farm. What if they're waiting for me there?'

'I think you should at least try to find out what's happening, otherwise you'll always be on the run. I'll be with you. I won't let anything happen to you.' It was then that Ben realised that he was still holding Jo's hand. He didn't let go.

~~~

Work on the fencing had continued throughout the day. Seeing the bandage on his employees' hand, Phil had suggested that Graham should steady the posts while he took over the hammering, for his calloused hands were far more used to the hard manual effort involved. It was clear to Phil that Graham was distracted by something on his mind, but didn't make any comment. *The man is entitled to his privacy so long as it doesn't slow him down.*

The work was interrupted mid-morning when Sergeant Edwards was seen puffing up the hill toward them. Wiping his brow
~~~

with his kerchief as he approached the two men, he enquired, 'I assume your daughter hasn't returned, Mr Simons?'

'I would have notified you straight away, had she done so, Sergeant,' replied Phil abruptly.

'Thought not, as we've not heard from you. It's been some time now, since she took off. Sorry to say, we've had no luck with our enquiries. I'm even more sorry to say that we're having to tone down the search. She's on the books as a "missing person", along with many more, I'm afraid.'

'Does that mean you've given up?' asked Phil sharply.

'Well, I wouldn't say that exactly. We haven't given up as such, just reduced the focus a bit,' replied the embarrassed officer while stroking his earlobe.

'Sergeant,' Graham interrupted. 'Have you considered that she might have taken to The Basingstoke Canal? She could have stowed away on one of the boats.'

'Yes, we thought of that, but it's all army on that canal now. There's no way she would be able to get aboard one of their barges. No, that line of enquiry won't help us, I'm afraid.'

'But worth a try, surely?' piped in Phil, who was slightly lifted from his despondency by this turn in the conversation.

'I'll tell you what, Mr Simons, I'll call the station in Odiham and see what they have to say. But I wouldn't build up my hopes on that line of enquiry if I were you.'

Later, as darkness descended, Graham was walking more slowly than usual along the lane in the direction of his lodgings, his thoughts in turmoil. *What can I say to her? Will Polly have regrets about last night? Will she want me to leave? What sort of welcome home can I expect?* Approaching the side door into the kitchen, he was surprised to hear Polly singing. He paused on the path for a moment before giving a loud cough, sufficient to warn her of his approach. The door had then swung open before he had time to reach for the latch.

'Hello Graham, dinner will be ready in twenty minutes, smiled Polly. 'Plenty of time for you to wash and change if you need to. Had a good day?'

'Hello Polly. Yes, um .. busy but okay.' There followed an awkward moment when neither knew what to say. The silence was broken by Polly.

'How is the hand? I see you've removed the bandage.'

'Oh, I'm afraid it didn't survive the rough work. It's okay though.'

'Better let me look at it, let me see?' Graham first removed his knapsack from his shoulders before holding out his hand, palm uppermost.

'Looks okay. Is it sore?'

'No, in fact I'd forgotten it,' he lied.

'Okay, give it a wash, I'll put some of my ointment on it just to be sure.'

Dinner, and the remainder of the evening was just as though yesterday hadn't happened. Later, Graham waited for a while before following Polly up the stairs, having locked up. He was relieved to see that Polly's door was closed as he passed it. Sleep took Graham into its warm embrace earlier than normal that night, as he gave in to his weariness.

~~~
~~~

At the same time that Graham was allowed himself to slip into his restful sleep, just a few miles away in his kitchen, which had not seen a duster or broom for over a week, Phil was sitting by his empty fireplace. He was slowly polishing his boots and remembering his last evening with Jo. That evening that changed his world. Every so often he glanced at the empty chairs drawn up beneath the table. None were being used now. Whatever simple meals he had been preparing for himself he had eaten in this, his favourite chair. His troubled mind conjured pictures of the three people he loved and missed so much.

His late wife, Ethel who had died in Jo's second year, back in the year 1902. A happy vivacious girl whom he had sat alongside at school for four years before he had bucked up the courage to ask her out. That first date when he had tried to impress her by climbing an apple tree to pick her one of the not-quite-ripe apples. How he had pretended to be stuck so that she had to reach up and help him down, leading to that first tentative kiss in the shade of the tree. That wedding night when feeling shy, they had separately changed into their unromantic night-clothes in the corner behind a screen. Both of them ending up as naked as the day they were born, as they joyfully consummated their marriage hours after creeping into his creaking narrow bed in his room, which was inconveniently and embarrassingly next to his parent's bedroom.

John, their first-born. A happy smiley baby and child. Always curious, often getting into mischief. Loved the farm and every animal within it, whether chicken, cow, goat or horse. It made no difference, they were all deserving of his love, attention, and interest. If he had allowed it, he had no doubt that one or more of the animals would be found in the house at any time day or night. John had been devoted to his sister from the moment she had made her first sound. How he loved to hold her, to watch her feeding at the breast, to help with the nappies no matter how disgusting they often were. All of this had been so helpful when Ethel had succumbed to pneumonia that dark winter. John had, at first, been distraught at the death of his mother, as any five-year-old would be, but soon he was being as helpful as he could, making the bringing-up of his baby sister his personal task in his young life.

And what about Johanna? A beautiful baby, a beauty she carried into adolescence. Slender but strong, A shy nature but not to be crossed. Practical. Organised. A good farmer. Phil had not realised until now quite how much he had grown to depend upon her. For sure, John was the more dominant of the two on the land, but Jo was the undisputed boss around the house, in the milking parlour and in all matters horse related. As Phil looked around the kitchen, he was aware of the lack of the woman's touch. An empty vase on the window ledge where there would normally be beautifully arranged flowers, no enticing aroma wafting from the range, an untidy shelf where gleaming pots would normally be neatly arranged, the usually gleaming butler sink, now stained and cluttered with dirty cups, plates and an assortment of cutlery. He would take any amount of his daughter's nagging if she would only walk through that door right now. *Please come back, Jo. Did you manage to take to the canal and if so, where are you now, my love?*

Chapter 14

Not knowing whether she would be returning to *Red Rose* with Ben, Jo faltered as she prepared to step out of the cabin. Addressing herself to Ed and Marge, she said ‘You have been so kind, I don’t know how I would have got on without you.’

‘Now you take care of yourself, luvvy,’ said Marge while trying to hold back her tears. ‘Everything’ll be alright. You’ll see. You’ll soon be at ‘ome with your Pa, and all of this will be just a memory, a good one I ‘ope, whenever you think of us.’

‘I’ll never forget you,’ said Jo, as she threw herself into the arms of the woman who had come to mean so much to her. ‘You’ve been like the mother I’ve never known.’ Jo was unable to hide her tears as she pulled away.

‘Get on with you, girl. You’ll ‘ave me blubbering next. Now, get yourself up them steps and don’t keep our Ben waitin.’

Turning to Ed, Jo said, 'What will you do if Ben decides to go?' Last evening, Ben had recounted the remark made by the policeman, about him nor being in the army, and had said that the officer might be right. Ed had become annoyed by the suggestion that Ben should go, and reminded his son of the important work they were doing. Ben had then left the cabin without a further word.

'We'll manage, Lass. Anyhow, it may never happen once he's really thought about it,' Ed replied with less conviction than his words suggested.

'Come on, Mouse! We've a way to go. We should be getting on!' Ben was calling from the bank and was clearly anxious to go.

A few minutes later, Jo gave Beth a firm hug as the three of them stood on the humpy bridge. 'Remember what I told you about looking after Skippy, Beth.'

'I hope you come back,' replied the tearful six-year-old, with a sniff. 'I like having a sister.'

‘And I like thinking of you as my younger sister too,’ replied Jo as she fought to conceal her tears. ‘I don’t know when, but we’ll meet again, who knows? It may even be tonight.’

‘Oh, I hope so,’ exclaimed the girl. Then realising her mistake, said, ‘I’m sorry, I didn’t mean I wanted you not to be able to stay on the farm with your dad, I just meant …’

‘I know what you meant, Beth. Thank you. Now we must be going.’ Jo quickly turned away from the confused girl and looked toward *Red Rose*, nestling against the quay below, her home and refuge for the last ten days. With a lump in her throat, she returned the wave that Ed, with his arm around Marge’s broad shoulders, gave her. Walking up the street away from the canal, Jo was reminded about the encounter with the policeman the previous evening, suddenly realising that she had dropped her guard while on the canal and that she must, once again, be on the alert.

Ben was quiet. He hadn’t spoken as they passed through Odiham which was soon left behind. Although the day had started with a chill in the air, the sky was clear and the warmth of the sun began to revive Jo’s spirits as she considered the real possibility of seeing her father that afternoon. Walking beside her silent friend, Jo reflected upon how strange it now felt not to have the canal alongside them. She was already missing the regular sound of Skippy's feet, and the quiet swish of the water as it became disturbed by the passing, brightly decorated, narrowboat. What would they discover at the farm, she wondered? How had her father been coping? How were the animals? She thought fondly about Blacky and Champ, and wondered if they had missed her.

Jo was snapped out of her thoughts as Ben suddenly broke the prolonged silence between them. 'I'm going to sign up.' Jo remained silent, waiting for more. 'Did you hear what I said? I'm going to sign up. Do my bit.' He awaited Jo's reaction which was not forthcoming. 'Well? Say something.'

'What do you want me to say, Ben? You know how I feel about that. You're needed here, on the boat, especially if I don't come back with you. They won't be able to manage without you.'

'Yes, they will. Maybe a bit slower but they'll manage. Everyone's having to make sacrifices these days and …'

Jo stopped walking and spun round before saying, 'You don't have to sacrifice yourself, Ben. *It's pointless!'*

'I *have* to go,' said Ben quietly. 'Why can't you see that?'

'No, I *can't*. I've already seen my brother go, and I don't know if I'll ever see him again. He might already be dead, or wounded for all I know. I can't bear the thought of losing … of thinking of you over there.'

'I'll be all right. They say it'll all be over by Christmas, anyhow. I know you can't understand. It's a man thing.'

'Oh, why do men have to be so *stupid?*' uttered Jo as she stormed off.

'Jo, wait!'

Catching her up, Ben said, 'Don't be angry, Mouse. One day, you might understand, perhaps when you're older.'

Now, he's really done it. Does he think I'm a little girl? 'If that's how you feel, Ben, why don't you leave me alone and just go back? I can manage without you. Go on. Go back!' With folded arms, Jo increased her pace along the road as she tried to blink back her tears. For a moment, Ben stood still and watched her go. *What the heck, why should I care what she thinks?*

~~~

'Where am I?'

Startled by the whispered words, barely heard above the constant noise of the Casualty Clearing Station, Nurse Farley paused from her work of replacing the dressings, to look at the face of the young soldier. His sunken eyes, now partly open, peering up at her, the tip of his pink tongue running over dry cracked lips amidst the stubble on his grey face.

'Where …? What's happ ..happened to me?' Bending forward to hear what the soldier was trying to say, the middle-aged nurse took John's hand and, giving it a squeeze, said, 'You're in the CCS. You were transferred here from the FA last night. Too soon in my opinion, but they need the space. You took a bullet in the chest over a week ago. You had a collapsed lung among other things. You're very lucky to be alive, young man. The good thing is that you've earned your ticket to dear old England. You will, no doubt, be rested in a temporary hospital for a while, before being allowed home. Where is …?' Nurse Farley got no further as she became aware that her patient had drifted into a healing
~~~

sleep. *That's right, you poor boy. Sleep. That's what you need now. I imagine you're quite good looking under all that stubble. I dare say you've more than one lass back home setting her eyes on you.*

~~~

Not for the first time that morning, Polly glanced at the telegram which was now tucked behind the clock on the oak dresser. She had finished her washing and had just returned from the garden where she had been hanging various items of bedding on the line. In an instant, her life had changed. She was suddenly free to do whatever she wanted with her life. Her marriage to Len had been a predictable failure. She had had no choice once the reality of her pregnancy could no longer be ignored. It had all been such a silly mistake. Len had been walking her out for several months before the relationship started taking a serious turn. Her mother had constantly warned her of the folly of allowing any man to press his attentions beyond a chaste goodnight kiss, even then, only after a reasonable period of courting. Len had been patient
~~~

up to a point, but as time went on, his demands became more difficult to resist, even if she had wanted to. The first tentative touch of his hand on her breast, on one of their walks through the woods, was at first, alarming. She had not been prepared for her own reaction, which, she had to admit, was one of pleasure. She had felt ashamed as she became aware of her hardening nipples beneath her bodice as his hand gently moved over her breast. It was as his thumb passed over her engorged nipple that Polly had managed to find the strength to forcefully remove his hand before rising from the log upon which they had been sitting. That night, she had felt even more ashamed as she allowed her hand to caress her naked body.

It had been just a matter of time before Polly had finally given in to Len's pent-up desires. That first intimate touch had soon led to further exploration beneath their clothing by both of them. This went on for weeks until, that fateful day in which her life was to change, they had walked hand-in-hand across the heath on a warm sunny day and had found a secluded spot amongst the blossoming heather. Kisses led to caressing, then to fumbling with clothing, then each slowly undressing the other until the warmth of the sun caressed their skin. Polly had surprised herself with the utter abandonment she felt as she jumped up and ran naked through the heather, with Len chasing her. The inevitable penetration, when it came, was momentarily painful for Polly. However, both were beyond caution as they gave themselves up to their heightened quest for indescribable pleasure and ultimate release.

Eventually, when the pregnancy could no longer be concealed, both were confronted by Polly's father, a bank manager based in Guildford. There had been no question that Len would have to do the right thing and marry his daughter. The word "Love" had never entered the conversation. An early date was settled with the vicar who asked no questions beyond those that were legally required. The newly-wed couple had lived for a while in Len's parent's home, before the rented cottage became available. Polly's father helped the couple financially with the advanced payment of the rent and with the purchase of second-hand furniture. Beyond that, her parents didn't want to see them, or the unborn child ever again.

There was little love, if any, shared between the couple, and when Polly miscarried in her fourth month, Len had made it clear that he had done his duty by her, but beyond that, she should not expect anything other than a home to look after and meals to cook.

Again, she looked at the telegram. Although she would never have wished this to happen, her new found freedom overpowered any sense of guilt she may have harboured in respect of her growing feelings for Graham. She would certainly miss the small amount of income she had received from the Army, but with her washing service and now that Graham was to have a regular income, as long as he continued to board with her, she would be able to manage. Thoughts of Graham remained in her head as she made a start on the ironing from yesterday's washing. She marvelled at his restraint as she had slept naked in his bed the night before last. He had made no reference to it yesterday. It seemed that he was an honourable man who would never take advantage of anyone. She asked herself why she had removed her night clothes before slipping into his bed. She supposed it was because he had said that he was naked and she had wanted the comfort of his warm body against hers. Nothing more than that.

The more she thought about Graham, the more she looked forward to his home-coming that evening. She decided that she would make an extra special meal for him, as a thank you.

~~~

The sour mood remained with Ben as he continued walking. He could see Jo up ahead and became a little agitated each time she went out of sight around a bend in the road, or over the brow of a hill. Knowing that his father had trusted him to look out for Jo, he eventually picked up his pace in order to catch her up.

‘Wait, Jo,’ he called. The road had been skirting some woods and as Jo emerged into a clearing, he saw her disappear through some bushes. He hurried to the spot where he had last seen her and followed the pathway she would have taken through the bushes. As he emerged onto a ploughed field beyond the bushes, he was relieved to see Jo, with hands on hips, standing facing him.

‘You took your time,’ she said scornfully. ‘We haven’t got too far to go now. We need to cross this field then we take a lane into the village. The farm is half a mile beyond the village.’

‘Best be careful then,’ replied Ben. ‘We need to make sure there are no cops around as we go through the village, and
~~~

particularly at the farm. Is there anywhere we can check it out before going in?'

'Yes, there's a small wood behind the barn. We could go through that and watch from there.'

The field presented no problems for the couple and soon they were climbing the stile leading to the lane. Fortunately, the lane was empty of traffic, or people, apart from a lady in her garden gathering washing from her line, who gave them a friendly wave as they passed. However, as they cautiously entered the village, Jo became immediately concerned when she saw people who would know her. First, the baker who was standing at his open door chatting to a customer, then the postman passing on his bicycle in the opposite direction. Although both looked at the young strangers passing through, it was fortunate that neither seemed to recognise Jo in her disguise as a boy. She had done her best to hide her face on both occasions. She was just coming to the thought that passing through the village had been a big mistake when, to her horror, she saw a policeman cycling up the side street they were about to cross. She remembered, too late, that the police house was in that street. Grabbing Ben, who was still unaware of the danger, she pulled him into the doorway of the hardware shop, which stood on the corner, where she quietly said, 'Policeman coming, pretend to be window-shopping.' In the reflection of the shop window Jo watched as he turned into the main street and continued his slow progress in the direction they would need to take.

The couple watched the policeman drawing away while waving to various folk who greeted him as he passed. Suddenly, the door of the hardware shop opened with the tinkling of its overhead bell. 'Can I help you?' enquired the overall-clad figure who emerged. 'Oh, hello Jo, it's you! You're back then? Your dad's been so worried about you, how is he?' Before Jo had time to respond, the kindly man continued, 'So, he's sent you down to ask about the wire, has he? Well tell him I'm still trying, but wire is difficult to come by these days. I often see his new man passing by on his way home, what's his name? Oh yes, Graham, that's it. I'll let Graham know if I have any success with that wire. I must admit, I didn't recognise you at first, dressed like that. What's the world coming to?' The tinkling bell was still ringing in her ears for several seconds after the owner had slipped back into the shop, closing the door behind him.

Chapter 15

It would have been easy for the horse-drawn caravan to be unnoticed as it nestled amongst the bushes beneath the canopy of a large wooded area on the north side of Guildford. There had been no visitors since they had set up the camp on arrival in the secluded spot, carefully chosen by Patrick Stibbs. However, this day was to be different. The soldiers, a subaltern leading three old-time regulars, had come upon them after spotting smoke rising above the trees. The designated task of this team was to acquire horses and mules by whatever means possible. These animals were badly needed in France for the transportation of men and supplies, as well as the hauling of heavy guns, ambulances, barges and broken-down vehicles of all sorts. The life expectancy of these creatures was short, not so much due to gun-fire and explosives, but mainly through sheer exhaustion and malnutrition.

Mavis, who was in the process of tying sprigs of heather, looked up as the four uniform-clad figures emerged from the bushes. ‘Okay lads, untie the horse,’ barked Subaltern Grey.

Addressing himself to Mavis, he said, 'Madam, I am authorised by the War Office to commandeer your horse. I assume it *is* your horse?'

'You can't take our 'orse,' expostulated Mavis as she dropped the heather and jumped to her feet. 'It's private property.'

'Not any more, madam. It belongs to the army now. If you care to give me your name and permanent address, I'll write you a receipt so that you can be compensated in due course.'

'We ain't got a permanent address! *This* is our 'ome,' wailed Mavis. 'You can't do this to us, it ain't right.'

During the brief encounter the soldiers had untied the horse and placed a rope around its neck. 'Okay, men, take it away. Turning back to Mavis, he asked, 'Name?'

'The 'orse belongs to Patrick Stibbs. You wait till my 'usband gets back from his work. He won't let you get away with this,'

Slipping a notebook from his tunic pocket, the subaltern wrote the name and said, 'Shall we say "Care of woodlands north of Guildford?" I suggest he takes it up with the King. Good day madam.' As the subaltern pushed through the bushes in the wake of his men, the irate woman shouted, *'A curse on you!'* before sinking down and bursting into a mixture of tears and muttered curses.

~~~

Sergeant Edwards arrived at Meadow Farm, pushing his bicycle which had a very flat front tyre. He was not happy and continued cursing the misfortune of getting a puncture from one of the many pot-holes along the lane. He passed through the gate into the yard where he carefully propped the bicycle against the wall at the front of the house. His frustration increased as his knocking at the front door of the house remained un-answered.

'Hello? Anyone about?' The loud call had no result, apart from the fluttering wings of a disturbed pigeon which had been pecking at something on the ground nearby. Looking in all directions as the studs of his size ten boots rang on the cobbles, the irate policeman crossed the yard, heading for the barn. It was at that moment that Graham, holding a walking stick, stepped out into the sunlight. 'Ah, someone at last,' said Sergeant Edwards.
~~~

'The boss is up on the top field, can I help?' asked Graham.

'When do you expect him to return?'

'Won't be long now. He sent me on ahead to fetch his stick as his leg has started playing him up. It's been a bit of a search, finding it in that barn. If you would like to wait here, I'll go up and let him know you're here. We've finished what we were doing up there.'

Removing his helmet for a moment, to scratch his head, the sergeant replied, 'Okay, I'm in no hurry. I'll wait here then.' With Graham gone, Sergeant Edwards, with helmet back in place, and hands clasped behind his back, slowly walked around the yard while peering at the various buildings that enclosed it. It was as the policeman entered the open shed which housed the heavy equipment, that Jo and Ben came to the edge of the wood through which they had been silently and cautiously walking. Having crept from the shelter of the trees and along the side of the barn, Jo gave a quick glance around the deserted yard. She breathed a sigh of relief and was about to step into the open when she spotted the bicycle propped against the wall of the house. She quickly took a pace backward and, in doing so, accidently stepped on Ben's foot.

'Ouch!'

'Shh! The policeman is here! I think it's his bike I saw,' whispered Jo.

'What do we do now?' asked Ben, quietly.

'Wait and watch, I suppose. They must be in the house.'

A moment later, the police sergeant emerged from the shed and continued his slow amble around the yard. Startled by the sudden appearance of the policeman patrolling the yard, Jo turned and grabbed Ben, pulling him back toward the woods. 'He's on the lookout. We'll need to move further round to see what's happening.' Having found a spot amongst some bushes where they could clearly see the yard, they cautiously watched the policeman who, at that moment, was checking his pocket watch. A few minutes later, Jo's heart leaped as, with bated breath, she saw her father limping into the yard while leaning heavily on his stick. He was accompanied by a man she instantly recognised from their encounter in the darkness, so long ago it now seemed to her. The policeman stepped forward as the two men approached, but unfortunately, they were too far away for Jo to be able to hear what was being said.

'Good afternoon, sergeant,' said Phil. 'Have you come with some news?'

'Only to let you know that our men have been checking the canal. No luck, I'm afraid, although one of the constables reported his suspicion's concerning two youngsters, he encountered in Odiham last night. He thought one of them, although dressed as a boy, could have been a girl. They said they were working on a boat named ..' pausing to retrieve his notebook from his breast-pocket, he flipped it open and continued, '*Dancing Lady*. However, it has been established that no such boat has ever called into Odiham Wharf. They did investigate another narrowboat currently moored there,' glancing again at his notebook, '*Red Rose*, a family-run boat, apparently. A married couple with a son of around seventeen and young daughter of about six or seven. They say they haven't seen anyone fitting Johanna's description. They were kind enough, apparently, to allow our man on board to look around.' For a moment Sergeant Edwards paused before clearing his throat.

'Well?' said the exasperated farmer anxiously.

'Mr Simons, I must inform you that it's now unlikely that we will find the runaway, and that we will no longer be pursuing active enquiries. I'm sorry.'

There followed a moment of stunned silence as Phil let out a long breath while taking in what had just been said, Graham noticed the vein thickening on his boss's neck and the colour of his face becoming purple as anxiety turned into anger. *'What? You mean to say you've abandoned her?'* demanded the angry father. *'You know why she went away, man. It was plain and simple fear. She's not a runaway!'* Calming down slightly, he muttered, 'She's a frightened girl who doesn't know it's safe to come home.'

'Well, of course,' responded the embarrassed policeman. 'Needless to say, we will let you know of any developments should they crop up in the future.'

'So, that's it, then!' demanded Phil. 'Well, I would thank you for leaving these premises, *now!* And be assured, that I will never give up on my daughter. Good day to you, sir!'

Both men watched as Sergeant Edwards silently walked over to his bicycle. Lifting the machine upright from the wall and looking at the front tyre he turned in Phil’s direction and asked, ‘You wouldn’t happen to have ….? Oh, never mind’ wheeling the bicycle, he started his thoughtful walk through the gate and back toward the village. None of the three were aware of the youngsters who had already slipped away, having been convinced that the police must be closely watching the farm and not having heard any of the conversation they had just silently witnessed.

~~~

‘What ya mean, they took the ‘orse? Who took it?’

‘Them soldiers, four of ‘em. Just walked in and took him. Said ‘e was needed for the army.’

‘What did they pay for ‘im?’

‘Nothin’. They said we’d be compensated, though ‘ow and when that might be, gawd knows.’
~~~

'So, you just let 'em take him, you stupid mare. *Now we're stuck 'ere!'*

'How could I 'ave stopped 'em? Four of them with guns, and just me on me own. If you'd bin 'ere instead of rolling around with one of yer floosies, I doubt you would 'ave done anything to stop 'em either.'

'What do we do without an 'orse? It's all that girl's fault. Back at the farm. If she 'adn't pitchforked me we'd still be there.'

'Well, I'll tell you this, Pat. I ain't gonna stay stuck 'ere in these bushes while your off stickin' yer cock-robin into places where it don't belong. I'm off to our Lil's where I can 'ave a proper bath and a knees-up. Yer on yer own.' It was at that point that Patrick noticed the bulging bag resting on the top step.

'You go now, and you don't never come back!' shouted Patrick as his wife picked up the bag and descended the steps.

'That's alright with me, I'm done with you anyhow. This life ain't the life I wanna live anymore. If you wants an 'orse, go join the army. I 'spect they'll 'ave plenty that needs lookin' after.' Having said that, Mavis heaved the bag onto her shoulder and headed for the gap between the bushes.

'Mav? *Mav!* I never meant it. *Come back, Mav!'* She was gone.

'She'll be back,' muttered Patrick to himself. 'And as for that snotty-nosed girl. If ever I see her again…'

Chapter 16

It was a week later when *Red Rose* started loading at the coal depot in London. Marge, with Jo's help, had carefully secured all hatches and windows and placed old towelling in the gap beneath the cabin door. She was aware that, even with those precautions, coal dust would inevitably find its way into her clean and tidy cabin.

'Well, luv, that's all we can do,' said Marge with a sigh. 'Just have to try and keep on top of it.' She was not unduly perturbed however, for such was life on a working narrow boat.

It had been with mixed feelings that Jo had arrived back at the boat that evening after the failed visit to the farm. She had been broken hearted as they had walked away from the yard, having seen her father looking so sad and weak, and very much dependent on his walking stick. The walk back had been hard, although Ben had done his best to reassure her that things would work out [illegible] the end. The one uplifting factor for Jo was the fact that Gra-[illegible] the poacher, had followed up on her advice and gone to work at the farm. When they arrived back at the boat, Jo had been overcome by the welcome she had received. Still smothered in Marge's arms she had been amused to see Beth's grinning face peering round the drawn curtain of her parent's bed. During that time, Ben had remained outside with his father, where he gave Ed an account of all that had taken place at the farm. It was not long before Marge had prepared a simple meal of potato and carrot soup, with freshly baked bread, for the couple, although Jo had found that she had little appetite, following her disappointing day. Apart from any other concerns playing on her mind, she had also been aware of an undercurrent of emotion passing between Ed and Ben.

Later, after the table had been cleared and stowed, and Beth's tiredness had finally overcome her excitement, they all retired to their respective beds. For Jo, sleep had been far off, as her mind dwelt upon all that she had witnessed at the farm. It was clear by the policeman's presence, and the heated discussion that had taken place in the yard, that she was a wanted person. Jo remembered thinking, *if only I could have let dad know that I'm okay.*

That thought had repeatedly rolled around in her mind as she had tossed around in the confined space of the side-bed that night.

Jo had been about to roll into a more comfortable position that night, when she had heard Ed's whispering voice behind their bed curtain, 'Ben's intending to sign up when we get to London.'

'Oh, the daft bugger,' whispered Marge. 'Couldn't you stop him?'

'He won't listen. He says he has to do it.'

'Rubbish! He doesn't have to do any such thing. We needs 'im 'ere; didn't you tell 'im that?'

'I did. He just said that now we've got Jo to help, we'll be no worse off.'

'What if Jo's discovered, or just wants to leave? What could we do?'

'If she's discovered, we'll stand by her. If she wants to leave us, and I hope she won't, we'll just have to let her go.'

The whispered conversation had stopped at that point, although Jo remembered Marge sobbing for a long while before sleep overtook her.

That had been a week ago. True to his word, yesterday Ben had walked to the nearest recruitment office once the unloading of timber had finished. She could still remember that stupid grin on his face when he returned three hours later. With his head held high and his chest pushed forward, he told them triumphantly, ‘They’ve accepted me. When I told him I work the canals, the sergeant said I would probably go straight over as they desperately need experienced hands for those French canals. I’m to report back tomorrow at ten.’

It had been a strained evening as they finally sat down for their meal. The little cabin, which Jo had come to love, with its friendly and cosy atmosphere, suddenly seemed gloomy and cramped within the silence that had descended upon the family. Ed was still fuming, while Marge constantly fought back her tears. Beth, frightened by the strained atmosphere, remained unusually quiet. Looking across the space at Ben, who was perched on the second tread of the steps, giving his full attention to his plate, Jo was confused by her feelings. She felt hurt, in the same way she had when John had marched away. She had long since, given up arguing with her friend. However, when it came to the time to face the fact that Ben was actually going, she was surprised how much she cared. She knew that she would miss the company of her new friend, his knowledge of the wildlife they encountered, his confidence and strength, his patience in the early days as he had taught her all that she should know about his way of life. Okay, he didn't waste his words or laugh as much as she would like, but that didn't matter, or distract her growing affection for him.

If Jo had been harbouring a determination to move on, she now felt that she should stay with the family who had so readily taken her in. Was it out of a sense of obligation or the thought of losing contact with Ben all together? She didn't know.

After a restless night, Jo had watched Ben walk away until he disappeared around the corner of a warehouse fronting the quay. His goodbyes had been brief. A handshake for his father, a hug for his mother, a pickup and squeeze for Beth, and a nod for Jo whose day had just become much darker, although not by the clouds of coal-dust that filled the air and filtered into the cabin.

~~~
~~~

‘You have a visitor, John.’

‘Peering around Nurse Farley, John was both surprised and delighted to see Sergeant Langley, arm in a sling, standing close behind her. ‘You can have ten minutes Sergeant, no more,’ said the exhausted nurse as she turned away. ‘He’s still weak and the infection has returned. I’ll be back soon.’ Pushing a camp chair behind his knees, she said, ‘Sit here,’ and was gone.

‘Hello, Sarge,’ greeted John. ‘It’s good of you to find the time to come.’ Glancing at the sling he enquired, ‘What’s happened to your arm?’

‘Oh, just a flesh wound, nothing to write home about. What about you, young man? It sounded serious when I asked about you.’

Collapsed lung apparently. Breathing’s a bit hard. A bit of infection, they say. Feeling a bit weak. Soon be back with the lads I shouldn’t wonder.’

‘No, Lad. You’re on your way to Blighty just as soon as they can move you on. You won’t be much use to the platoon now.’

John thought about that for a moment, with mixed feelings, then said 'I'm sorry, Sarge. I never wanted to leave like this.'

'Nothing for you to be sorry about …. apart that is … I should tell you that your mate Norman never made it, along with so many other good men, I'm sorry. I know you were close.'

Remaining silent for a moment, John eventually said, 'He worked for us … on the farm. A good hand, as well as a friend. He fancied my sister, Jo. He might even have become my brother-in-law one day. I would have liked that.'

'I'm really sorry to bring you such sad news, but thought you should know before returning home. Now you just concentrate on getting well again, so we can share a drink in the sergeant's mess one day when you've got your third stripe.'

True to her word, Nurse Farley returned at the end of ten minutes and gently took the sergeant's good arm to lead him away. It was only then, that John realised the sergeant was blind. He was not to know that he would never see his solid mentor again, a brave man who was soon to lose his life when the troop-ship taking him back to England was sunk by a German submarine.

~~~

Life for Polly and Graham continued in domestic harmony. The shock of losing her husband had diminished as Polly buried herself in her work. She was comforted by the routine of Graham's comings and goings each day, and pleased that her lodger seemed a lot happier now that he had a regular job with a steady income. Polly had argued when Graham insisted upon paying extra for his rent, saying that she had kept him without complaint when things had been tough for the ex-poacher.

Nothing was said about the one night when Polly had slept in his arms, although she often thought about it as she went about her work. Would she have resisted if he had wanted more than to comfort her? She didn't know, although she sometimes wondered what it would have been like to feel his hands on her nakedness. Polly was aware that Graham still worried about the missing girl. As much as she told him it wasn't his fault, he continued blaming himself for not being more forceful in convincing the girl to return
~~~

home. He even blamed himself for finding the encounter a little amusing at the time.

Last evening, while they had sat eating by the light of the oil lamp, Graham had said that he was thinking of going off to search for the girl, if only he could be spared from the farm. However, during the sowing season would not be a good time for him to leave Phil on his own. It worried Polly that this good man should be carrying such a burden, so much so, that she had reached across the table and taken his hand into hers, caressing it as she said, 'You're a good man, Graham. I know you will always do what is right, and I love you for it.' The words were out before she fully realised what she was saying. 'I just meant …' flustered, she faltered for a moment before continuing, 'I just meant, I'll support you in whatever you decide to do.'

That had been last evening and she had had time during the day to think about what she had blurted out. *Do I love him? I suppose, in a way that I do, but am I "in" love with him? No, It's not possible, it's not appropriate, it's too soon. Anyhow, he's never given me any indication of a relationship beyond friendship. Be sensible, must be sensible. It's just my hormones being upset after losing my husband.*

~~~

Graham had spent a long day sitting on the hard saddle of the tiller which was effortlessly pulled across the field by Blacky and Champ. After discreetly knocking on the door, he entered the farm house to let Phil know that the horses were fed and settled for the night. Looking around the untidy kitchen, his concern for his boss increased. It was easily apparent that he was not coping. The kitchen sink and draining board were cluttered with a variety of dirty dishes, the tiled floor was mostly hidden by drying mud. The table was hidden by empty bottles and unread newspapers and mail. His concern increased as he saw Phil slumped in the easy chair by the empty fireplace, his stockinged feet resting on the guard, with his muddy boots dropped on the floor in front of him.

'All finished, Phil. Is everything alright? Have you eaten, or even made yourself a drink?' It was at that moment that he noticed the buff letter held in Phil's hand. 'Not bad news, I hope?'
~~~

'It's from some officer in my boy's regiment, telling me he's been seriously wounded and will be transferred home once he's fit enough for the journey. Doesn't say how serious though.'

'Oh, I'm sorry to hear that, Phil. At least he'll be out of it for a bit, possibly for the duration.'

'I suppose you're right, the daft thing is, I'm hoping it's so serious, he can never go back. What sort of father am I, to want his son to be permanently disabled?'

'Phil, it's just your heart taking over your senses. At least, you'll be seeing him again, and hopefully, soon.'

'Yea, I suppose you're right,' replied Phil. 'That's not all though. I had a visit from the mother of my labourer, Norman, this afternoon. To let me know that he won't be coming back. She was quite matter-of-fact, even apologised. I felt useless, didn't know what to say to her.'

'You've had quite a day, Phil. Do you want me to tidy up in here and knock you up a meal before I go?'

'No, you're a good man, Graham. It's been a long day, I'll be okay.'

'Tell you what, Phil, get those boots on and come back and eat with us. Polly won't mind, she often says she'd like to meet you. Then we could go to *The Feathers* for a pint or two.'

At first, Phil had declined the offer, but Graham's insistence won the day. Polly was indeed pleased, an hour later, when Phil turned up with Graham. She had no difficulty in stretching the stew. Her lively conversation had the desired effect of lifting Phil's black mood. By the time the two men stepped through the doorway of the cheerful public bar, he was even managing the odd smile. Friends were quick to greet him and it wasn't long before they were on their second free pint as they stood at the crowded bar. One of the men who had been playing Dominoes at a low table near the fire, eventually came over to Phil with a half-empty pint of ale in his fist, and said, 'Evening, Phil. Glad to see your Jo's back, did she give you the message about the wire?'

'Jo? Back? What are you talking about, Frank?'

'She came to my shop over a week ago, her and a lad. I told her I was still trying to get that wire you ordered,' replied the mystified man. 'Didn't she come home?'

'No. Are you sure it was her?' asked Phil as he placed his jug down on the bar-top.

'Oh, it were her alright. Dressed like a boy, but it was certainly your Jo. I would know that sweet kid anywhere.'

'What day did you say that was?' enquired Graham, butting in on the conversation.

'Let me see … yes, it would have been Tuesday week, I know that because that's the day I do my morning deliveries and I hadn't long been back in the shop.'

Turning to Phil, Graham said, 'Hang on a minute! If I'm not very much mistaken, that's the day the police sergeant called to tell you they've given up. If your Jo saw him at the farm …'

'She wouldn't have come in,' Phil quietly finished the sentence. 'Oh, my god, she was so close. *Damn the man!* Why did he have to come on that day of all days?'

'At least you know she's safe,' said Graham, 'and it would seem, she's got a friend, she's not on her own.' For a moment neither of the men spoke, as both were lost in their thoughts. Placing down his empty jug, Graham broke their silence, saying, 'Phil, I wouldn't want to get your hopes up too much, but I'm becoming more and more convinced she's on the Basingstoke Canal. Do you remember that policeman saying a narrowboat had been berthed in Odiham Wharf when they were searching that morning? He said there were just two adults and a child on board. Don't you think that's a bit short-handed? What if Jo's friend was one of that family and she's living with them? It fits. The police wouldn't have seen them on the boat because they were on their way here. I wish I could remember the name of that boat,' continued Graham. 'Phil, if it's alright with you, I'll pop in to the police house tomorrow and ask the sergeant if he can tell me the name of the boat. He had it written down in his notebook.'

Chapter 17

It was Friday, two days later, when Graham arrived at Odiham Wharf. Driving the farm wagon over the humpy bridge, he noticed a large open-decked barge tied to the quay but no sign of a narrowboat. With a feeling of disappointment, he turned into the wharf and was soon in conversation with one of the workers, an elderly toothless man who was busy stacking timber.

'*Red Rose*, you say? Why are you asking?'

'I have a friend who works on her and he mentioned that they are often down this way.'

'Well, we're not supposed to give out information to anyone concerning movement along the canal. What with the war on and everything. For all I know, you could be an enemy agent.'

'But I'm not,' replied Graham while trying not to let his frustration show.

'How would I know that? No, I'm sorry, I can't help you.' The man made no attempt to carry on with his interrupted work as he waited expectantly.

'Would ten shillings make any difference?' asked Graham while reaching into his pocket.

'A pound!' replied the man without hesitation.

'Seven and six and that's it,' said Graham firmly.

'By my reckoning, *Red Rose* is due to return after the weekend. Can't say for sure. She's most likely on her way back from London by now.'

'Do you know the family?' asked Graham hopefully.

'A pound might help me to remember,' came the reply.

'Ten shillings.'

'Family by the name of Simons. Husband's a Number One, which means he's the owner. Wife and two kids, a lad and a little girl. Had another lad with them last time they were here. Never seen him before.'

My god, it has to be her, thought Graham. *I was right, she's on the canal and what's more she's on that boat!*

'Thank you, you've been most helpful,' said Graham.

'Not me, mister,' replied the old man with a wink. 'Never said a word.'

It was late in the afternoon when Graham steered the horses into the farm yard where Phil was leaning on his stick, as he had been for several hours, waiting for Graham's return. 'Looks like I was right, Phil,' he called as he pulled on the reins and applied the break with his foot. 'That boat family has apparently gained a new crew member, according to a chap working on the wharf. I think it's possible that the new lad on that boat is your Jo. With your permission, I intend going back to the wharf over the weekend, and will stay until *Red Rose* returns. I noticed the pub overlooking the canal has rooms to let, so I can stay there for as long as it takes.'

'Thank you, Graham.' replied Phil. 'I'm much obliged to you. I do hope you're right and that it is Jo on that boat, and that she stays with them till they get back. I'll pay you any out-of-pocket expenses of course, whichever way it goes. Get yourself home, Graham. I'll see to the horses.'

'No, we'll do it together, Phil.'

Passing through the village, on his way home, Graham called into *The Feathers* and purchased a bottle of white wine. He was elated with his success and intended celebrating with Polly that evening. *With luck, Phil will have his two children back home on the farm. But what about my own future?* he asked himself. He had settled at the farm which had given him a new life, and purpose, as well as self-respect. He liked Phil, a fair man and a hard worker when his leg allowed it. He could be about to lose it all, then what? Poaching. The thought of that possibility was enough to dampen his spirit. But then, hadn't they employed an extra hand before the war? The one who had been killed? If Phil's son wasn't able to go back, because of his injuries, whatever they were, they would definitely still need him. Suddenly his mood revived, *Yes! They will still need me on that farm. With my help, I know it has the potential of bigger and better things. They have land that's not even being used.*

At last, the welcoming light of the cottage came into sight. He had much to tell Polly about the day's events. He felt the final burden lifted from his shoulders as he pushed open the door into the warm kitchen.

'Hello love, you're a bit later than I expected, dinner's in the oven, I hope it hasn't spoiled, it's a bacon roll with roast potatoes.'

'It certainly smells good,' replied Graham as he suddenly realised how hungry he was, after his long journey that day. I've bought a bottle of wine, I hope you like it, where celebrating. I think I've found Jo.'

'Really! So, she *is* on the canal, as you thought? Go and get changed while I dish up, then tell me all about it. And yes, I do like wine, although I haven't had any for ages.' With a smile, Polly turned back to the oven to lift out the pan of potatoes to give them a final turn.

With the plates cleared, and glasses refilled, Graham finished his account of the day's events. 'So, I'll be returning to the canal straight after milking tomorrow morning. If I have to stay there for a day, or two, I'll get a room at the local pub, till my boat comes in, as they say.'

'Let's hope you're right, Graham. That family's been through so much. I've just had a thought. You said, the other day, that the farmhouse is in a state.'

'Still is,' responded Graham.

'Well, why don't I come over there with you in the morning and offer to give it the woman's touch, ready for Jo's return?'

'Are you sure you want to do that?'

'If you think he won't be offended?'

Rising from his chair, Graham stepped around the table and placed his hand on her shoulder as he planted a kiss on Polly's cheek. 'You're a treasure, Polly.'

Just for a moment, they remained still, with Graham's hand resting on Polly's shoulder, before she lifted herself from the table and stepped into his arms. It all happened so suddenly and unexpectedly. Polly lifted her head to look into Graham's eye for a brief moment before their lips met. Graham marvelled at the softness of her warm inviting lips. He could taste the wine she had been sipping a moment before. Tenderly, she lifted her hand to the back of Graham's neck. His hair was thick as it cascaded over the back of her hand. As the kiss continued, Graham squeezed Polly's soft body closer to his own and allowed his hand to slide to the small of her back. It was all so natural, so right. Slowly, Polly drew back from the kiss and gazed into the single eye of this honest, caring man, in whose arms she felt so secure.

'Polly, I love you, have done, for a long time,' breathed Graham.

Stepping away from the embrace, Polly continued looking into Graham's eye. She saw uncertainty, integrity, desire. Slowly she took his hand and, without a word, led him to the stairs.

In her bedroom, Polly walked over to the dresser and lit two candles before turning back to Graham who was standing uncertainly in the doorway.

'Close the door,' she said quietly.

As he started to do as he was told, Polly smiled and said, 'With you on the inside, silly.'

The climax, for both, was intense and somewhat sooner than either of them expected. Polly, in her simplicity, would never have described it as something like breasting a hill in a glorious sunset, with birds singing their evening choruses all around them. No, for her, it was the consummation of a growing love for a man with whom she wanted to spend the rest of her life.

As the sated couple lay resting on the pillows in the soft candle-light, Graham said, 'Polly, I know it's too soon, but if at some point in the future you should consider the possibility of re-marrying, would you entertain a proposal from me?'

'No, Graham, I won't do that in the future, although if you were to ask me right now, the answer would be, "Yes!"

'Oh, Polly, I do love you, you forward huzzy. Will you marry me?'

'Yes, Graham, there's nothing I could ever want more. I will marry you just as soon as we can get things sorted with the War Office, or whoever.'

A simple breakfast of dripping on toast was eaten in the dimness of the pre-dawn light seeping through the kitchen window. Polly prepared a packed lunch for both of them, while Graham washed the dishes which included those that had been left from the previous evening. Polly was quietly humming a tune which was not familiar to Graham. 'You sound happy this morning, Polly,' he observed. 'Has something special happened?' he asked with a grin.

'No, nothing particularly.' she replied. 'Just an ordinary evening ravishing my lodger. A little more interesting than knitting I suppose.'

'Is that so? I hope you enjoyed it?'

'Well, it helped to pass the time.'

'Well, in that case, I'll have to find something equally interesting for you to do this evening, won't I? Can't have you moping around while I seduce my landlady, can I?'

'Sir! You are an uncouth beast, and I love you.'

'And I, you.' Graham dried his hands as he spoke and before taking Polly into his arms. 'You have made me so happy, my love. Let's hope that very soon, Phil will know happiness again with his two children at home by his fireside.'

With the sky behind them changing from deep purple to red, Polly felt that she wanted to skip like a child as she walked through the still deserted village alongside Graham. The desire to do such a thing would have been rather difficult in reality. For in one hand, she was carrying a bucket which contained all that she felt would be required to get that kitchen looking as all good kitchens should. In the other, she was holding a small suitcase, last used for a holiday in Normandy with her parents before the unfortunate event which was to change her life for ever. Within the case were her night-clothes, a change of underwear, and basic toiletries. It had been Graham's idea that Polly could accompany him to the canal, thinking that female company might further encourage the girl to return to the farm. Although, if he was being totally honest, the thought of spending two or three nights away with his fiancé may have been a contributing factor to his suggestion. At first, she had declined the invitation, thinking about the cleaning waiting to be done. It was the possibility of a complete change in her dull routine that finally persuaded her. The thought of spending time with Graham, seeing new places, spending a night or two in a cosy Inn by the canal like a married couple. The temptation became too great.

Walking beside Graham as they left the village behind them, she thought about last evening, the tender love-making, Graham's proposal of marriage, her future with this lovely man who had entered her life and captured her heart. Regardless of the many cruel blows life had dealt him, he had matured into a good trustworthy and confident man with a caring and gentle nature. His proposal had been a surprise in the afterglow of their lovemaking, but she had had no hesitation in accepting. Her love for this man walking beside her had taken a while to grow. In the early days of his boarding in her cottage, she had enjoyed the warmth of his company, his good humour, his interesting accounts of his former life, his willingness to help around the house. The seeds of love were resting beneath the surface, not visible, undisturbed. The growth of that seed was slow but sure. At first, hardly noticed amidst the easy conversations during the evenings before Graham had to leave to go about his nocturnal work. The seed had slowly matured into a comfortable friendship, each living their separate lives but happy to relax in each other's company when time allowed. The seed had developed into a visible plant, a plant with tender leaves of concern, of trust, of interest, loyalty and support. The bud was detectable to the discerning eye, tightly closed as the faithful married woman silently prayed for the husband who was away over the sea fighting for his country, the husband who had little time for his wife beyond taking all that she had to offer, and giving nothing in return. That bud grew larger, but remained closed. The time for its revelation was still to come. Within the tightly closed folds of that bud was a woman whose passion had slept for too long, who had so much warmth to share with the right person. In a brief moment of total abandonment, the bud had opened to reveal its beauty, its colour, its fragrance and its strength as it blossomed into fulfilment. How had she been so unaware of the true depth of her feelings for this solid man walking beside her? They say, "Love is blind," she could now see the truth of that statement. She had indeed been blind to the reality of her feelings for this man who had not only come into her life, but had now *become* her life.

They were greeted by Phil as they entered the yard in the first light of dawn. He showed his surprise as he took in the sight of the grinning couple. 'Good morning, Polly. What brings you here so early in the morning? Are you looking for more customers? If you are …'

'No, Mr Simons,' Polly quickly replied. 'I thought you might like a little help tidying the house before your daughter returns. I'm free for the day and happy to help, if you will allow me.'

'Well, I must admit, the place is far short of my Jo's standards,' replied Phil as he removed his cap to scratch his head. 'But what's with the suitcase? Are you planning on staying?'

'No, Phil,' interrupted Graham. 'I suggested that Polly could accompanying me to meet *Red Rose*. We both feel that Jo, if she's on board, will be more comfortable with a woman for company when she returns with us. We'll be setting off later this afternoon if that's okay with you? We may be gone for a couple of days. If you like, I can pop down to Farmer Gill's to see if he can spare someone to help you while I'm away.'

Turning to Polly, the grateful man said, 'How can I ever thank you? First, the meal on Wednesday, now giving up your time in this way. Come into the kitchen and have a warm drink, have you had breakfast, my dear?'

'Yes, we've both eaten,' replied Polly with a smile. 'Actually, I wonder if, before starting work, I can watch the milking?'

A short while later, the cows having found their own way to the milking shed, as they did every morning, had each taken a separate stall where they were contentedly munching fresh hay. Polly stood back as Graham took his place on a low stool beside the rump of the first to be milked. She was fascinated by the deft movement of his hands as he gently squeezed the teats, at the same time she felt her cheeks flush as she remembered all that had passed between her and Graham long into the previous night.

'Fancy, having a try?' Graham looked up with a huge grin on his face as he addressed his startled fiancé.

'Yes please,' she replied hesitantly, 'I don't know if I'll be any good at it, though.'

'You'll be a natural, I'm sure,' Graham replied, still grinning as he stood to allow Polly to take his place on the stool. 'It's as simple as …'

He didn't finish whatever he was about to say, as Polly quickly interjected, 'Move over, let's have a go.'

Chapter 18

Jo hadn't realised just how much she would miss the companionship of Ben. Walking along the bank, windlass in hand, she reflected upon the fact that, when she had been talking and listening to her friend, she had completely forgotten the fact that she was a wanted person. At those times, she had felt alive and normal. Now, trying to distract herself with her observation of the wildlife along the bank, didn't have the desired effect. Ben had always been there to tell her about all the plants, animals and insects they came across. The colour of her life on the canal was gone. Handling the locks took twice as long unless Ed came forward to assist, which he often did.

'You've done really well, Jo,' said Ed a while later when the last lock before Odiham came into view. He had joined her for this last one. 'It's just as though you've spent your life on the canal. Lucky for us you were here to take Ben's place. It's a good life, out in the open, away from crowds and folk hurrying all over the place.' With a sigh, he continued, 'I just don't know how much longer it'll last. The railway's taking over. Much faster than the canal, by far. Companies don't want to wait for their goods anymore. Some of the canals are already being neglected and silting up. This one's only surviving because of the war, and the army needing it. I just don't know what the future holds for the likes of us.' Shaking his head, he continued, 'I may even have to sell at some point in the not-too-distant future. Lord knows what'll happen to us then.'

Looking into his troubled weather-beaten face Jo replied, 'I'm sorry to hear that, Ed. I didn't realise things were so bad.'

'No, it's me who should apologies, lass. What with all your troubles, here's me banging on when your future's much more uncertain than ours. I'll tell you this though, you've got a home with us for as long as you need it, no matter what, or where. My Marge and little Beth love having you with us.' He briefly paused before saying quietly, 'And so do I.'

Touched by Ed's embarrassment, and what he had said, Jo stopped walking and gave the startled skipper a big hug.

'Thank you, Ed, and I love being with you all. You're my second family now.'

Following that shared moment, they continued walking together, in companiable silence until they arrived at the lock.

~~~

They had registered at *The Swan* as Mr & Mrs Stephens the previous afternoon, having stabled the horses and checked that there were no narrowboats resting at the quay. Polly had been in her element earlier that day before they left the farm on the wagon. She had been quietly singing most of the time as she had washed, dusted and swept throughout the farmhouse. It had given her some satisfaction knowing that she was working close to Graham who was busily repairing some equipment in the lean-too next to the milking shed. Every so often throughout the morning, Phil had popped in to enquire if she needed anything, and to compliment her on the singing and the progress being made in his home. At first, he had been embarrassed with the state in which he had allowed the house to become. Following Polly's reassurances of her understanding, he began to relax and allow her to do what she had come to do.
~~~

Sunday was a cold clear autumn day in which, after a hearty cooked breakfast served by the jovial landlord, they were free to wonder along the canal towpath, kicking the dried leaves as they did so. Polly had marvelled at the fact that she had had no idea that all of this tranquil beauty was so close to her home.

With amusement, they had enjoyed watching the antics of a group of mallards and the gracefully regal movement of two swans which had swum over from the opposite bank to investigate the passing of the visitors. Graham could still hardly believe that the delightful woman holding onto has arm, was soon to be his wife. His life had so dramatically changed over the last few weeks, from an unsuccessful poacher, to an employed farmhand who had become engaged to a woman who had declared her love for him.

Later that day, the happy couple, were standing on the parapet of the humpy bridge watching the ever-changing colours of a beautiful sunset. Their first full day together, had had a magical quality to it. They had enjoyed a relaxed pub lunch in the village of Broad Oak, before, hand-in-hand, slowly making their way back along the towpath to Odiham wharf. On return to *The Swan,* they had booked a further night before meandering down to the bridge to watch the sunset.

Turning his back to the dipping sun, Graham leaned back onto the parapet wall as he looked at Polly's face, now glowing in the light of the setting sun. He took her into his arms and kissed her soft willing lips. As he contentedly pulled away, he was distracted by movement over her shoulder in the gathering dusk. 'It's a boat!' he stated. 'There's a narrowboat coming up. It has to be *Red Rose,* surely!'

Quickly, they both crossed the road to the other wall and peered into the distance. A short while later, Graham said, 'Looks like a man leading a horse with a child on it. There's a lad steering the boat.' A moment later, he quietly said, 'Can't see anyone else. That man told me there was a family of four on *Red Rose,* plus a lad who had recently joined them. I can only see three on this one. They continued watching as the boat came closer at its sedate pace. The silence was suddenly broken as a blackbird started its evening song. It would have been a perfectly romantic moment as the horse, which now took on the form of a mule, approached the quay, the boat silently moving through the calm still water, the beautiful melody of the bird, a couple, very much in love, with the red orb behind them. Graham however, was unable to appreciate the tranquil moment as disappointment dampened his previous excitement. *There are only three of them, it should have been five,* was all he could think.

Approaching the wharf, Jo held the tiller, while Marge was below starting her preparations for the evening meal. Ed was leading Skippy with Beth sitting astride. Jo was peering directly into the sinking sun, judging the moment when she should steer for the quay. Although shielding her eyes with her hand, she was unable to see the two silhouetted figures standing on the humpy bridge, watching their approach.

'Okay, Jo. Pass me the stern rope,' called Ed who had finished securing the bow line a few minutes later. *'Beth wants you to go with her to the stable, do you mind?'*

'Not at all. I'll enjoy that,' replied Jo. As she stepped onto the bank where Beth, already walking Skippy, was calling, *'Come on Jo!'*

'Coming' called Jo as she picked up her pace to catch up with the girl and mule before they had gone too far down the lane.

Graham had suddenly come alive as he heard the man call out to Jo to pass a line.

'It *is* them, and that's Jo, it must be!' he said with renewed excitement. I can't see her clearly in this light, or the boat's name, but I bet that's our girl and *Red Rose* down there. Come on, Polly, let's go and see.'

Approaching the gate, Jo was surprised to see two people in the gathering darkness barring her path. Her heart leaped as she recognised Graham the poacher stepping forward, instantly realising that her hiding place had been discovered. What did he want, and who was that woman? Her immediate instinct was to run. She swiftly turned to do just that.

With his voice raised in alarm at the possibility of losing her, Graham called, *'Wait!'* before Jo had taken her first step of flight. 'It's me, Graham. I'm the poacher you bumped into that night over three weeks ago. It's all right, Jo! You didn't kill that man!

He’s not dead? Jo hesitated, still poised to run. She was unable to process what Graham was saying to her.

‘What’s going on here?’ Ed, having heard Graham’s raised voice, had run up the slope with his windlass clutched in his fist. ‘Is this man bothering you, Jo?’ Turning to Graham, he demanded ‘What do you want with my son, mister?’

‘Let me explain,’ replied Graham quickly. ‘I know who Jo is. I know she’s a girl, and I know she is innocent of any crime. The man she thought she killed is very much alive according to the police. Jo’s father is waiting for her to come home to Meadow Farm. She’s not in any sort of trouble.’

With emotions running high there was a tense pause before Jo suddenly buried her face in her hands and burst into tears. Polly, who had been keeping back, swept forward and took the shocked girl into her arms as tears flowed unchecked from both women.

The two men, at a loss for what to do next, stood and watched for a brief moment before Ed asked, ‘How did you find her? It seems you knew she was on my boat. And who exactly are you?’

'I came across Jo late in the night she ran away,' explained Graham. 'She was dressed as a boy, but I knew she was a girl. I was between jobs and out poaching. I told her how to find her way to Odiham. Before she walked on, she told me about Meadow Farm needing workers. I guessed that was where she had come from. It was none of my business so I didn't think much of it at the time. That was a big mistake on my part, and I'm sorry for it. Well, to cut a long story short, I ended up working on the farm, always thinking of the owner's daughter. Remembering that I had pointed her in this direction, I couldn't get it out of my mind that there was the possibility she had somehow taken to the canal. Then, a few days ago, the local police sergeant mentioned that one of the coppers here had encountered a couple of youngsters one evening, acting suspiciously by a shop window. They said they were living on one of the boats. Apparently, one of their men searched your boat sometime later, but didn't find anything.'

'I remember.' interrupted Ed. 'My son, Ben had gone with Jo to the farm to find out what was happening, and to see her dad.'

'Well, it seems they never got there,' replied Graham.

'Oh yes they did,' replied Ed, 'But the police were there, so they came away sharpish. It seems heated words were being exchanged between the constable and Jo's father.'

'Oh, my god! So, Jo was *there* that day! Watching the discussion.'

'Yep. It convinced her she was still wanted by the police.'

As Graham was talking, Marge, having realised something was wrong, had walked up the slope to see for herself what was going on. Seeing Jo's distress, she immediately nudged Polly aside and took Jo into her own arms, which caused more tears to flow from the confused girl as she buried her face into the ample bosom of this woman she now loved as a mother. 'There, there, my little lamb, I'm here, I won't let nuffink bad 'appen to you. You 'ave a good cry, you needs to let it all out.' All the time she was soothing the girl she now regarded as a daughter, she was looking toward Ed and Graham for an explanation.

'She's free, luv,' sighed Ed. 'These are friends who've come here to tell our Jo she can go home. That the man who attacked her, isn't dead after all. She's never been wanted by the police.

They were just looking for her to get her home safely to her dad. That's all. Seems we've all been making mistakes.'

Noticing Beth who was still holding Skippy a short distance away in the gathering darkness, Ed left the group and walked over to her. 'Has something bad happened, Daddy?' asked the worried child who looked as though tears were welling. 'I don't like that man. He looks like a pirate.'

'No, sweetheart. It's good. Jo can go home to her father now.'

'But, Daddy! How can that be good? She's my sister now. Does that mean I'll never see her anymore?'

'I don't know, my luv.' replied Ed who was trying to swallow the lump in his throat. 'She belongs with her own father, you do understand that, don't you?'

'I don't want her to go!' cried Beth as her tears could no longer be held back.

'I know, I know,' repeated Ed as he stooped to hug the distraught girl. 'We don't want her to go, but we have to let her. It's where she belongs, just like you belonging with us.'

With his back to the group, trying to sooth his little girl, Ed was unaware of Jo approaching them, having eased herself from

Marge's arms. 'Don't cry, sweety,' she said as she knelt down to hold Beth. 'You won't be losing me. You'll always have your big sister, you'll see. Now, why don't we go together and get Skippy settled down. We can leave the grown-ups to talk.'

Later, with the mule settled for the night, Jo, with Beth clutching her hand, approached the warm glow of the lamp-lit cabin window. All was quiet in the darkness of the wharf. Jo shuddered with the momentary memory of having been emersed in the cold blackness of the water that night three weeks ago. So much had happened in such a short period of time. She thought she had lost a family, now she had two. She had thought she was wanted for murder, now she was wanted, not by the police but by both families who needed her. She had never before contemplated a relationship with any man, other than her father and brother, now the image of Ben walking away from her on that quay in London, remained in her mind. She had never before been on the water, now she could handle every aspect of life on a working narrowboat. She had never had a mother with whom she could confide, now she had a mother in Marge.

Stepping down into the familiar warm, snug cabin which had become her home, Jo felt truly safe for the first time. The mixed aromas of cooking, polish, and burning lamp oil met her over-stimulated senses. How could she ever leave this haven, she wondered?

'Ah, there you are,' said Marge. 'Dinner's ready, wash yer 'ands, both of you.'

'Your friends are over at *The Swan,*' said Ed as he tamped his pipe. 'They'll be staying there for the night. They said there are more rooms if you want to stay there with them?'

'No, I'd rather be here with you, if that's okay,' responded Jo who hadn't even thought about leaving.

'That's what they thought you would say. They're coming over after breakfast in the morning, assuming you intend returning with them,' continued Ed.

'Yes, I will be going with them, I want to see my father,' replied Jo. 'If I can be sure he's okay, I'll be coming back to *Red Rose* though.'

'Well, don't decide anything now,' said Ed. 'See how things go, and how you feel once you're safely home.'

'It'll be a big day for you tomorrer, what with seeing ya Pa, an' all,' said Marge while placing the plates on the small table and trying to remain positive for both Jo and herself.

'Can I come with you, tomorrow?' asked Beth as she looked pleadingly at Jo. 'Then we can come back together.'

'Best you stay here, Beth,' replied Jo, 'How can your mum manage on her own without you?'

'Oh, I suppose you're right, she does need me, doesn't she,' sighed Beth with resignation.

Laying on the small bed that night, Jo played over in her mind, all that had happened, and how she was to move forward from this moment. She found her loyalties split between the farm and *Red Rose.* They both needed her, with John away from the farm and Ben away from the boat. It was a dilemma that she had been unprepared for. Her over-riding thought though, was the fact that she was not a fugitive and murderer. She could be her true self again. Sleep was a long time coming, a sleep that was to be filled with strange dreams, all of which hinted at a loss that she couldn't understand.

Parting with the family she had become so much a part of over the relatively short time she had been with them, had not been easy for Jo the following morning. This however, was nothing compared with the joy of falling into her father's arms later that day. Once away from Odiham Wharf where she had sadly waved farewell to the little family she had come to love, her excitement had grown with each passing mile. During that long ride, she had spent much of the time conversing with Polly, who she instinctively liked. She learned much about Polly's life up to the point where she had proudly informed Jo of her recent engagement to Graham. In return, Jo shared with Polly her dilemma of wanting to be with two families, both of them needing her as much as she wanted to be with them. There seemed to be no answer to Jo's emotional problem that Polly could advise.

Upon reaching Meadow Farm, Polly and Graham remained seated on the wagon, arm-in-arm as Jo jumped down to fall into the arms of her father who had been watching and waiting for so long now. Eventually, Phil released himself from Jo's strong embrace and addressed himself to Graham. With a voice filled with emotion, he said, 'I don't know how to thank you, Graham. We are in your debt. You never gave up and now my daughter is safely home because of your determination. You will always have a job here, for as long as you want it.' Looking at Polly, he said, 'As for you, dear lady, I can't thank you enough for rescuing me from the wrath of my daughter had she ever seen the mess in her beloved kitchen. If my Jo had never come home, heaven forbid, I would have begged you to come and work for me, and to keep me in order. As it is, you are welcome here at any time.'

'Yes, please come and call on us whenever you can,' interrupted Jo. 'I would like to get to know you more and there's such a shortage of female company on this farm, apart from my beautiful Blacky and the cows. Do say you will come.'

'I would love to, Jo. But my work, doing other people's laundry keeps me busy. I promise I will come as often as I can.' Saying this, Polly, in her wildest imagination, was not to know that Meadow Farm would become her new home in the very near future.

PART TWO

Chapter 19

Dapdune Wharf, on the River Wey, in the city of Guildford, was an industrious centre in which facilities were available for the repair of barges. Within the relatively small area, was a dry dock where barges could be hauled from the water by use of two large capstans which required four strong men to handle. There was also a barge repair shed, built over a backwater channel, where work could be carried out undercover with the vessel still afloat. There was also a smithy where iron implements could be forged. It was alongside this building that Patrick was working on the day after Jo had returned to Meadow Farm. Although the earlier rain had ceased on that cold Monday morning, the traveller was in a bitter mood. He had had to walk the half a mile from his camp in the rain, and his clothing was still clinging to his body. To top it all, he had been allocated the task of learning how to mix goat hair with hot tar. The result of this would create caulking for sealing gaps between the planking of one of the barges currently resting on the dry dock. The one redeeming feature of this exacting and smelly task was that he, and his damp clothing, were warmed by the very hot tar chest.

Patrick had been readily taken on by the wharf foreman soon after he and Mavis had arrived at Guildford. The shortage of labourers during the war, had been the only reason Patrick had been accepted, although he had no intentions of staying long in this place, where manual work was so hard, and the foreman, harder still. He had, so far, been quite successful in his attempts to help himself to any tools and metal that could be sold. He cursed as he thought about his callous wife who had left him three weeks ago. He had expected her to return before the end of that day, with her tail between her legs, begging for his forgiveness. However, that hadn't happened. *How can an 'onest man live without his horse and wife?* He muttered to himself as he continued his unpleasant task, under the watchful eye of the smithy who was constantly gauging the temperature of the tar. Every so often, with a gleam in his narrow eyes, Patrick would glance at the stable. *How difficult would it be,* he wondered? *Wouldn't hang around here if I ever managed to nab one. I'd soon be on my way west, with or without, that stupid fat woman. I wonder if they still hang horse thieves? If it weren't for that jumped-up, snotty-nosed, kid at the farm, I wouldn't be in this mess.*

'Come on, man!' yelled the smithy. 'More hair. Stop your muttering and get on with your work!'

If I could ever get my hands on that girl, I'd finish what I started, and this time, no pitchfork. I'll teach her not to stab me in the back!

~~~

Nurse Farley, had become hardened to the suffering that surrounded her from one day to the next. Occasionally her spirits would lift when a severely injured soldier showed signs of recovery and possible improvement, but more often it was a case of holding the hand of a dying boy. It was a slippery slope to allow herself to become emotionally involved. She had seen it happen too many times with young colleagues who had broken down under the weight of caring too much for young soldiers who had little hope of recovery. She had vowed not to let that happen to
~~~

her. She was a highly skilled and respected nurse who often found herself advising newly qualified doctors when they were at a loss as to which way they should turn when all looked so hopeless.

It was the lad she was looking at now, who was breaking her resolve. *It was less than a week ago when that blind sergeant came to visit this boy,* she was thinking. *He was propped up talking to the man. How is this happening?* Having carefully removed the final strip of bandage from the moaning semi-conscious boy, she let out a sigh as she lifted the sterile pad away from the wound. She didn't need to lower her nose to the yellow and purple flesh to identify the unmistakable smell of corruption. Amidst the noise and organised activity around her as medics fought to save lives, limbs, and eyes, Nurse Farley's world had shrunk to this one moment and this one bed. *We're going to lose him,* was her only thought. Catching the eye of the harassed senior doctor who was busily writing notes on a board, she beckoned him to come over.

'How is he, nurse?' he enquired as he approached. He didn't need an answer as he took in the sight, and noticed the putrid smell. 'If it were a leg or an arm, we would take it off in order to save him, as it's his chest, there's little, or no hope I'm afraid.'

'A little hope means there's some hope,' retorted Nurse Farley. 'It seems clear to me that not everything was removed from the wound. There must be residue from his clothing still in there, causing this regression. He needs an immediate operation!'

'So, it's *Doctor* Farley now, is it? There are other patients who need your urgent attention, *nurse.* I suggest you make this one as comfortable as possible and let nature take its course.'

'I can't believe you're saying that, Doctor Jennings. I think this young man can be saved, and I believe you have the skill to do it,' retorted the nurse.

'I dare say,' replied the doctor as he turned to leave. 'But my time must be spent on those who have some chance of survival. You must understand that?'

'I only understand that this boy will die within the next day or two without your skill and compassion. He still has hope, doctor. If anyone can save him, *you* can … Please?'

The doctor paused, having already taken a step away from the bed. Nurse Farley watched as his shoulders suddenly slumped.

‘Prepare him for op, and get the orderly to bring him to the waiting area. I make no promises, but I suppose I owe it to you for all the assistance you give my team.’ He quickly walked away.

Looking at the feverish face of Corporal John Simmons, she breathed, ‘I’ve done my bit, John, now it’s up to you to fight, and keep on fighting, for your life.’

The operation was over in less than fifteen minutes. To the surprise and horror of Doctor Jennings a second bullet had been found lodged below John’s breast bone. ‘How this man has survived so far, is beyond me,’ he exclaimed as he stood back to enable a junior doctor to stitch the incision. ‘Keep an eye on him Nurse Farley, and let me know the minute there’s any change in his condition. I want to make sure this young man returns home to his family.’

~~~

‘Okay, Private. You’ve proved that what you have told us is true. You’re a natural, all right. No need for canal training in your case. We’re shipping you out immediately. They’re desperate for
~~~

competent boat handlers over there. You are to report to the quartermaster and get kitted-up, you're leaving tonight at twenty-one-hundred, that's nine-o-clock for the uninformed.'

'Yes, Sarge. Twenty-one-hundred,' repeated Ben. It had been only four days since Ben had left *Red Rose.* He recalled the moment he had walked away from Jo and now regretted that he had felt unable to give her a friendly hug as he left. He had noticed the slight disappointment on her face as he had given her a brief nod. His first day in the Aldershot camp had been both confusing and tiring. He had always taken pride in his fitness, but one day under the watchful eye of the sergeant designated to the squad of new men, now convinced him otherwise. The squad was earmarked for working the French canals after a period of induction and training, although it had seemed to Ben that the ability to march correctly and to get a mirror shine on his boots, was the secret to winning the war against Germany. It was on his third day with the squad that Ben had had the opportunity to impress the sergeant with his knowledge and ability when they spent the day on one of the barges on The Basingstoke Canal. Although the barge was considerably larger than *Red Rose,* he had had no difficulty in adjusting to the larger craft. His handling of the horses and deft handling of the locks made him stand out amongst his fellow recruits. Needless to say, he was not popular, due to the sergeant's obvious approval of his efforts, while they themselves were constantly receiving the sharp edge of his tongue.

Ben's first ever experience of leaving England was a mixture of excitement, apprehension, curiosity, and boredom. The journey to Dover with seven other men from Aldershot was in the back of a covered Y-type Daimler on roads clogged-up with slow moving army vehicles. They were not allowed to show themselves for any logical reason that Ben could make out, so the uncomfortable four-hour journey was made in total darkness. Upon reaching the port of Dover at two-o-clock in the morning, they, with several hundred other soldiers, were filed up a steep and narrow gangway onto the open deck of a paddle steamer where they were to spend the remainder of the bitterly cold night as the vessel made its way to the continent. As he sheltered in the lee of a deck-housing, Ben's thoughts returned to his family, and in particular, Jo. He had no idea when, or if, he would ever see them again. The irony of his situation was that without Jo being there, although he wanted to, he would probably never have left, and now that Jo *was* there, he didn't want to leave but felt that he must. As he sat on the deck shivering with cold, he found himself wishing that he could re-play that moment of parting, so that he could hug Jo and even kiss her good-bye. As he sat, shrugged into his army great-coat, he longingly pictured Jo tucked up in the side-bed of the only home he knew.

In his wildest imagination, he would never have considered the possibility that Jo, rather than being asleep at that moment, was in fact walking across the farm yard in the pre-dawn darkness. The yard which, less than two weeks ago, seemed to hold so much danger for the girl who now crowded his imagination.

~~~

The previous two days had been something of a roller-coaster for Jo. The sadness of parting from her new family, all be it for only a matter of a few days, the joyful arrival at the farm and into her father's waiting arms just a few hours later. The relief of knowing she was innocent of any crime, conflicting with the pain
~~~

her needlessly hasty departure from the farm had caused, both to herself and to her father. Then there was the concern of hearing that John was seriously hurt and would be returned home when his injuries, whatever they were, allowed. On top of that, the sad news of Norman's death. She had liked the cheerfully efficient farm-hand and had been only too aware of his fawning looks whenever they had worked together. She was saddened by the fact that she had enjoyed the chase and, no doubt, would have agreed to walk out with him should he ever have bucked up the courage to ask her. Her sadness had increased tenfold when, on the first evening home, her father had reached up to the mantle and lifted a sealed British Forces envelope addressed to her. Thinking it might be from John, she had excitedly torn it open, only to discover that the folded letter within, was in fact from Norman. The pencil of the dead man, had revealed for the first time, the depth of his feelings for her. It was all so sad, so painful, so late. Life during that month of October had been overwhelmingly emotional for the farmer's daughter, who's predictable routine had not prepared her for such life-changing events.

Later, on her first evening home, work done and sitting opposite her father beside the fire, Jo had been confronted by her dilemma. Now that Ben was gone, Ed needed her on the boat. Of that, she had no doubt. He had assured her before she left that morning, that they could cope, but she knew that it would be at a price. Apart from that, she enjoyed being with the family as well as the hard life it offered. Without it, how would she ever see Ben again? On the other hand, looking at her father that evening, as he sucked on his pipe, she had realised how much he had aged in the relatively short time she had been gone. How could she leave him? She had learned, with gratitude, how Polly had cleaned and tidied the house the day before, and dreaded to think about the mess it might have been in beforehand. It was too much to expect him to cope with both farm and housework, even with Graham’s firm support.

Her first night at home had not provided any easy answers. Before cock-crow she was dressed and on her way to the milking shed, as she had done since she had been a child.

‘Morning, Jo,’ called Graham as he entered the shed ten minutes later. ‘I see the old habits have kicked in already.’

‘Good morning, Graham. Hope you don’t mind me getting started. It wasn’t my intention to do this, but old habits die hard.’

'That's fine, I had a feeling it wouldn't take you long to get back into milking.'

Jo was in her element as she revelled in the task of milking, with its familiar noise and smell, combined with the comforting warmth permeating from the munching herd on this frosty morning. 'I didn't realise how much I'd missed the girls. It's nice to see them again. How's the yield?'

'Oh, it's been pretty constant since I've been here, though I imagine it'll drop off as winter approaches. Right then, if you want to carry on, I'll get the churns ready.'

'Thanks.' With Graham gone, Jo turned back to the stalls. 'Now, let's see who's next.' Moving the stool to the next cow in line, Jo said, 'It's Marigold. Now, old girl, let me see those tits of yours. Yes, healed up nicely, Graham must have a nice touch.' As Jo worked along the stalls, she could feel herself relaxing into the familiar work, as though she had never been away. With the milking done, and with the sun appearing above the stable a short while later, Graham and Jo worked together, hoisting the filled milk churns onto the carter's wagon.

'Are you intending to go back to the boat, Jo?' enquired Graham as they watched the horse-drawn wagon exit the yard.

'I can't decide,' replied Jo, glancing at the house as though expecting to see her father. 'I'm torn both ways. Dad needs me, and, although Ed wouldn't say it, so does he. They were so good to me and I feel as though I'd be letting them down if I don't go back. Apart from that, I feel as though I belong there. But then again, we don't know how badly injured John is. He may need me here to look after him when he gets home. Oh, why does life have to be so complicated?'

'I see your problem,' said Graham. 'If it helps, your father and I can run the farm between us, although the housekeeping's a different matter. Can't help there, I'm afraid. Thinking about it, I might be able to persuade Polly to come over occasionally to sort things out. The real problem is that your dad's not been taking care of himself. I'm sure he's not cooking proper meals. He certainly tucked in the evening he came over to us to eat.'

'Yes, I must thank Polly for that when I see her again,' replied Jo thoughtfully.

'Well, must get on, I've still got some machinery to service. If you do decide to return to the boat, I'll drive you over there in the wagon, as long as your dad can spare me.'

'That's kind of you,' replied Jo. 'Will Polly come with you again?'

'I doubt it. She'll be busier than ever, catching up after missing two days. She works so hard, for a pittance. I wish she didn't have to do it, but my rent alone isn't quite enough. Doing other folk's dirty washing isn't something I'll be happy for Polly to do once we're married.'

Jo suddenly had a thoughtful look on her face as she said, 'Graham, would you and Polly care to come and join us for dinner this evening?'

'Thank you, Jo, that would be really nice, but not possible I'm afraid. You see, Polly will have a meal ready for me when I get home and I won't be able to let her know.'

'Well, tomorrow then,' replied Jo while looking as though she would brook no argument.

'That would be great,' responded Graham with a huge grin on his face. 'I know Polly will be delighted.'

'That's settled then. Tell Polly not to worry about dressing up. Because I won't be,' said Jo, thoughtfully, as she didn't want Polly worrying if she had nothing suitable to wear. 'Now, I think it's time I collected the eggs and cooked dad some breakfast.'

~~~

It had been a cold uncomfortable night crossing the channel, particularly as the steamer frequently slowed down. On one occasion, Ben's excellent sense of direction convinced him that, for a while, they were heading back toward the English coast. Men around him were wrapped in their overcoats, heads on kit-bags, soundly asleep on the deck. Ben had managed to doze while sitting with his back to the steel housing, until another change in the threshing of the paddle-wheels told him something was happening again. This time however, opening his prickly eyes, Ben was surprised to see the deep red sky of a glorious sunrise. *Red sky in the morning, shepherd's warning,* was his first waking thought. However, he didn't have time to dwell on the depressing thought, as he noticed a sailor stepping over the prone figures cluttering
~~~

the deck, before reaching a coiled line which he deftly picked up before standing by the rail, waiting. Now fully awake, Ben stiffly rose to his feet to take in his first sight of a foreign land. It was surprisingly flat, with few buildings of any significance. The part of a harbour he could see coming into his view was packed with shipping of all sizes. Had he expected to see evidence of fighting? He was not sure. It all looked peaceful enough. The men around him were stirring. Several were lighting cigarettes. Most were yawning, stretching, scratching, farting, or coughing. He could see that the squad of men with whom he had left Aldershot were still close together, as they had been instructed. They each had their marching orders packed within their kit-bags, which informed them that their small squad of canal soldiers were to muster on platform 2 at the railway station, immediately on disembarking. There, they were to board a train to Saint-Valery-sur-Somme, wherever that was, and report to a Major Fielding in the port HQ.

Upon stepping from the bottom of the gangway, over an hour later, bewildered by the organised chaos surrounding them, the small group gathered together, leaving Ben to ask a smartly turned-out army lieutenant the way to the station. 'May I see your orders, please?' asked the lieutenant with surprising politeness. Upon handing over his papers, which Ben had had the foresight to remove from his pack, the officer said, 'Ah yes, St Vals. That train's due to leave on the hour.' Checking his watch, he continued, 'You have twenty minutes, best get a move on. There won't be another until tomorrow. It's along the quay, turn left, over the road, you can't miss it, good luck, you may need it where you're going.'

The train ride was cold but a comparative luxury after their uncomfortable night. Ben was mostly unaware of the passing flat scenery as the rhythmic sound of the train wheels clacking over the rail joints, and the fact that he had had so little sleep, soon enveloped him in much needed slumber. All too soon he was rudely awoken as the journey came to an abrupt end with the loud hissing of escaping steam and the kerplunk of closing carriage doors.

Saint-Valery-sur-Somme turned out to be a small town on an estuary overlooking the channel. Having reported to Major Fielding, who, much to Ben's relief, was expecting them, they were directed to a mess tent where the hungry men each received a, less than fresh, roll with a cold bacon filling, along with an enamel mug of hot sweet tea. As he ate and drank, with his hands wrapped around the mug, Ben watched the comings and goings of the uniformed men milling around his group. They all appeared to know what they were doing and where they were heading, all of which added to his concerns and confusion in respect of the immediate future. Throughout his short life he had always had a clear understanding of what was expected of him on the canals. There were few surprises that might have weakened his confidence and he regarded himself as competent in all that was required of him. Now, watching the activity around him, he disliked the feeling of not being in control and being at a loss as to what to expect next. However, having finished the mean but welcome meal, the immediate future became apparent as a harassed subaltern, who was cradling a clip-board in his arm, directed them to a large barge which was moored alongside the busy quay. On inspection, the vessel, which displayed large red crosses on top and sides, offered warmth in its extensive interior. Much to Ben's frustration, the squad of new men were to be confined to a small cabin throughout the two-day journey. It became apparent that the barge, which was clearly hauled by a steam tug, was to be the final mode of transport that would complete the journey to their designated base in war-torn France.

Chapter 20

It had not been easy for Jo to tell her father, the previous evening, that she was intending to return to *Red Rose* at the end of the week. He had sat and listened as she had tactfully explained her dilemma, and the possible solution. Although unhappy with the thought of Jo being away from home for days, or even weeks, at a time, he could see the sense in what she was proposing. Whether, or not, it would work, he was uncertain. Then there had been the question of her safety. The attack on his daughter had shaken him more than he had realised. How vulnerable would she be, working on a canal with all those locks, and with tough men working in the wharfs? Would he be failing as a father to let her do such a thing? Eventually, he had reluctantly allowed himself to be persuaded until such time as John's injuries made it necessary for her to return home.

Determined to make this evening's meal a success, Jo worked in the kitchen throughout the afternoon, having warned her father to be home, washed and changed by six-o-clock at the latest.

Delightful aromas permeated the air as the stove worked overtime and various saucepans bubbled or simmered on top of the range. Phil, amused by all the fuss, kept away from the house and warned Graham to do the same while they sat together with their pre-packed lunches in the comparative warmth of the barn. Eventually, as the hour of four drew closer, Phil stepped into the equipment shed and told Graham to go home.

'Okay boss, Polly's been looking forward to this evening, we'll see you later then.'

'Don't be late,' warned Phil. 'Jo won't be happy if the food spoils. I know that, to my cost,' he added with a grin.

The meal turned out to be a resounding success. Jo had pulled out all the stops with the three-course meal, supplemented by the bottle of red wine and some bottled beer brought along by Graham. Jo had welcomed the help Polly had given, both before and during the meal, knowing how she herself would have felt not being useful. Apart from being a means of thanking the guests for their help during the weekend, the main purpose of the evening was left unspoken until after the meal was over.

Placing a tray of tea cups on a low table in front of the roaring fire, Jo addressed herself to their guests who were still seated at the dining table, saying 'Would you like to come and sit by the fire? I have something I would like to talk to you about.' Having poured the tea, she carefully outlined her proposal. Jo was very much aware of the changing expressions on their guest's faces as she was speaking. Concern? Confusion? Surprise? Doubt? None, or all of these, or more. She wasn't sure. 'You don't need to give me an answer now. Please talk it over and let us know what you think in the morning. I know it's a big decision for you both.'

The couple had a lot to talk about as, arm in arm, they walked home later that evening. 'Well, that was a bit of a surprise,' said Polly. 'I didn't see that one coming.'

'I agree,' replied Graham. 'How do you feel about it?'

'Well, for a start, it would mean giving up the cottage. I just can't get my head around the fact that they are prepared to give us full board and meals, for nothing other than for me to be the live-in housekeeper. Effectively, we would be moving in to a new home and more or less become a part of their family.'

'Not to mention a small wage for you and a salary increase for me,' chipped in Graham with a smile.

'It all sounds too good to be true,' mused Polly. 'What if Jo wants to come back from the canal permanently? She might resent me being in charge of the house. Then again, what happens if and when the son comes home? How will he feel about it?'

'I see what you mean, luv.' replied Graham, who's smile was suddenly replaced by a frown. 'Could be awkward on both counts. I know Jo is doing this because she feels obligated to that boat family. Also, it seems, she loves being on the boat with them. She confided to me yesterday that it was a dilemma for her, although to be fair, it's also partly to do with the fact that I said I didn't like you working for a pittance on other people's washing.'

'I wouldn't like to think it's all charity, Graham. I couldn't bare that. If we accept, and I'm not saying we will, I think I would take them up on the idea that I could still take in washing, so that I still have a bit of independence.'

'It's clear there are still issues to iron out.' replied Graham. 'Phil did say you can come in with me in the morning to discuss any concerns. Apart from anything else, I want to see what accommodation they're offering. I would expect to be treated as a married couple straight away, if you get my meaning.'

'Okay, I'll come with you tomorrow, it'll put me back in my work a bit more, but it's important to get this right.'

'Does that mean, you're open to the idea, Polly?'

'I like Jo, and I know I could become fond of Phil. This could be the beginning of a new life for us all. Let's sleep on it. That's a point, Mister Lodger, are you expecting to be treated like a married man tonight?'

'Well, since you ask ….'

~~~

The back-breaking work of unloading the coal from the hold had taken three days. Now, Ed was relaxing his aching back as he sat by the warm stove contemplating the future. He was still cursing Ben's decision to sign up for a cause he didn't understand. A feeling of hopelessness had descended upon him as he had also watched Jo walking away on Sunday. He had done his best to
~~~

convince her that they would be able to cope without her, but the reality was that it would be nigh on impossible to continue without her or Ben. He needed Marge to handle the steering while he could single-handedly manage the locks. That left only Beth to handle Skippy. It would not be fair on the girl, and the working days would be necessarily long with only the three of them to handle everything. Then there was the fact that the evenings had drawn in and much of the swimming would have to be done in the dark. The last thing they needed was for little Beth to “take a look” if she, or Skippy, heaven forbid, lost their footing on a wet and muddy towpath in the dark. He had told Jo that, with luck, they would be ready to leave with their cargo of timber on Saturday. As much as he wanted the girl’s life to get back to normal at the farm, it was with a sense of guilt that he hoped Jo would return.

Almost as though little Beth was reading his mind, she stopped her cutting-out, in which she had been quietly occupied at the table, and asked, ‘Daddy, when will Jo be coming back? She’s been gone for three days now and I want her to see what I’ve been doing with all my cutting-out.’

'I don't know, child.' replied Ed with a sigh. 'Maybe tomorrow, or the next day. We'll have to wait and see.'

'But I really, really want her to come back. She likes talking to me and telling me all about the animals on her farm. Can we go to her farm one day, Daddy?'

'Now, you stop bothering your father, Beth.' said Marge while continuing with her embroidery. 'If she comes, she comes, if she don't, we'll 'ave to get used to it. It's time for your bed, go and get yourself ready, your nightclothes are on our bed, and make sure you put it on the right way round this time. You're a big girl now.'

As Beth did as she was told, Marge stopped her work and asked quietly, 'Are we gonna to be able to manage on our own, Ed?'

'We'll manage, he replied, 'But it won't be easy. Hopefully, it won't come to that. Why that boy had to go, beats me. Let's hope this ruddy war will soon be over, that's what I say.'

'I can't stop thinkin' about 'im, Ed,' said Marge wistfully while packing away her embroidery. 'I just 'ope 'e's safe and eatin' well, that's all.'

~~~

When Ben had signed up, he hadn't been sure of what to expect. He'd heard about the trenches, the bombs, the gas and the thousands of men killed, on both sides. However, two days after leaving Saint Valery-sur-Somme, nothing had prepared him for the sight of so many suffering wounded and dying soldiers packed into whatever space could be found for them at the Casualty Clearing Station. Most of the beds occupied by casualties within the cluster of three huts were nothing more than camp-beds, while many, still awaiting treatment, were on canvas stretchers exposed to the elements in the open, some on scrappy grass while the less fortunate, on mud. Most were simply lying quietly, as though they were already accepting their imminent demise.

Although unsure of his expectations, Ben had assumed that he would be equipped with a rifle, for such a weapon was always present in the many pictures he had seen of infantrymen. What he had not expected was the lack of any weapon, and Red Cross armbands added to his battledress. He was an experienced canal man,
~~~

what did he know about first aid? There must have been a mistake, he imagined. However, all was soon made clear to him and the other members of the squad soon after arrival at their new base at Ovillers, which was close to the River Somme. They were to be crew-members of the barges, such as the one in which they had travelled upriver during the last two days. In addition to the railway, these barges were used to transport the "Blighty" casualties to the coast where they were to be transferred to a seagoing vessel for the onward crossing of the channel and on to a Base Hospital somewhere in the South of England. The new men were attached to The Queen Alexandra's Imperial Nursing Service in which barges were used for the slower but smoother transport of casualties as their treatment continued in the care of the nurses who accompanied them. Each of the barge convoys were capable of carrying up to three hundred casualties and the journey could take anything from twenty-four to forty-eight hours. These barges were pulled by steam tugs and had, for the duration, been converted from coal-carrying vessels to floating hospitals.

Ben was surprised with the situation in which he found himself. He had imagined that he would be in charge of a horse-drawn barge much smaller than these, transporting equipment and soldiers. Instead, he was under the command of a RAMC Non-Commissioned Officer on one of two hospital barges which were to swim together behind a smelly steam tug. His quarters were no bigger than the one he had so recently left on *Red Rose.* The barges were normal looking, apart from the grey paint and the clearly painted red crosses. However, once he stepped below, it was as though he had stepped into a small cottage hospital, minus windows. It was painted white throughout and contained a number of small spotlessly clean wards, each with a row of iron beds and a stove. To his surprise, the barges even boasted hand-operated lifts to enable stretchers to be lowered into the converted hold.

Stepping onto the deck of No.107 for the first time, Ben was met by an unusually cheerful sergeant. 'You must be Private Ben Fraser. Welcome aboard, lad.'

'Yes, Sarge!' replied Ben as he came smartly to attention.

"Yes" that you're Private Fraser, or "Yes" that you're welcome aboard?' replied the grinning sergeant.

'Err, both, I think, Sarge.'

'Okay, ye can cut out the "Sarge" malarkey. Ye can call me "Jock" when there's no brass around. For my sins, I'm the skipper of this excuse for a boat, which, as ye can see, is neither a barge nor a hospital, but somewhere between the two. I expect you thought you would be on a wee narrowboat pulled by a horse, didn't ye? As ye can see, we are towed by that 'orrible kettle contraption up forrard. So, apart from the few manual locks we'll come across from time-to-time your duties as a barge handler will be light. However, just so's to be sure ye won't be thinking you're on a cruise, you'll be mainly engaged as a medical orderly. We travel by daylight and moor at night. Ye may be pleased to know ye won't be seeing much hostility, apart that is, for an occasional bastard novice Hun pilot who fancies being a brave hero by dropping a bomb or two on a clearly marked hospital ship. Doesna happen very often thankfully, but if it does, it can be nasty. One of your jobs is to see that we're not showing a glimmer of light during the dark hours. In addition to following my orders, ye'll be at the call of all and any of the medical staff. We're a close, well-oiled machine, Ben. Generally, a happy team of dedicated personnel who support each other, as well as the casualties. If ye think ye can fit in, ye'll be a greet asset, if ye don't like what you're seeing and hearing, say so now, and ye'll be on your way to the front. It's up to you. Well?'

'I can fit in, Sar .. um Jock. Where do I put my kit?'

'Good man! I knew my instinct was reet. Follow me, and no eyeing-up the bonny nurses, ye can do that later, if ye ever find the time, which you won't. We load up in the morning, then we're on our way to St. Val. I suggest ye turn in to your wee cabin now and get a good night's kip. I'll introduce ye to the team first thing in the morning. It'll be a busy day.'

~~~

It was on the third day that John slowly emerged from the coma that had engulfed him. Blinking in the brightness of the light that pierced his eyeballs he became aware of the dreadful pain in his chest, his groan immediately attracted the attention of Nurse Farley who was tending a middle-age soldier whose head was covered in bandages, leaving holes for his mouth and nostrils. 'Nurse Wilks, would you mind taking over here. Try to keep him quiet
~~~

and reassured,' she whispered to the young VAD who was new to the ward.

Stepping around the bed to position herself next to John's head, she leaned forward and asked, 'Can you hear me, John? It's Nurse Farley. You've been asleep for a while. John? Can you hear me?'

'It hurts,' gasped John through the pain. 'What's happening to me?'

'We had to do a second op, three days ago. Your wound was infected. It *will* be painful for a while, but you *must* try to lie still.'

Tossing his head from one side to the other, John asked through clenched teeth, 'Can … can you give me some …. something to reduce this …. It bloody hurts.'

'I'll go and fetch Doctor Jennings, he operated on you.'

A moment later, Nurse Farley returned, accompanied by the surgeon who looked as though he hadn't slept for the last three nights. 'Hello, young man,' said the latter, 'So you're back in the land of the living then? Good, it was touch and go for a while back there. Worst is over now. May be able to get you shifted tomorrow. We'll see how you are in the morning. Your war is over young man. You've done your bit. Well done.' Turning to Nurse Farley he said, 'Two Morphine tablets, I think, nurse.'

Left on his own, sweat soaked his entire body as John continued to battle with the pain. His entire world had shrunk to this moment and this bed. For him, nothing else existed other than his determination to be ready for the start of his journey home.

~~~

Work on the farm, that day, had been difficult for Graham. He and Polly had been unable to make up their minds, regarding Phil and Jo's proposal the previous evening. Polly had informed Graham that she wouldn't accompany him to the farm that morning, as planned, as she wanted to have the day alone to think about it. It was a potentially life-changing decision with many facets to consider.

Upon his own arrival at the farm, for milking, Graham could feel the tension emanating from Jo as they worked together. He was aware that *Red Rose* might be leaving Odiham tomorrow, or
~~~

on Saturday at the latest. He had slowly come around to the opinion that they should accept the offer, but was mindful of the fact that it was Polly, who's life would be totally turned around. She would be giving up a secure rented cottage, not to mention her independence. For what? To be a housekeeper with only a small wage of her own. The main attraction for him was that they would be seeing more of each other and he would have a larger vested interest in the farm which would become his home. Also, it would mean Polly could be free of laundering if she chose. Apart from anything else, he had become fond of Phil as they had worked together.

It was just after four in the afternoon when Polly unexpectedly walked into the dimly lit farm yard. She was carrying a wicker basket in which she had placed a cake which had clearly been baked that morning. Graham had just finished packing his tools away in the barn. 'Hello Polly,' he said. 'I wondered if you would come.'

'Hello Graham,' she replied as she lightly kissed his cheek. 'I've made up my mind. What about you? Have you thought any more about it?'

'At the end of the day, it's your decision, luv,' he replied. 'After all, you'll be most affected.'

'Yes. But it's important that we both agree. If it helps, I've decided to accept, but with conditions.'

It was at that moment that Jo appeared from the stable where she had been tending the horses. 'Hello Polly, this is a nice surprise. Come on in and I'll put the kettle on. Dad should be back soon; it's getting dark earlier now. Have you come to give us an answer?'

'Yes,' replied Polly while glancing at Graham. 'But I would prefer to wait till your dad is with us. Do you mind?'

'Of course not. Is that a cake I see in your basket?'

'It's a carrot cake, I baked it for you and your dad, as a sort of thank you.'

'Oh, that's kind of you, Polly. Thank you, it'll go well with a nice cup of tea, I'm thinking.' Placing her arm round Polly's shoulder she continued, 'Come on in and warm up, it's getting chilly now.'

Polly and Graham took their seats at the kitchen table, while Jo put the filled kettle on the range. 'Would you like to cut the cake, Polly? The bread knife is right in front of you. I'll get the plates.' It was at that moment that Phil came in from the yard.

'Company, tea and cake!' he exclaimed. 'What more can a hard-working man want? Hello Polly. Good to see you again.'

'Hello Mister Simons.'

'Cut out the "Mister Simons", it's "Phil" to you. I imagine you're here to talk over our suggestion, is that right?'

'Yes, it is,' replied Polly as she finished cutting the cake. Looking at Graham, she continued, 'only I don't know what Graham's decided yet.'

'If you think it would work, I'm okay with it,' Graham said as he took Polly's hand into his own.

'Good, I thought you would say that,' replied Polly with a grin. Turning to Phil, she continued, 'I'm happy to accept your offer, but I have to make some conditions.'

'Okay,' replied Phil. 'We're all ears, what are these conditions? I'm sure they're nothing we can't agree to.'

'I hope so,' replied Polly. 'Firstly, I will want to have total freedom to work as I feel fit. Second,' she continued while glancing at Jo, 'at such times as Jo is free to come home, I will still be in charge of the kitchen. Third, I would want to help out with the animals from time-to-time, even with milking. Fourth, should your son come home and not like the situation, we should terminate the arrangement immediately. In case of that eventuality, I will keep the cottage as a stand-by until such time as everyone is happy, and I *mean,* everyone! Meanwhile, I may have to continue taking in laundry to help cover the rent. Fifth, Graham and I are to have our own room, although we would expect to take our meals with the family.'

'Agreed,' said Phil with a laugh. 'I'm used to having a bossy woman in the house. One more won't make any difference.'

'I agree, Polly,' said Jo. 'I expect to come home each time *Red Rose* returns to Odiham. That arrangement gives me more time to work on the farm, as I've always wanted.'

'It's all settled then,' said a beaming Phil. 'When can you move in?'

'I imagine Jo will be wanting to return to the canal tomorrow?' asked Graham while glancing at Jo.

'I think *Red Rose* will be ready to leave on Saturday,' replied Jo. 'I would like to go tomorrow if possible, to be sure to get back in time.'

'In that case, if I can borrow the wagon in the morning, we can bring a few things over before I drive you to Odiham. Polly can start getting settled in while I'm gone,' said Graham. 'How does that sound?'

'Sounds good to me,' replied Phil. 'Now, where did you put that bottle of wine I've been keeping for a special occasion, Jo? Let's drink to the future for us all.'

Chapter 21

'Mummy! It's Jo! She's come back. She's got that man with her, the one with the funny eye who took her away.' In her excitement, she forgot all about the window cleaning she was half way through, as she scampered onto the bank and ran to the gate leading to the humpy bridge. With no hesitation, she ran into Jo's outstretched arms and hugged her hard enough to squeeze the breath from her lungs.

'Hello, Beth. Would you mind letting go so that I can breathe?'

Doing as she was asked, slightly, Beth asked, 'Are you back to stay? Oh, I so want you to say you are. Are you?'

'Yes, Sweety. I'm back to stay, now if you would kindly let go, your mummy and daddy have come to say hello.'

'You're back then?' was all Ed could think to say as he approached. 'Not a day too soon, if you ask me,' he continued gruffly in order to hide his relief and pleasure.

'Yes, I'm back, Ed. If you'll have me.'

'If we'll have you? Come here, girl.' Before Jo realised what was about to happen, she was being crushed for a second time that morning, this time in Ed's arms. 'You're family now, Jo. And don't you ever forget it.'

'What's this then?' Marge was puffed-out having climbed the slope as fast as she could. 'Do I need to be concerned, our Ed? You look as though you're about to eat that poor girl. Hello Jo. I knew you would come back to us, 'ere give us an 'ug.'

Graham, still seated on the wagon and holding the reins, was looking on, bemused by the sight of Jo enfolded in the huge woman's ample breasts. 'Looks like they're pleased to see you, Jo,' he called with a chuckle. 'I can see I'm definitely riding back on my own. I'm glad.'

'Oh no, you're not goin' orff yet, young man. Not till you've been fed. You looks like you need it. Come on down to the boat all of you, lets 'ave some grub. 'Orses can graze on the bank.'

The loading of timber was nearly complete as the sun dipped behind the bridge. Ed expected to be casting off early in the morning. Graham had bid farewell to Jo and the family soon after he had eaten a lunch of home-baked bread with cheese. With a satisfied look on his face, Ed said to Jo, ‘Soon be able to cover up. I’ll show you how we do it, cos that’s part of your job while you’re with us. Ben always used to help me, so you’ll be taking his place. Is that okay with you?’

‘That’s fine,’ replied Jo. ‘I want to learn all that you can teach me, including the trading. So that I can truly feel I’m earning my keep.’

‘Good girl. You’re a marvel. It’s pie and mash in *The Swan* tonight. We can celebrate your return.’ Turning to peer at the wharf, he continued, ‘Here comes the last of the load. We’ll be done in an hour and I’m ready for a beer.’

Jo was pleased to be back among these people who had so readily accepted her into their family. On the other hand, she felt sad having left her father again, although she was certain he would be well cared for. Polly was a gem and Jo had no doubt that she would become a very good friend. Yes, her father would be okay, but what about John? It was now over a week since their father had received the news of his having been injured. How serious was it? she wondered. When would they hear more, or see him again? They said he was to be transferred to a hospital in England somewhere. *Oh, I wish we knew more. Where he is now. Why is it taking so long? I so much want to see him. How will he feel about the changes in our lives? I hope it won't all be too much of a shock for him.*

~~~

With mixed feelings Nurse Farley watched as the stretcher bearers, headed for the door with their patient firmly strapped down. John had squeezed her hand as he thanked her and bid her farewell. He looked so thin and vulnerable, and was clearly in a lot of pain. She was pleased that he was considered well enough for his journey to England, but knew that in normal circumstances a patient in his condition would never be subjected to such a difficult, not to mention, dangerous journey. *He's just a boy. Please let him be safe,* she thought as she swept away a tear. *Why did I have to go and let this one touch my heart? Must remain detached, otherwise I'll never get through this horror.*
~~~

‘Nurse Farley! There’s a new patient being brought in,’ said matron. ‘Gas, I’m afraid. Be careful as you strip him. There’ll be gas in his clothing, hair, everything. We don’t want you becoming a casualty as well. Best put your mask and gloves on. I don’t expect him to survive, but see what you can do.’

Life and death go on, she thought to herself as she looked toward the closing door. *Good bye, John. God keep you.*

John was only vaguely aware of being carried out to the waiting barge. His world was so full of pain which increased with each step the bearers took through the grounds and down to the river. At one point it felt as though a knife had been driven into his chest when one of the bearers slipped in the wet mud. Looking beyond the rounded belly, unshaved chin and hairy nostrils of the closest bearer he could do no more than focus on the blue sky which, every so often, was partly masked by the overhanging bare branches of trees which had now shed their leaves. He was willing for this torture to cease as the blue of the sky above was replaced by a white wooden ceiling which seemed to be rising further away. Before his stressed mind had time to work out what was happening the, now distant, ceiling was replaced by a closer one, no more than six feet from his head. Having descended into the hold of the hospital barge by means of the lift, which had been cranked by the cook, the bearers were directed to a bed which was covered with recently laundered sheets and pillow-cases. An involuntary groan escaped him as the stretcher was firstly placed on the bed before being eased from below his prone body. He had closed his eyes with the increased intensity of pain the manhandling had caused him, but his determination prevented him from passing out.

'Let me see who we have here,' a soft female voice with an Irish lilt broke into his awareness. 'Ah yes, Corporal John Simons, chest wound. Prescribed two morphine tablets at ten-fifteen. Can you hear me, John?'

John listened to the soothing tone of the young voice and forced his body to relax sufficiently to be able to open his eyes, only to be confronted by an angel bending over him.

'Am I dead?' he gasped through dry lips. 'If I am, why is it hurting so much?'

'No, not dead by a long way, John.' replied the warmly smiling angel. 'You're still in the land of the living, no doubt about that.

You're not in heaven yet, to be sure. You're on a hospital barge with many other lucky soldiers, on your way home. You're the last to come on board and we'll be on our way at any moment. As for the pain, it should get a little better now that you're no longer being manhandled. Try to relax a little, you're all tensed up. I'm Sister Francis, a nurse who is also a Novice from the Convent of St Angela in Northern Ireland. So not an angel, I fear, at least not in this world, according to Mother Superior. The Chief Medical Officer will be along shortly to check you out and make you more comfortable. I must go now, but won't be far away.'

As his angel seemingly floated away, John slowly became more aware of his surroundings. There was a mixture of single and bunkbeds, all occupied by patients, some quiet and still, others propped up, talking to a neighbour, a nurse, or an orderly. There was quiet laughter at the far end of the room. His own bed was positioned next to a partition and he could see another similar room through the wide opening. Apart from his angelic nurse, there were several others tending patients or unhurriedly passing through, carrying trays, or bowls of something he would rather not think about. Unlike the Casualty Clearing Station, there was a sense of orderly calm in the room. It was good to hear the laughter and see smiles on the faces of a few of the staff and patients. He could hear the sound of a mouth-organ on the far side of the partition playing a familiar popular tune which, in his confused state, he was unable to put words to. There were, of course, inevitable groans added to the background noises. He became aware of the sound of a distant steam-whistle, followed by some thumping on the deck above him.

'Good morning, welcome aboard. I'm Doctor Russel. I see from your notes that you stopped two bullets with your chest, not a wise thing to do, is it? Severe infection, now decreased. How are you feeling?'

John thought about it for a moment before replying, 'As though I've been kicked by a team of horses, otherwise, just glad to be on my way home.'

'That's the spirit. You'll be with us for at least two days, then transferred to a ship which will take you back across the Channel. No reason why you shouldn't make a good recovery in time, although they'll keep you in a base hospital for a bit, to keep their eye on you. Could even be home with your family for Christmas I shouldn't wonder. Now, let's give you something for that pain.'

Soon after Doctor Russel had moved on, Sister Francis, accompanied by another nurse, returned to prop up his pillows sufficiently to enable John to take some pills with a glass of water. ‘You won’t be feeling the movement down here, but we’re on our way now,’ said Sister Francis. ‘Soon have you back home, isn’t that grand? This is Nurse Becket, she and I will be looking after you until we get to St.Vals. Where is your home, if you don’t mind me asking?’

Regardless of the nagging pain in his chest, John felt that he welcomed conversation to take his mind off his discomfort. ‘It’s in a small farm in the county of Hampshire. I’m the son of a farmer.’

‘Sounds grand. Do you have any brothers or sisters?’

‘A sister, Johanna, we call her “Jo”.

‘Older or younger?’

‘Younger than me in age, but older in maturity, you might say.’

‘Why would you say that?’

‘Well, mum died when we were kids, Jo became mistress of the house as she grew up, right from a very early age. She’s amazing and I love her to bits. I can't wait to see her, although she may not have forgiven me yet, for signing up.'

'Well, hopefully you'll be seeing her soon, I expect she'll be at home on the farm waiting for you to return. Now, get some rest, I've kept you talking too much.' It was a wise and experienced nurse who knew that talk of home was like a tonic to these wounded men who were in her care. The short conversation had exhausted John and soon, in spite of the pain, he slipped into a dreamless sleep. Meanwhile, lashed together, barges 107 with 103 moved quietly west in the wake of the steam tug.

Ben was finding it a novel experience to be swimming without the aid of a mule on the bank up ahead. Jock had handed the large tiller to him soon after casting off from the quay, with the instruction to remain mid-stream until told otherwise. To his surprise, he found that he was enjoying the task as he watched the slowly passing banks for signs of wildlife. There was little scenery to take his interest as the land was mostly flat and devoid of trees and buildings. There was no sign of fighting, although he noticed many military vehicles slowly crawling along the lanes whenever the river came close. It was mid-afternoon when he spotted a biplane heading in their direction from across an open field. It was low and coming fast. At first, he couldn't see any wing markings as he watched the helmeted head of the pilot coming closer. It wasn't until the aircraft flew directly over them that Ben saw the black crosses on the underside of the wings. *Hell's teeth, it's a Hun!* The pilot was peering down at them through his goggles as he passed some two hundred feet above. Instinctively, Ben ducked down as low as possible while still holding onto the tiller.

'Keep your eyes ahead, laddie.' Ben had not noticed Jock standing alongside him, having just come up from the hold. 'He'll not harm us, he's a scout spying on the movement of our troops and weapons.' The aircraft was now half a mile away and turning. The turn continued until it was heading straight back toward them, this time head-on along the river. *'Bliddy hell! The sod's coming in to attack!'* shouted Jock. *'Get down everyone!'* The air was split with the chattering of a machine gun which was mounted on the nose of the oncoming plane. As he watched, Ben could see that it was the tug it was after. He had little time to think before the plane climbed steeply with the crackling snarl of its engine filling his ears. It was at the moment the plane started another turn that Ben saw a second aircraft swooping down from the low clouds. This one however, was not aimed at them. It was heading directly for the Hun. With a rattle of its machine gun, the pilot, who was wearing a bright yellow scarf which was streaming behind him, continued chasing the Hun until both aircraft were out of sight.

'That was a close one,' said Jock. 'He was trying to cripple the tug. He wasn't aiming for us. You did well, laddie, kept your calm under fire. Well done, your first encounter with the enemy I suspect. At least the cheeky bugger didn't drop a bomb on us.'

Looking forward, Ben was relieved to see that the tug appeared to be unharmed as it continued towing its charges along the river. He felt breathless with a combination of fear and elation. He had actually been under fire by the enemy. He could imagine telling his father about the experience. His thoughts turned to the glamorous English pilot with the long yellow scarf. *What must it be like,* he wondered, *to be up there amongst the clouds, engaging the enemy man-to-man?* His Jo would be so proud of him if he was one of those men fighting in the air. *My Jo?* He held that thought as a slow grin spread across his face. *Yes, she's my Jo. I must be in love, to be thinking of her in my hour of danger!*

'My word, Laddie!' said Jock who was observing the new man. 'You're a cool customer, smiling at danger. You're okay in my book. I'll take over, you can go below and get some lunch in the crew room.'

It was late in the afternoon before the tug master signalled, by hand gesture, that it was time to moor up for the night. Jock, who was on the helm, instructed Ben to stand ready on the bows with a long steel pin and a sledge-hammer. It would be his job to step onto the bank and drive the pin into the soil in time to catch a thick rope which Jock would toss from the stern as it came level. The rope was then to be coiled around the spring. In this way, forward movement could be taken off the barge as it settled into the bank for the night.

'Mind your fingers, laddie.' called out Jock. 'Don't want to lose any of the buggers, do you?'

As darkness descended, Ben walked around the barge to ensure there was no tell-tale glimmer of light to be seen, although it was highly unlikely that any aircraft would be aloft in the cloud covered darkness.

Stepping below into the warmth of the hospital wards, Ben was detailed to report to the galley where he was to assist with the distribution of food to those patients who could eat. From steering the large vessel to working in the hospital environment was quite an emotional leap for him. The medical staff were going about their business both efficiently and cheerfully. The up-beat atmosphere was supported by the buzz of conversation and occasional laughter. These were men who had come through their own personal nightmares with the knowledge that they were on their way home. The cook was a fat jovial man in his forties who introduced himself to Ben as "Butch". 'Okay, young man, take this trolly to room four at the other end. The nurses there will tell you who can eat what. You may need to stay there and help.'

Having helped to prop up several patients, and served their meals, Ben was asked by Sister Francis to lend a hand to a patient on a single bed at the far end. The man was already trying his best to sit up a little when Ben got to him. 'Here, let me support your back as I rearrange your pillows,' he cheerfully said to the man who was close to his own age.

'Thanks, I suspect you're not a nurse, judging from your uniform,' replied the young man.

'No, I'm a member of the crew, just arrived from England. My name's Ben. Can you manage with a fork, or shall I feed you?'

'No, I'll manage, I think. My name's John.'

'Expect you're glad to be going home, John. Where would that be?'

'I live on a farm in Hampshire, north of a town called Petersfield.' replied John. 'Not many people know it.'

'I don't know Petersfield, but I've heard of it, believe it or not, said Ben. 'I come into Hampshire a lot. My family owns a working narrowboat on the canals. At the moment we are regularly travelling between London and Odiham, near Basingstoke.'

'I know Odiham,' replied John who was delighted to be talking to someone from his own part of the world. 'You must be on the Basingstoke Canal then.'

'That's right, although I'm not sure for how much longer. The army's taken it over, and they don't really want us on it.'

'I've been there fishing sometimes,' replied John, 'with my friend Norman, whenever we could get a day off, which wasn't very often. Never caught anything worthwhile though.' He paused for a moment as he thought of Norman, before asking, 'Do you do any fishing?'

'No, not really. Though we did manage to fish a girl out at Odiham four or five weeks ago. She'd taken a look in the dark and was freezing when we got her out.'

'Taken a look in the dark? She wouldn't have seen much, I imagine.'

'No, in our canal jargon, "taking a look" means to fall into the water. If you've finished, I'll take your plate. I can see you're in a lot of pain. Shall I fetch a nurse?'

'No, don't bother them. There are men a lot worse off than me, I reckon. It's been good talking to you Ben. Made me feel closer to home. Thanks.'

'My pleasure, mate. I'll look in later when I'm all finished for the day.'

~~~
~~~

The night had drawn in by the time *Red Rose* had settled at Frimley quay at the end of Jo's first day back. The day had been uneventful with very few locks to impede their progress. In Ben's absence Ed had worked with Jo along the bank. As much as she enjoyed Ed's company, she found that she was missing Ben enormously. His knowledge of wildlife and nature, his sense of humour, his teasing, his presence. Ed had been unusually quiet throughout the day and Jo suspected that, amongst other things, he also was thinking about Ben. Trying to draw him out as they waited for one of the locks to empty, Jo had mentioned how much she was missing Ben. Leaning back against the thick timber arm of the lock gate, Ed had thought about what she said for a while, before replying, 'I noticed you were getting fond of him, and I suspect he feels the same way. Would I be guessing wrong if I were to think there could be a touch of romance in the air?'

'No, of course not!' Jo felt her cheeks burning as she denied the suggestion rather too sharply.

'Ah, I thought so,' said Ed with a chuckle. 'Well, well, well, we might even have you as a daughter-in-law one day.'

‘Ed, you’re letting your imagination run wild. Yes, I like Ben as a friend, but beyond that, it’s …’

‘Okay luv, I understand it’s all too soon for you, I guess the future will tell what it tells.’

Later that evening, with Beth tucked up in bed and Ed somewhere on the bank, Jo asked Marge, ‘Why does Ed always want to tie up here in Frimley. I’ve noticed that we could get a bit further sometimes. What’s so special about Frimley?’

‘There are some things it’s best for a wife not to ask ‘er ‘usband, Luvvy,’ Marge replied with a wink. ‘E works ‘is socks off lookin’ after us. In my way of thinkin’, ‘e deserves a bit of pleasure when ‘e can get it. ‘E loves me and the children and would do anyfing for us. That’s good enough for me, so let’s say no more on the subject, all right?’

~~~
~~~

True to his word, Ben found time to sit with John for a while that evening. 'What was all the excitement about today?' enquired John. 'I heard a machine gun and what could have been a plane passing overhead. Were we under attack, by any chance?'

'Yes, a Hun pilot having a bit of a pot-shot at the tug that's pulling us. Didn't have much chance of hitting anything before he got chased away by one of our fly-boys. Nothing to worry about, John.'

'Oh, I'm not worried, mate. I've already received the two bullets that had my name on them, and I'm still around. Stick close to me, you'll be alright.'

'You're looking a lot better than the first time I spoke to you, How's the pain?'

'I can stand it,' replied John 'If you've ever sat on the iron saddle of a plough for three days on the trot, you would know what pain is, so don't worry about me,' he continued with a grin. 'I'm on the mend. Now, tell me about life on a canal boat.'

John listened with interest as Ben talked about life on a narrowboat, describing the hardship, the stigma, the cargoes carried, and the conditions on the boat, among other things, before asking John, 'Have you got a girl to go back to?'

'As a matter of fact, I have, though she doesn't know it yet.'

'How's that?'

'Her name's June. She works in our local post office. Often comes to our pub to play the accordion. I've had my eye on her for some time now, and the signals I'm getting are encouraging. I've been shown that life's too short now, so I'm going to ask her out just as soon as I get back home. How about you? I imagine the girls are all over you with your smouldering looks?'

'Yes, I've got a girl. As a matter of fact, the one we fished out of the canal. I call her "Mouse" cos she looked like a drowned rat when we pulled her out, but I didn't think she would go for "Rat".

'Well, here's to the folk at home, including June and Mouse,' said John as he raised his glass of water.

Chapter 22

Polly missed the sound of church bells in the village, which had ceased ringing at the beginning of the war. On that Sunday morning she and Graham had finished packing various bits and pieces from their respective bedrooms and were placing them, along with various other essential items, by the kitchen door, ready for collection later. Polly had not previously been in the habit of regularly attending church, that is, until Graham had come to lodge with her. It was he who had originally suggested that she might like to accompany him to the morning services, and this had become a habit ever since.

As they made their way to the church on that brisk frosty morning, Polly looked forward to the time when it would be acceptable for them to arrange their wedding service and the calling of the Banns. Meanwhile, a suitable time of mourning would have to be observed, for the sake of her reputation in the village. She was saddened by the thought of Len's death. She would never have wanted him to be hurt, or killed, but she couldn't honestly say that she was in mourning. He had long since forfeited any love she may once have had for him.

'Well, now that it's all happening, how do you feel about it, luv?' asked Graham as they walked side-by-side through the lychgate while trying to ignore the inquisitive stares of one or two ladies.

'I'll miss the cottage, although certainly not the laundering,' she laughed. 'I like the room Phil has given us, and I like him and Jo. I'm actually looking forward to getting started properly on the housework and cooking. I think it could work out. How about you, Graham? What are your thoughts?'

'I'm happy with it. I certainly won't miss the walk to and from the cottage. It was a good idea of yours to keep the cottage on for a while, Polly. With my increase in wages, we should be able to afford it, especially as we won't be paying any rent on the farm. Thinking of the farm, there's a lot of land not being used. I think I'll have a word with Phil some time, and find out what his plans are in that respect.'

Standing at the church door, Reverend Perkins, stood greeting his parishioners as they walked up the gravel path. 'Good morning, Polly, somewhat chilly but pleasant enough. I hear that your husband has been killed in France. I'm sorry. So many of our men have fallen. The village will feel so much different once it's all over, and I'm a bit concerned about the cricket team, apart from anything else. Would you like me to call in for a chat during the week?'

'Thank you, Reverend,' replied Polly. 'As a matter of fact, Graham and I are moving in to Meadow Farm today. As you know, Graham's working there and I have been invited to become the live-in housekeeper. It's a large house, so there's plenty of space for us both. I don't feel it necessary for you to put yourself out, I'm fine now that the initial shock has passed. Thank you all the same.'

'Quite a change for you, then,' replied the vicar with a frown. 'If you should ever want to talk about it, the offer is there. I must admit, I don't know the family from that farm. Please give them my regards.' Turning to Graham, he asked, 'Are you enjoying life on the farm, Graham?'

'Yes, thank you Vicar. Working the land is right up my street and I'm in my element.'

'I wanted to ask you, have you considered my suggestion of agreeing to be nominated for Deputy Church Warden at the next AGM?'

'I've thought about it,' replied Graham. 'Thank you for the compliment but I don't think the time is right at the moment. Perhaps in the future?'

'Pity. You would be an ideal candidate, given your previous experience. If you change your mind, there's still plenty of time. Now, if you will excuse me, I must greet Mr and Mrs Villiers. Did you know they're celebrating their sixtieth anniversary in December?'

'I think we both got off lightly there,' said a grinning Polly as they entered the cold half-filled building to take an empty pew at the back of the church, next to the font. 'Just think, one day we'll be standing down there in front of the alter, saying our vows. I do love you, Graham.'

'And I, you,' responded the smiling man as he squeezed Polly's gloved hand briefly before anyone should happen to notice.

~~~
~~~

At the same time as Polly and Graham were awaiting the start of the service, *Red Rose* was silently swimming along Deep Cut, a straight section of the canal which had been cut directly through a hill and was totally overlooked by a canopy of trees. Marge and Jo were together on the counter while Ed was walking alongside Beth who was mounted on Skippy. A variety of birds were flitting between the trees on both sides of the cut and Jo was wishing Ben was here to identify them for her. Up ahead, she could see the first of the many locks they would tackle that day. Jo had been telling Marge about the arrangement that had been agreed with Polly and Graham and how pleased she was that it enabled her to join them on the canal. A whistle from Ed suddenly interrupted their conversation as he alerted them to the fact that he was about to jog on to set the lock, leaving Beth to handle Skippy.

'Okay luvvy, I think it's time you handled *Red Rose* through the lock. I'll step back and leave it all to you. Remember to check that we're well clear of the sill, we wouldn't want our arse end to get hung up on it as the level goes down. Don't worry if you nudge the gate as you goes in, we all do that from time to time and it won't do any 'arm. Looks like it's in our favour, so's we can swim straight in. Keep 'er as she is, it looks good. Beth's gonna stop the mule to take way off before we pass through the gate, and Ed'll be standin' ready to catch yer line and pass it back to ya.'

Jo watched the opening as it drew closer, not realising that, in her concentration she was inadvertently running her tongue over dry lips. She could feel her heart beating faster, her sweaty hand, in spite of the cold, was clenched into a tight fist as she gripped the tiller.

'You're doin' fine, luvvy. Try to relax,' encouraged Marge.

Jo was partly relieved to see Ed standing by the open gate grinning at her. She was vaguely aware of passing Beth who was standing alongside Skippy, then realised that *Red Rose* was already slowing as she cleanly passed through the opening without contact. Letting go of the tiller, she lifted the coiled line from the counter and tossed it across to Ed who deftly looped it around a bollard before passing it back to her. Taking the strain, she took way off the boat, ensuring that it was well clear of the sill beneath the gate which Ed was already closing. It had all gone like clockwork.

‘Well done, luvvy, ‘andled like an expert,’ exclaimed Marge. It was only then, that Jo noticed the small group of overall clad German Prisoners of War clapping her efforts. They had been doing some maintenance work on the pathway alongside the lock, and were happy to be diverted by the appearance of the familiar narrowboat coming through the lock. With the upper gates now closed behind them, Ed was soon at the other end raising the paddles which would lower the water level in the basin to match the level on the lower reach. It was now Jo’s job to pay out the line as *Red Rose* sank between the wet lock walls. Meanwhile, Beth started leading Skippy to the other end of the lock, ready to take the strain once the gates were opened. It all happened so suddenly there was no time to react until it was too late. A fox darted out of the undergrowth immediately beneath Skippy’s feet. The mule panicked and side-stepped several paces, enough to drive Beth to the edge of the basin.

‘Beth!’ shouted Ed, but the damage was done. The girl hovered on the lip of the basin, arms swinging to try to catch her balance, then, with a loud scream, she was gone. Franticly Ed swung the windlass to close the paddles for fear that the girl would be drawn

to them in the current, or trapped beneath the lowering boat. Before Jo had time to react, she saw a sudden blur of brown as one of the POWs jumped into the swirling basin. In panic she stepped to the side of the counter to peer into the gap between the boat and the wet slimy bricks. She could see no sign of either Beth or the man. *Oh my God! They've gone underneath the boat!* With the paddles closed, Ed dashed back to the spot where Beth had gone over. Seeing no sign of the girl, or the POW, he shot across the counter and looked down between the narrower gap on the side where the line was still looped around the bollard.

'She's down here! Jo, let that line out and help me push the boat away from the wall! Then let the line drop into the water right here. I'm going over!' Jo rapidly did as instructed and as the gap widened Ed dropped over the side. Beth appeared to be unconscious and the POW was trying to hold her head above water. Jo heard Ed telling the man to hold onto the line as he took the unconscious girl onto his chest and back-paddled to some rust-caked iron steps set into a recess in the lock wall. Meanwhile, the other POWs had crossed the lock via the closed gate. Upon reaching the steps Ed called up to the POWs to form a chain to haul Beth out, as he attempted to lift her. In a matter of seconds Beth

was lying face up on the grass. Her skin was white and there was a deep gash on her forehead. It was clear that she was not breathing.

Before Ed had stepped off the iron ladder, one of the POWs was already turning the girl over and thumping her between the shoulder blades. Ed leaped forward, only to be grabbed by another of the POWs who firmly held him back. 'Heinrich is a medical student,' he said. 'Let him do as he must.' Having thumped Beth's back several times, the POW roughly pulled her over and tilted her head back, at the same time he pinched the girl's nose and breathed into her half open mouth.

'What's 'e doin' to our Beth, Ed?' It was Marge, standing on the cabin roof and peering across the gap.

'He's trying to save her life, Marge,' replied Ed, who was being supported by the man who had held him back.

The man continued his breathing action for several minutes while everybody stood like statues, watching and waiting. Suddenly the girl coughed and retched before being manhandled on to her side, where she continued coughing up water as the man started thumping her back again. Suddenly, the statues came alive amidst the sound of cheers and laughter.

'He's done it, Marge!' cried Ed. *'He's bloody well done it! He's brought her back!'*

It was then that Jo, having hurriedly stepped from the boat onto the iron ladder, swept forward and, falling to her knees, took the coughing girl into her arms. 'Oh, Sweety, you're alright, Sweety. Your sister is here. Keep coughing, get all that water out of your lungs. It's all okay now. You took a look, but now your safe, thanks to all these kind soldiers.' Calling across to the boat, she said, 'Marge, can you come up and bring your emergency box, Beth's got a bad gash on her forehead that needs some attention.'

While Marge and the medical student worked on Beth, Ed approached the POW who had brought Beth out from beneath the boat. 'How can we ever thank you enough for what you did. You risked your own life to save our little girl.'

'I do vhat any man vould do, ya? Ve Germans are not bad men. Ve are just like your young men who are caught up in this cvazy var.'

'I understand. My son is over there also. I only hope he never has to kill good people like you. I still can't quite believe your friend breathed life into my little girl, I didn't know that was possible.'

'Heinrich is clever man, has new ideas, much better than the old methods, I am thinking. Ve have to go now, before our guard returns to escort us away. It was good to meet you. Ve often see your *Red Rose* passing us, and you alvays vave to us. Ve, how you say? app .. appre ..'

'I think you are trying to say "appreciate", and let me tell you, mate. We will always appreciate what you did for us today. All of you.'

Returning to where Beth, now wrapped in a blanket, was being cradled in Jo's arms, Ed, with tears in his eyes, said, 'Let me have her. I'll carry her down. Marge, you give her some hot sweet tea and put her to bed, while me and Jo gets things sorted up here.' When, a few minutes later, Ed emerged from the cabin onto the counter, he was a little surprised to see the POWs lined up and being methodically counted by an elderly soldier whose ill-fitting uniform left much to be desired, and whose rifle was propped against the fence. Satisfied that his charges were all present and correct, he turned and started leading them toward the next section of towpath needing to be cleared. He was clearly somewhat embarrassed when all the men started laughing as one of the grinning POWs stepped out of line and handed him the forgotten rifle.

With Jo on the counter paying out the wet line, Ed completed the emptying of the lock and lowering of the paddles before walking back to where Skippy was contentedly munching grass back along the bank.

'Okay Jo. All set. Let's go,' he called down to her as he walked past while holding on to the mule. 'More locks ahead. We'll have to manage with just the two of us for a bit.'

It wasn't long before they drew level with the group of POWs who stopped their work as they cheerfully waved. As Jo, in her position at the stern, passed the group, one of them called out, *'You are very pretty girl, I come back after the var and marry you, ya?'* Jo felt herself blushing as a few of the men clapped their friend on his back, while others whistled the wedding march.

The usual lunch of bread and cheese was eaten at one of the locks as it emptied. 'How's Beth?' enquired Jo as Marge handed her the bread.

'She's asleep, but she's okay. I should be able to come up and take the tiller, if you could walk with Skippy. With our Ed trotting ahead to the locks, we'll get along faster. I can keep an eye on Beth as we swims along.'

It seemed a long day, with so many locks to pass through, and Ed wanting to continue working through the dark evening to make up lost time. By the time Jo had returned from stabling Skippy at Sheerwater quay, the evening meal of stew was ready and Beth was sitting up at the small table with a bandage tied firmly around her head. 'Hello, little one,' said Jo as she took her place beside Beth. 'How are you feeling?'

'My head hurts a bit, and my chest and throat both feel sore. I don't remember being in the water, I can only remember being knocked over by my Skippy. But I forgive him.'

'Well, it's a day in bed for you tommerer,' said Marge. 'And no arguments, do you 'ear?'

‘Yes, Mummy. But can I get up the next day?’

‘We’ll ‘ave to see, won’t we,’ replied Marge while winking at Jo. ‘It’s an early night for us all, I’m thinkin’. I’ve ‘ad about enough excitement for one day. And as to what our Ben will ‘av to say about ‘is girl marrying a German, ‘eaven knows.’

‘But I …’

‘Just teasing,’ said Marge with a grin. ‘Although …’

Had they known what was about to happened to their son on that Sunday 5th of November, Bonfire Night, they would not have been joking in that way.

Chapter 23

Sunday 5th November, Ben's second day on Barge 107, was not to be as smooth as his first. Shortly after casting off, the tug was clearly having problems. Speed through the water was reducing with each passing mile. 'Something amiss, I'll be bound,' muttered Jock who was peering ahead. 'Here, take the tiller, laddie. I'm going forward to find out what they're up to on that old kettle.'

After much calling and listening, Jock returned to the aft deck to say, 'Losing steam from one of the joints. It took a hammering from one of the spent shells from that plane yesterday. They're patching up the best they can, but insist upon reducing steam pressure for the rest of the journey down river. It'll add a day to our journey for sure. I'm going below to warn the SMO.'

'Should have stuck to mules, said Ben with a grin. 'The only steam that escapes from them is a fart after an apple.'

As predicted, the day was turning out to be long and frustrating, with frequent stops for more repairs. There was a moment of excitement during the afternoon when two British aircraft did a low formation fly-pass. Ben noticed that one of the helmeted pilots was streaming the familiar yellow scarf. As the planes circled around to fly over the stationery convey again, Ben removed his hat and waved it in the air. He was elated when the machines turned again to fly even lower over them while waggling their wings in salute, before climbing away in a steep turn with engines crackling and snarling.

'Cocky bastards!' said Jock dismissively. 'They think they're the cat's whiskers, but I don't begrudge their moment of glory. Their life expectancy is just three or four weeks, if they're lucky, that is. We've had a few of them with us, mostly serious burns. Faces their own mothers wouldn't recognise. Ye'd never catch me up in one of those things.'

It was much later in the day, an hour before sunset, when the attack came. The tug's engine had died yet again, so that the convoy had had to moor alongside the bank for the night, while more repairs were carried out by the frustrated engineer. Ben, who was still on the upper deck carefully stowing equipment, first heard the familiar clattering sound of an aircraft engine before spotting it coming low over nearby trees. He instinctively knew that it was an enemy aircraft and that it was about to attack them. *'Get down, everyone,'* he yelled. *'It's coming in to attack!'* Before any had time to react, the plane was upon them, machine gun chattering. Without hesitation, Ben ran for the stern locker from which he took a Red Cross flag. As the plane returned for a second pass Ben held the flag between his raised arms and stood his ground as bullets whistled around him.

Noticing what the new man was doing, Jock's voice rose above the sound of the engine, the machine gun, and the whistling and zinging of bullets as he shouted, *'Get down, you stupid idiot!'*

Ben however, continued waving the flag as the plane swept past and started another turn. It was at that moment that a second aircraft appeared. Ben immediately recognised the yellow scarf and started cheering his hero as the two pilots entered a deadly ariel battle. The evening sky was filled with the sound of straining engines and chattering machine guns as the planes climbed, turned, rolled and plummeted in their attempts to gain advantage and deliver the killing blow. Several members of the medical team had put on their capes to join Ben and Jock on the upper deck to watch the ariel gladiators testing their individual skill to the limit in their desperate attempt to survive their fight to the death. It was the German who was to end his day telling his comrades about his victory. With a feeling of dismay, Ben watched as smoke started pouring from the cowling of the British plane while the engine started to misfire. One of the nurses let out a scream as the plane went into a twisted dive from which it would never recover. As the plane plummeted to the ground, Ben caught a glimpse of the yellow scarf, but had no way of telling if the pilot was dead or alive. With a sickening thud the doomed machine hit the ground and immediately burst into flames, no more than two hundred yards from the moored convoy.

'*We've got to get him out!*' yelled Ben as he leaped for the bank.

'Come back here, you fool!' responded Jock. *'He won't have survived that crash and it could go up at any moment!'*

Now on the bank and running through the gathering darkness for all he was worth, Ben shouted back, *'We can't just leave him to burn!'*

Before Jock had time to jump ashore and pursue Ben, whom he could no longer see against the backdrop of flames, there was a violent flash of light and an ear-splitting sound as ammunition and petrol exploded in the heat of the burning aircraft. Jock was thrown to the deck as a wave of heat hit him. Recovering from the fall and through slitted eyes, he watched with hope, only to be replaced by despair, as fire filled the night. Nobody emerged from the conflagration.

Half an hour later, with yet another temporary repair completed, the skipper of the steam tug decided that they should risk moving further downstream in the dark, to be away from the fire which would be a beacon to the enemy. The fire was to continue burning for many hours during that long night while the convoy slipped further away.

Chapter 24

He peered into the flames as heat from the fire warmed his face and hands. There was nothing but bitterness in his very being. Why had it come to this? he had asked himself over and over. Nobody cared about whether he lived or died. Mav had deserted him, all because of the horse. Is that all he was worth to her, owning a horse? *Well, I'm better off without the bitch,* he tried to console himself. And as for this lousy job, they could stuff it. If he wasn't working his butt off preparing this stinking material for caulking, they had him doing the most menial tasks such as tidying the wharf, painting the shed doors and windows, or mucking out the stable. He had no friends on the wharf as none of the men were as interested in loud-mouthing the bosses as he was. On the plus side, he had managed to pilfer various tools such as chisels, saws and spanners, all of which he had managed to sell to dealers.

He was still having no luck with female company. His last attempt to indulge in a bit of a snog in *The Four Horse Shoes* had ended up with a slapped face and expulsion by the landlord. 'Why does everyone have it in for me?' he moaned under his breath.

While these black thoughts were running through Patrick's head, he failed to notice the foreman heading in his direction.

'Stibbs! Get a move on with that goat's hair! I'm fed up with warning you. If you don't pull your finger out, you're on your way out! I've got my eye on you. Funny how tools started going missing after you started working here. If I ever catch you at it, I'll call the law in. Now, get on with that job, or else.'

If I ever get him alone some night, I'll show him who's boss, he thought to himself as he sifted the smelly goat's hair, ready for the next mix in the hot tar. Once again, the obsessive thought of that bossy girl from Meadow Farm filled his head. *I know she wanted it. Why did she have to play so innocent with me? Stuck-up cow. If it weren't for her, I wouldn't be in this stinking place.*

'Come on, you.' The voice of the smithy, who was stoking the fire, intruded into his lustful thoughts. 'You heard what the man said. Get that goat's hair sorted, and be quick about it.'

~~~

It was three days later, when *Red Rose* picked up her mooring at the London wharf. Beth had made a full recovery from her earlier encounter with the cold water in the lock. She had been allowed out of bed by her mother yesterday and was going about her business of unhitching the rope, or "snubber" from Skippy as though nothing had happened. Marge had been keeping an eye on the girl and would continue to do so for a while, for who knew what damage may have been caused in her head? She had noticed how restless the girl had been in bed last night. *Best keep 'er busy, although there's no point cleaning and polishing in 'ere till the coal's all loaded. I'll use the time teaching her 'ow to make ear protectors for the mule, or do some spiderwork to make 'er dad some new braces. Maybe tomorrer I could take 'er bankside to buy some food and maybe 'av a look around. Praps our Ed will agree to Jo coming as well, if 'e can spare 'er.*

At that moment, Jo was on deck helping Ed remove and stow the heavy canvas covers, thus exposing the timber which would soon be hauled out of the hold. As she worked, she found that she was continually looking along the quay, toward the corner, the
~~~

last place she had seen Ben. *When was it?* she asked herself. *Just two weeks ago, seems much longer.* She had not realised at the time just how much she would miss him. Once again, she tried to imagine where he was at that moment, and what he was doing. Was he in danger? Had he made any friends? Was he regretting his decision to go? Did he ever think of her, and if so, what was he thinking?

‘Are you alright, lass? You looked as though you were miles away.’

‘Sorry Ed. Was I slowing down? Just thinking about Ben. Being back on this quay started me off.’

‘Yea, I know what you mean. I imagine it’s hard for you to find yourself falling in love so quickly then losing him even quicker.’

‘You are very perceptive, Ed’

‘Don’t know what that means luv, but I know love when I sees it. When I first met my Marge, she and her little sister were riding on one of them whirligig things at the Banbury fair. She was so young and pretty, carrying a bit of weight, mind, but pretty all the same. I watched her going round and round that thing while the steam organ played some tune I can't remember, couldn't take my eyes off her. She looked so happy and full of life. Then I realised she was looking straight at me every time she came round. At first, I wasn't sure, so next time she was on the other side I quickly moved further round to see what she would do. Sure enough, as she came round, I could tell she was looking for me over the heads of the crowd. That was enough for me. When the ride finished and as she helped her little sister to get off, I went right up to her and said the most romantic thing I could think of.'

'What was that, Ed?' asked Jo who was captivated by this story.

'I said to her, "Fancy some candyfloss, miss?" just like that, bold as brass, I was.'

'Do you mean to tell me that was the best you could do?'

'Well, it worked, didn't it? Then when I found out she was a "boater" that did it for me. She had gone to the fair with her Pop, as she called him. He was over at the horse sale at the time. Turned out he was a Number One and owned the boat moored up close to ours. I reckon we fell in love then and there. In this life of ours there's no messing. Who knew if our paths would ever cross again, and if so, when? So, I walks Marge and her little sister home to her boat later that afternoon and I asks her Pop if Marge and me can be wed and for her to become my “Best Mate”. Course, my dad was still around then, so I wasn’t a “Number One” at the time, although I would become owner of *Red Rose* one day. Anyhow, Pop goes and has a chat with me dad, and the next you know, Marge is transferring her few belongings into *Red Rose* and I have to move into the fore-cabin till a ceremony can be arranged a couple of days later.’

‘That was quick!’ exclaimed Jo in amazement. ‘How did you organise a church service so fast?’

‘Oh, it wasn’t done in church. We had a gathering of all the boaters who happened to be moored there, and we made our promises in the middle of a circle on the green. Someone had lent Marge a posh dress, although I noticed after, that the top buttons at the back didn’t quite reach. Didn’t matter though, cos it was covered by a shawl. Lots of beer and pies and things, all donated by the other boaters. It was right grand; I can tell you. Children enjoying the fun and games. Women doing what they like best, gossiping. Men doing stuff like arm-wrestling. There was even a tug-of-war using one of the snubbers. It were a grand affair. My parents moved out that night, I can't remember where they slept. So, we had the boat to ourselves just for that one night. Nice clean sheets, ribbons tied around the cabin. We didn't know anything about what was expected, but we worked it out between us, if you see what I mean.'

'That's all so romantic, Ed,' said Jo. 'How did you manage after? There's not a lot of room in the boat, is there?'

'We just about fitted in the fore-cabin, a bit cold and damp, but it was okay. As it turned out, it wasn't to be too long. Mum and dad died within a year of each other. Dad first, he had a heart attack about six months after we were wed, while hefting a heavy load of chalk. Then mum went with some kind of virus not so long after.'

'I'm so sorry, Ed. Life on the canals is hard, I can see that.'

'Yes, luv. It's hard and you don't want to be doing this for ever. You need to be back on the farm. I know you're doing this because of Ben leaving, but you don't have to, you know.'

'Ed, I'm doing this because I know I'm in love with Ben, and I'm afraid I might lose him. I've also become fond of you all.

You’re like a second family to me now. You need me, Ed, and I need you. Now that Polly’s moved into the farm with Graham, my dad’s going to be okay. So, this is where I want to be, at least till my brother comes home, then I’ll have to see.’

‘Well, none of us can be certain about the future,’ mused Ed while removing his cap to scratch his head. ‘As I said before, trade isn’t so good now. I quite fancy the idea of settling down on the bank somewhere. We’re not getting any younger, me and our Marge. Added to that, I’d like Beth to have some proper schooling like you. We’ve got some savings, and the boat’s still worth a bit. Might be able to afford to rent a small-holding, a few pigs, chickens, that kind of thing, who knows? I’m going to have a chat with Ben about it when he comes back, see if he’s interested in taking on *Red Rose,* though I wouldn’t expect him to, now he’s been in the army and seen a different life, if you can call it that.’

‘My word, you *have* been thinking about it, Ed.’

‘Yea, me and our Marge often talk about it. Now this war has come along, I reckon we’ll stay as we are for the time being. Okay, luv. Let’s leave it there for the moment. We must get on with this, so they can start unloading that timber.’

~~~

John was sitting in a deckchair on the lawn, as were several other patients, enjoying the fresh air and the distant view of the Hampshire Downs. The large imposing manor behind him had been converted into a convalescence hospital for injured servicemen at the outbreak of war. He was wrapped in a blanket at the insistence of the duty nurse. In his hand was a novel that he had yet to open for the first time. He could feel the weak sun on his face as he thought about Jo and his father, and wondered how they were coping and how soon he would be able to start work on the farm. He had been checked over by the SMO that morning, to be informed that his right lung would never fully recover, and that he would suffer breathlessness if and when he ever over exerted himself. In the same breath, the man abruptly informed him that he was of no further use to the army. In his weakened state there was no argument.

As he sat there, breathing cool air that thankfully didn't smell of disinfectant, his mind took him back to the trenches. The
~~~

hardship, the companionship, the sense of achievement and purpose. The men who looked to him for guidance, support and reassurance. It had been a hard existence, but in a strange way, he had enjoyed it. His more recent memories however, were vague and mostly filled with pain and confusion. Images and voices had come and gone, making no sense to his tortured brain. Two of those images had however, broken through to his awareness. Even now, as he sat in the quietness of this brisk November day, he could feel the gentle touch of Nurse Farley who had willed him to survive. He was convinced that, without her, he would have died.

The other image had developed into the solid form of a man close to his own age. A soldier on the hospital barge with a Red Cross emblem on his arm. He would never forget him and the conversation they had enjoyed together. When he asked why Ben hadn't come to see him that evening, as promised, the angel nurse had had tears streaming down her cheeks as she told him what had taken place and how Ben had died.

Shaking off the depressing thoughts that had suddenly threatened to overwhelm him, John thought about the letter he had written this morning, to his father and Jo, informing them of his return to England, and that he would soon be home for good. The thought of Jo fussing over him, brought a smile to his face, a face that bore little resemblance to the one he had looked at in the mirror over the years. He had lost so much weight and his face was gaunt. His eyes were sunk and his hair was showing signs of grey, including the beard which had been growing since that dreadful morning when they had gone over the top. He had been shocked that morning when he peered at the stranger in the mirror. Would his sister even recognise him, he wondered? He had missed Jo more than he would ever have imagined. For her sake, as much as anything else, he would fight and overcome any weakness, as he returned to the peace of the countryside he loved so much.

At least he had come out of it all, alive, and in one piece. Many had not been so lucky. Again, he thought of his friend Norman and how much he was going to miss his cheerful presence both at work and at play.

Chapter 25

'Okay, Mr Fraser. Agreed. Once the timber is offloaded you can move along the quay and load with sand, to be shipped to Guildford for their iron works, at seven shillings per ton. No doubt you'll be able to pick up a cargo to bring back here. Possibly corn, or some other agricultural products. You should make a fair profit, I imagine.' Ed winked at Jo who had accompanied him to the Wharfinger's office so that she might learn and gain experience of the trading which was central to life on the canals.

Stepping from the cluttered office, which was the domain of the harassed wharfinger, and onto the busy quay, Ed turned to Jo and, with a grin creasing his face, said, 'That'll make a change from coal, and it'll give us a chance to haul *Red Rose* out at Dapdune Wharf to clean her bottom. We stick to the Wey Navigation all the way up to Dapdune. It's been a while since we were there. Marge will be pleased, she likes Guildford. Have you ever been there, Jo?'

'No, I've heard of it, but not been there. I'll look forward to visiting the shops with Marge.'

'Come on, let's go and give her the good news.'

Five minutes later, after hearing the news, Marge dropped the crochet hook and gave Ed a big hug, before saying, 'Oh, that's good, you know I likes going there, Ed. Last time we were there, I managed to buy some nice bonnets for me and the girls, from the market place. Never did see our Ruby in 'ers,' she tailed off as the smile slipped from her face, to be replaced by a faraway look.

Noticing the change, Jo quickly stepped over and gave Marge a hug, saying, 'I can't wait to see if we can find any bargains. I could do with a warm jumper now the winter's making itself felt. Dad insisted that he give me a large purse of money to "see me through" as he put it, so we can treat ourselves.'

'Yea, and some new boots would come in 'andy for Beth,' replied Marge as she shook off the moment of sadness. 'Right then, let's get dinner started. Jo, you can peel the tats and, Beth, you can shuck some peas, while I clears away all this wool.'

A short while later, Beth climbed the steps and slid back the hatch cover to step into the growing darkness. She was intending to throw the pea-shucks into the fast-flowing river when she became aware of being watched. Her voice could be heard down below as she said, 'Hello. What you doing here? Are you hungry? Where you from?' Without hesitation, Ed dropped the pipe he had been cleaning out and shot up the steps to investigate. 'It's a dog, Daddy. I think he's hungry.'

'Scat! commanded Ed, while stamping his foot on the counter. *'Go on! Get out of here!'* The dog quickly trotted off, tail between its legs. 'Come on luvvy,' addressing himself to Beth. 'Inside. We don't want you getting cold before you're fully recovered, do we?' An hour later, the four of them were eating their evening meal while talking about what they would do in Guildford. 'Can we buy some liquorice, Mummy? I haven't had any for ages and ages and simply ages, please? Can we?'

'We'll see if you're good enough,' replied Marge, amused to see Beth immediately sitting up straight and folding her arms. 'I'll be really, really good,' replied the hopeful child. It was as Beth closed her lips tight and sat up even straighter that the scratching noise could be heard.

‘What’s that?’ enquired Marge as she leaned her head to one side as though that would help her to hear better.

‘A seagull on the roof most like,’ responded Ed. ‘They fly up the estuary looking for scraps.’ They all listened for a while before concluding that the gull had flown off. Conversation picked up as Beth relaxed from the rigid pose which she had previously taken on to represent being “good”. Marge was regaling Jo with the delights of Guildford market when the scratching noise returned.

‘It’s that noise again,’ said Ed while holding up his hand to pause the conversation. They listened and for the first time, became aware of the constant gurgling noise of tidal water sweeping past the hull, and the distant clatter and hum of the London traffic, which never stopped. No scratching. As they sat in silence, in the dim light of the lantern, eyes were cast and met around the table. The silence within the cabin was suddenly broken by Marge who, in the creepiest voice she could muster, said, ‘Is anybody there?’ That did it. Laughter broke the spell in the warmth of the cosy cabin. ‘Last time I went to one of those I was in a tent and I was told I was soon to meet a tall, dark ‘andsome man, then ten minutes later our Ed offered to buy me some candyfloss. That’s when I knew it was all rubbish. Tall, dark and ‘andsome? More like small, stark and gruesome, if you asks me.’

‘Oh yea? Well, you were quick enough to shove that candyfloss down ya face, I seem to recall. I thought I was gonna marry a princess, and what did I get? Well, I’ll tell you. I ended up with the loveliest girl you could ever ask for. She ain’t no princess, but she is the queen of my heart.’

‘Oh, Ed, that’s the loveliest thing you’ve said since you told me you ‘ad weed growin’ out your bottom.’

‘The bottom of the boat, you daft bat …’ The rest of Ed’s comment was overtaken by the laughter from the other three, although it was doubtful that Beth knew what she was laughing about, apart from the cheerful moment in that confined, cosy space she was happy to call home. The laughter, which was self-generating, eventually died down, to be replaced by scratching at the top of the steps. ‘There it is again; I’ll have to have a look.’ Ed eased himself from the small table and reached up to slide the hatch cover and open the door. As cold air replaced the warm stuffy atmosphere of the cabin, Ed exclaimed, 'It's that bleeding dog again! The one I shooed off earlier. *Get off,* you stupid animal!' The small brown dog of uncertain breed, with no distinguishing features other than one white ear, was joyfully licking the face that had suddenly appeared at the top of the steps. *'Get off I tell you!'*

'Can I see it, Daddy?' asked Beth excitedly, as she hopped down from the side-bed. 'Daddy, can I see it?' she repeated.

'Looks like it's a stray. It's got dried blood on its neck. Looks as though it's bin in a fight, some time ago I would guess,' said Ed with a note of concern.

'Ere, let me 'ave a look,' said Marge as she pushed Ed to one side. 'Oh, you poor little mite. Come 'ere, let me see that neck of yourn.' There was a brief moment before Marge said, 'Can't see in the dark, I'm bringing it down.' It didn't take long for Marge to clean and powder the wound, all the while, the dog remaining still while Marge tut-tutted over her ministration. The dog turned out to be a smooth coated male, and was clearly half starved. The leftovers from their meal were very speedily consumed by the friendly animal who displayed his pleasure with a wagging tail, Marge found an old, rarely used, bowl which she half filled with water before placing it on the rug. The dog quickly lapped up the water before, to Ed's surprise, jumping up onto his lap and immediately curling up into a contented ball.

'Can we keep him, Daddy?' asked Beth plaintively.

'No!'

'Please, Daddy. I'll look after him.'

'I said, "No". We have enough problems feeding ourselves during this retched war, let alone feeding another animal. At least Skippy works for his keep, what could this dog do to pay his way? He's been fed and watered, and his wound's been taken care of, that's all we can do. I'm putting him out.'

'That's cruel, Daddy. Look, he likes you.' At that moment, the dog had uncurled himself and was licking Ed's hand.

'He's a bit of a chancer, I'll give him that,' muttered Ed as he looked into the dog's large mournful brown eyes.'

'Just like you, our Ed,' said Marge. I think 'e should stay, at least till mornin', to see how that wound looks.' There was no further argument from Ed, who always knew when Marge would get her way.

'Okay, just till the morning,' was all he could say as he attempted maintaining his authority. He failed to notice the wink Marge gave to Beth, as he distractedly stroked the dog's ears.

Jo had sat quietly throughout the discussion. Her intuition informed her that the family she had grown to love, had just acquired a dog. She was not to know then, in the comfort of that loving environment, how important the dog was to become to her and the family in the not-too-distant future.

~~~

Whilst Jo was settling down to sleep, with the dog curled up at her feet, many miles away Graham and Polly were lounging before the dying fire drinking their hot chocolate and gazing into the embers before retiring to bed. Phil had gone to his bed an hour or so earlier. In the distance, a barn owl could be heard, no doubt preparing for its nightly hunt for prey. The fire crackled just before a half-burned log dropped into the glowing ash. The couple were silent as they listened to the night sounds, each in their own
~~~

thoughts. The grandfather clock continued its rhythmic ticking, which went un-noticed during the day but which seemed to fill the quietness of the room at this late hour. It was a comforting homely sound, as was the occasional crack of burning wood on the fire.

The drawn-out silence was eventually broken by Graham who asked, 'What are you thinking, luv?'

'Oh, nothing much,' replied Polly with a contented sigh. 'Mostly about how nice this is. Nearly a week now, and every day has been such a joy. No washing for other people, apart from Phil's long-johns. getting used to a different kitchen, polishing such lovely furniture, planning how to decorate our bedroom.'

In addition to their bedroom the house was large enough for Graham and Polly to have their own bathroom. As for anything else, they were invited to share the family rooms downstairs, and for this purpose, the drawing room, which was previously rarely used, had been opened up, aired and heated with an open fire each evening. The kitchen was now recognised as Polly's domain, as per Jo's instructions before she left.

A few minutes later Polly broke into the contented quietness, saying, 'Phil has agreed to me resurrecting the kitchen garden, so I'm planning how and what to stock it with.'

'It seems Phil is more than happy with the new arrangement,' said Graham. 'It's had a positive effect on my relationship with him, which was always good, but now, even better.'

'I just worry about how his son will react when he finds his sister gone, and two complete strangers living in his house,' mused Polly. 'It'll be a bit of a shock for him, I imagine.'

'Well, Phil says not to worry about it,' replied Graham. 'Apparently John's an easy-going individual who will appreciate how much you're helping, both him and Jo. The only problem, as far as I see it, is how seriously he's been injured. We'll always have the cottage to fall back on, if necessary, although I don't think it'll ever come to that.'

'Speaking of the cottage,' replied Polly while moving to a more upright position and looking at Graham. 'I should have told you earlier, I went over there this morning to gather a few things from the last of the crop in the kitchen garden. Mrs Barker happened to call in while I was there. Although she knows why we want to keep it on for a while, she told me that she's concerned about the cottage being unoccupied for too long, in case of squatters, so she wants to terminate the rental agreement at the end of February if we haven't moved back in by then.'

'Okay, that's both understandable and reasonable,' replied Graham. 'I would imagine that we will have a better idea of our situation here long before that, so don't worry yourself over it. I'm sure it'll all work out fine. Now, if you've finished your drink, I'll put the fire guard on and lock up.'

~~~

'It makes a nice change to be wearing a frock,' said Jo. 'Although it can't be seen under this coat. How long is she going to be in there, do you think?' Together, she and Marge were sitting outside the fitting cubical of a small clothing retailer, in the High Street. Beth had slipped through the curtain, carrying three dresses ten minutes earlier while her mother continued perusing the various racks looking for anything that would fit her while, at
~~~

the same time, look "Posh", as she described it. It had taken a lot of persuasion for Marge to agree to Jo's offer of buying them all a gift, which she could well afford. After all, her father had been generous with the amount of money he had given her before she had set out from the farm the previous week. Jo had had to remind Marge that they were keeping and feeding her for no more than enjoying the experience of canal life. Beth had been so excited with the prospect of owning a new frock, something she had never previously experienced, hence the long wait while she tried all three garments on several times before finally swishing back the curtain and stepping out of the cubical.

'Oh, Beth, that looks lovely,' exclaimed Jo as she examined Beth's choice, with approval. 'What do you think, Mum?' The word was out before Jo had time to think about what she was saying 'Sorry, I meant …'

'I knows what you meant, luvvy,' said Marge with a huge smile. Squeezing Jo's hand she continued, 'I reckon "Mum" sounds just fine. Now then, turn round, Beth. Let me see the back.' After a brief pause, during which she surreptitiously wiped moisture from both eyes with the back of her hand, Marge exclaimed, 'Beautiful! A good choice. Now take it orff, carefully, so's I can try this on.' She had been nursing a crimson frock whilst awaiting her turn in the cubical. Turning to Jo, she quietly said, 'Thank you, luvvy. You didn't have to do this, you know.'

'I wanted to,' replied Jo. 'What about Ed? Any ideas as to what he may like?'

A while later, lunch for the three of them consisted of a hot potato, dripping with butter, which they were purchasing from a stall attended by an elderly gentleman dressed in an equally elderly army greatcoat. Beth was more interested in the man's black and white dog than she was the potato as they were being served. 'I hope Oddy's okay, and that Daddy's looking after him,' she said to no one in particular.

'Who's "Oddy"? enquired Jo and Marge simultaneously.

'Our dog, of course. I've named him "Oddy" cos of his odd ears.'

'Oh, so 'e's *our* dog now, is 'e?' asked Marge with a wink in Jo's direction.

'Yes, he likes us and wants to live with us.'

'Well, we'll just 'ave to see what yer father 'as to say about it won't we? Okay, this one's yourn. Don't get that butter all down ya.'

It was three weary boaters who eventually arrived back at the wharf several hours later. Jo could understand why that would be so for Marge and Beth, but she was used to being on her feet all day, hadn't she just walked all the way from London to Guildford over several days, working various locks on the way? It was the hours of ambling in and out of shops, carrying various parcels, that had taken its toll on the three of them. Beth had been about to complain as they entered the final shop until she realised that here, they would be able to buy liquorice, as well as a few other treats. What they were not expecting to see as they approached *Red Rose* at her birth along the quay, was her Number One sitting on the cabin roof with the dog's head resting in his lap. Unaware of their silent approach, he could be heard talking quietly to the dog as he caressed its ears.

'Just look at the daft apeth,' whispered Marge. 'Pretends to be 'ard but 'as an 'eart as soft as one of my fried eggs.' Then more loudly, ‘Ello Ed, ‘avin’ trouble with the dog? Got you pinned down, ‘as ‘e? Want me to pull ‘im orff?’

Startled, Ed struggled to his feet, as did the dog. ‘Stupid animal won’t leave me alone,’ complained Ed sheepishly.

‘Oh, is that ‘ow it is? I thought for a mo that you was ‘avin a nice chat wiv ‘im. Got you a present. Well, more like Jo’s got you a present. Show ‘im Jo.’

Needing no further prompting, Jo handed a brown paper-wrapped parcel up to Ed. ‘Thought you might like a new waist-coat now the winter’s coming on. I hope you like it,’ said Jo, feeling strangely embarrassed. ‘They said they can change it if it doesn’t fit.’

Ed took the parcel with a nod at Jo, before carefully untying the string. ‘We can save the string, and the paper,’ he gruffly said in an attempt to hide his pleasure. ‘Let’s see what we’ve got here.’ Holding up the bright yellow waistcoat Ed was silent for a moment. He then placed it back down onto the brown paper and, stepping off the roof onto the counter, took Jo into his arms. ‘I love it, girl. And I love you like you was my own. Thank you, luv.

I'll treasure it and keep it for the really cold days when I need a bit of extra warmth.'

'Daddy, can we keep Oddy? Please? asked Beth with her most pathetic voice, having waited patiently for the right moment.

'By "Oddy" I take it you mean the dog?' replied Ed now looking down at the animal who had already jumped down to greet his new friends.

For a moment, they all looked at the dog who seemed to be aware of the importance of the moment. He was now sitting on his haunches at Beth's feet, with his white ear raised and his tail slightly twitching. The dog made a sound somewhere between a bark and a growl.

'I think Oddy has already decided to adopt us, sweety. He's a part of the family now,' replied Ed with a broad smile.

With that declaration, Beth let out a loud yelp of joy while Oddy, sensing the moment, began running around his new pack, barking and licking any bit of exposed skin he could reach.

Chapter 26

With a contented smile on his face, Phil let himself out of the house and stood in the centre of the cobbled yard. The sun was shining, although there was a cold south-westerly breeze which encouraged him to turn up his collar before sinking his hands into his coat pockets. He had just enjoyed one of Polly's breakfasts after the milking which he and Graham had done together. Looking around the yard, he noticed and appreciated how much tidier everything had become since he had taken on the man who was fast becoming a friend. Strolling across to the barn door, he examined and admired the repairs Graham had done. He then turned around and looked across the yard to the machine shed where he knew that every piece of equipment was clean, well-greased, and fully serviceable. He had no need to tell Graham what needed doing. They had got into the habit of discussing plans for the coming day, every evening during the meal which was cheerfully served up by Polly. He had come to look forward to those moments, for it was just like the old times, as the same had happened when John and Jo were still at home. Thinking of Jo, he was expecting her to be home any day now. That, and the letter he had received from John the day before, was partly the cause for his good mood this morning. John was safely back from the war, apparently not as bad as he had feared, but enough to ensure he would never be going back to the trenches. His first thought, upon receiving the letter, was to go to the hospital and see his boy, to satisfy himself that he was indeed all in one piece. That was not to happen however, as John had written that visitors were not encouraged unless there was the possibility of death of a loved-one. *"An eventuality which is definitely not going to happen in my case!"*, he had written in large letters. The letter had finished with the cheerful words, equally as large; *"a great Christmas, all together"*. Disappointingly, there was no mention of exactly when John would be home, beyond the encouraging words about Christmas. There was also no return address, so Phil would not be able to let John know about Graham and Polly, or what Jo was now doing. *Let's hope it's not all too much of a shock for the lad.*

His thoughts were suddenly disturbed by the squeaky sound of one of the upper sash windows being opened. A glance revealed Polly, now leaning from her open window, as she hung out a bed sheet for airing. Spotting him in the yard, she waved to him, a huge smile splitting her handsome face. Yes, life was certainly good at that moment, he mused whilst returning the wave.

~~~

Life for Patrick was certainly not good as far as he was concerned. The work was relentless and the yard foreman was ruthless. There was never a moment when he could rest, apart from his forty-minute lunch break. He had had to help with the unloading of sand from a narrowboat that had arrived four days ago. He had watched the two women and the child, all bundled up in their coats and scarves, walk away from the yard later that morning. He remembered thinking; *they don't know how lucky they are. Poncing about on a boat all day, while the rest of us have to work.* Once again, he thought about the mule that had hauled the boat into the wharf. *Still got a lot of life in it. If I could only get my hands on it, I could hitch-up and be on my way out of here.*
~~~

On that afternoon four days ago, toward the end of Patrick's shift, the three members of the narrowboat's crew had reappeared, each carrying a bag, or parcel. He had been watching the man on the cabin top fussing with his dog for the previous hour while the others had still been away, when they had returned there was much excitement as one of the women handed a parcel up to him. The man had taken the parcel and immediately untied the string before examining a yellow garment of some sort. It wasn't long after, when the dog, amidst much laughter and screaming, had started going mad, jumping up and licking its owners.

Worth remembering they've got a dog, Patrick now thought to himself as he prepared to start his walk back to his caravan. To say that his camp site was untidy would be a gross understatement, for there was rubbish and rusty metal scattered all around the clearing. There was also a repugnant smell coming from the direction of the closest bushes. Patrick however, didn't notice any of this. For this was his life and he was used to it, although Mavis would certainly have had strong words with him had she returned to her husband.

~~~
~~~

It was on the following day that John was discharged from the base hospital. His chest wound had knitted with no further complications, although he was still aware of his shortage of breath with the least amount of exertion. He had been issued with a railway warrant with orders to report to his regimental base in Aldershot. A WD Thornycroft truck was laid on to take him, and several others, to the local train station. He was delighted to be travelling by train, although, throughout the journey, he discouraged any attempt by fellow passengers to engage him in conversation. He wanted to immerse himself in his private thoughts. He was looking forward to seeing his father and, of course, his sister, once he was finally discharged from the army. The cloud on his horizon however, was his inability to do the most menial task without severe loss of breath. How was he to be of use on the farm when he couldn't even pick up a shovel without feeling giddy? Although the doctor had assured him that his condition would slightly improve with time and practice, his natural tendency to become impatient when he was unable to progress, or achieve a set task, was likely be a constant battle for him. All these negative thoughts were going around in his head as he watched the passing scenery of bare trees, recently ploughed fields, and station platforms with warmly wrapped passengers boarding or leaving the train with its locomotive impatient to be on its way again.

At last, upon reaching the camp with its variety of brick buildings and wooden huts, he reported to the guardroom at the gate, where he showed his identity along with his orders.

"Corporal Simons," read the duty sergeant. 'The company Adjutant's office is along this road, pass block "A", turn left, three hundred yards and you're there. Got that?'

'Yes Sarge, got it. Thank you.' Pocketing his orders and marching in the appointed direction he was certain that the sergeant was watching him and would, at any moment, yell at him to *"Swing those bloody arms!"* His weeks of training and drill, in this place almost two years ago, all crowded in on his troubled mind. Without realising he was doing it, he found himself marching smartly, with arms swinging to the required height. Even this simple act was taking it out on him and he was relieved when he reached the door of the office he was looking for. In the distance he could hear the familiar sound of crunching feet on the parade ground as an unseen squad of new recruits was clearly not meeting their drill-sergeant’s exacting standards, judging by the amount of shouting and swearing he was directing at the unfortunate young men who were soon to exchange one form of hell for another.

‘My dear boy, you look all in. Here, take a seat. The duty sergeant rang to warn me you were on your way.’ The smartly dressed middle-aged Adjutant had stepped from behind his oak desk to place a chair behind John. ‘Bad, was it?’ he asked.

‘Sorry?’

‘Over there. Had a bad time I shouldn’t wonder.’ Returning to his chair behind the desk the adjutant placed a pair of spectacles on his nose before peering down at an open file, going through the motion of reading the report, which John had no doubt, he had already perused. ‘Let me see now,’ he said “Wounded whilst assaulting the enemy … Serious chest injury … A fine record and well thought of by both officers and men … Honourable discharge”. Looking up and removing his spectacles, he barked, ‘Good man! That’s the spirit we drill into the men passing through this base. Well done. You should be proud, as indeed we are.’

‘Yes, sir.’

Removing a form from the file and holding it up for John to see, he crisply said, ‘Well, it’s over for you now, young man. All that’s left for me to do is to sign this Form of Discharge and you can be on your way. I assume you intend returning to your home address, where was it now?’ Sifting through the pages in the file, ‘Ah, yes, Warningford, nearest town, Odiham. How will you get there?’

Taken by surprised by this turn of events and the promise of an immediate discharge, John replied with a grin, ‘It’ll have to be by road, hitch a lift, I guess.’

‘Tell you what,’ replied the Adjutant. ‘I’ll arrange for a car to take you. The least we can do for one of our own returning heroes. I know Odiham well, it’s not all that far away, five miles at the most. Can’t be much more to .. um, Warningford, can it.’

‘Thank you, Sir. That’s very kind’

‘Pop down to the Mess and I’ll arrange for your man to call in and collect you, shall we say, in an hour? Get yourself a cup of tea and a bun, you look as though you need it. That’s all, Corporal Simons. Or perhaps I should say, “Mister” Simons.’ Laughing at his own joke, the man closed his file and walked John to the door.

It was an hour and a half later, as the daylight began to fade, that John opened the front passenger door and stepped onto the cobbles, having thanked the private who had driven him to the farm. With the car gone, leaving a cloud of exhaust lingering in the chilly air, all was quiet apart from the murmur of a slight breeze passing between the bare branches of the surrounding trees and the clucking of a number of chickens pecking between the cobbles. He stood still as he breathed in the air and glanced around the familiar yard, his emotions running high. He noticed how tidy everything was, and how the barn door had been repaired. *Looks as though Dad's been busy,* he mused. Looking toward the house, he noticed the front door slowly opening and the silhouetted figure of a woman standing on the threshold.

'Hello Jo. The return of the conquering hero.' He called as, with heart hammering, he stepped across the yard to the open door. Much to his surprise, the only response he was aware of was the lifting of a hand to the startled face of a stranger.

'John?' asked Polly while knowing full well what the answer would be.

'Yes, who are you? Where's Jo?'

Flustered, Polly breathed, 'Oh dear. This is all going to be a bit strange for you.' Then, opening the door wider, said louder, 'Why don't you come in and let your father explain everything? He's due back from the bottom field any moment now. Are you okay, can I help?'

'No!' snapped John. 'I'm fine, thank you. Has something happened to Jo? Is she alright?' John asked with concern.

'She's okay. But she's not here at the moment. My name's Polly, by the way. I'm the new housekeeper.'

'Housekeeper? Excuse me if I'm being abrupt, but what's going on? Why isn't Jo looking after things, like she always has?'

'Please, John. Come in and I'll make you a nice cup of tea. You mustn't worry, everything's alright. I'm sure your father would prefer to tell you how things are. As I said, he and Graham will be back from the fields at any moment.'

'Graham? Who's Graham?'

'Oh dear … He works on the farm now. The previous hand left suddenly and your dad was in need of a replacement.'

'Okay, um .. Polly. I can tell this is all a bit awkward for you. Look I won't come in right now. If I can leave my kit here, I'll walk down to the field and meet Dad.'

'I'll take your things up to your room then,' replied Polly with a sense of relief. 'Your father has been so looking forward to having you home. I'll get on with dinner, I hope you're hungry.'

Phil and Graham had spent the last three days digging an irrigation ditch at the lower end of the bottom field. The dwindling light had forced them to call it a day, knowing there would be more to do the following day. 'We've done well, Graham. Another two days should do it. Come on, let's go and see what your Polly's cooking up.' As they started the walk up the slope a figure could be seen heading toward them from the direction of the yard. 'A soldier,' muttered Phil. 'What's afoot now?' As the uniformed man approached, he removed his cap and waved. It was at that moment that Phil realised who it was. 'It's John!' he exclaimed. 'My god, It's my son!'

Graham, stopped walking to allow Phil to meet his son alone. He watched as the sun finally dipped behind the two men who were embracing each other with a good deal of back-slapping. He gave them a few minutes before walking slowly up the slope to join the joyful father and son.

'Graham, meet my son, John. Home from the war at last,' said Phil with moisture in his eyes. John hesitated for a brief moment as he took in the sight of the piratical figure with one eye hidden behind a patch.

Holding out his hand, John said, 'Pleased to meet you, Graham. I'm looking forward to getting to know you.'

'Well, you'll have plenty of time to do that over dinner this evening,' said Phil who was unable to contain his excitement and relief, having seen his son, not only safe but standing unassisted on two sound legs.

'Oh, you're staying for dinner,' said John. 'Good, we'll have time for a good chat this evening, then.'

There followed a moment of embarrassed silence before Phil turned to Graham, saying, 'You go on, Graham. We'll take our time and have a bit of a catch-up on our way up.'

The meal that evening, was a little strained. John was still struggling to absorb all that his father had told him. The thought that overpowered all others however, was the news of the attack on Jo. How could his father be so careless as to take on a worthless traveller in the first place? If he ever got his hands on that bastard, he would … do what? What could a man who gets breathless holding a cup and saucer ever do in a fight? His feelings of hopelessness dominated any sense of happiness he should be feeling now that he was safely home. Then again, these two strangers taking over his home, because of Jo feeling under some sort of obligation to a family of canal-boat workers. What the hell was that all about? He made up his mind, there and then, to get Jo back to where she belonged.

In an attempt to relieve the strain, Polly asked John if he felt able to talk about his experiences in France. *'I'm not ready yet!'* he snapped. After an embarrassing moment of silence John said apologetically, 'Words can never describe the things I've seen and experienced. The last few weeks are just a blur. I know that I owe my life to the skill of the surgeon who operated on me, and the dedication of the nurse who always seemed to be there, holding my hand, whenever I returned from the blackness that surrounded me, or tried to lift myself above the pain and torment.' He paused for a moment while the others remained silent trying to absorb what John must have been through. 'There was also a young soldier,' he continued. 'He tried to protect the hospital barge we were in when we were on our way to the coast. He was apparently killed while trying to save an airman from his crashed aeroplane. Funny enough, he was from around these parts. So many I knew, and became fond of. All dead now.' Lifting his moist eyes to his father, he gently said, 'Norman won't be returning, Dad. He copped it at the same time I was wounded.' Turning to Graham, he added, 'He was my best friend who worked for us. We were together, most of the time out there.'

'I knew about Norman, son,' said Phil softly. 'His mother called round to let me know.'

'Oh.' John was silent for a while. 'Did you know he had a thing about our Jo? He said he was going to write to her, just before ….'

They were all silent around the table, none of them able to think of anything appropriate to say, until John suddenly pushed his chair back, saying, 'If you don't mind, I think I'll pop down to *The Feathers*. There's someone I want to see. Don't wait up.'

The three of them looked blankly at each other as the door slammed behind the departing figure.

Chapter 27

The rustling of curtains stirring in the light breeze that filtered through the slightly open window was enough to rouse John from his troubled sleep. With half opened eyes, he became aware of the pillow alongside his own. The indentation left by June's head was evident. Instinctively, he moved his arm to the cold space where, such a short time ago, so it seemed, the girl had been asleep in his arms. Glancing at the clock on her bedside cabinet, he was surprised to see the hour-hand pointing to the figure ten. This was enough to rouse him from the last vestige of sleep. With a sense of guilt, mixed with a feeling of warmth, he allowed his mind to dwell upon their tender love-making the previous evening. He had slowly consumed two jugs of draft beer in *The Feathers*, as he listened to June playing one popular tune after another. He had politely responded to the greetings of the few men who recognised the young lad they had known, and who was now replaced by the husk of a haunted uniformed man who had lost any trace of his previous youthful enthusiasm. Left gratefully alone, he had watched and listened as the woman, four years his senior, continued pressing the black buttons and white keys of the ungainly accordion. He had noticed that she was watching him as he watched her. Each time her glances moved in his direction, which was often, a knowing smile touched her face. At the end of the evening, well after the landlord had called, “Time gentlemen, *please*”, June had placed her instrument in its case before moving across the emptying room. Without a word being spoken by either of them, they left the pub and walked in the direction of the Post Office, where she was accommodated in the rooms above. As he stood, with the heavy instrument case propped against his leg, she had retrieved her keys from her shoulder-bag and unlocked the side door. Following her through a door at the bottom of the stairs, he had asked himself what he was expecting of this moment. At the top of the stairs, he found himself in a small but tidy living room where, for the first time since leaving the pub he opened his mouth to speak. ‘June, I ....’

‘Shhhh.’ She had placed her finger on his lips. ‘Come.’ She took his hand and led him into her bedroom where she silently lit the wick of a small oil lamp which was sitting on a chest of drawers. 'John, I've been waiting for you … for so long.'

Entering the small kitchen, having splashed his face from the bathroom tap before dressing, John immediately noticed the handwritten note propped up against the teapot on the table. *"Didn't want to wake you. You were sleeping so peacefully. Thank you for last night. Am working downstairs in the Post Office. Make yourself some tea and toast if you want it before you go. I'll be playing at The Feathers again this evening. Love, June xx"*

On the table, June had thoughtfully left a loaf of bread, some butter, and a pot of marmalade. Now feeling extremely hungry, John helped himself, as invited. Letting himself out through the side door, he turned his coat collar up before walking round the corner and straight into the Post Office where he saw June serving a customer, an elderly lady wrapped in a brown fur coat.

'Good day, Mrs Atkins, mind how you go, now,' she was saying as the lady turned to leave. Not looking at John, the lady shuffled past him to the door, leaving a strong smell of mothballs and talcum powder in her wake.

Before the lady had closed the door behind her, June politely addressed John, 'Good morning, sir. What can I do for you?'

'Um, a packet of razorblades please.'

'Certainly, sir. Would there be anything else?' Before John had time to answer, the door closed with the tinkle of the bell. John was now free to speak. 'Thanks for last night, June. I just wanted to tell you that I've been thinking about you a lot since being wounded. It wasn't just a spur of the moment thing. I really like you and …' The door had swung open to the tinkling of the bell.

'If that's all Mr Simons,' said June quickly. 'It's good to see you home again. Perhaps I'll see you in *The Feathers* some time. Give my regards to your father.' Before John had time to answer, June addressed herself to the new customer. 'Good morning, Mr Golding. A cold one, but nice to see the sun shining.'

With a grin, John turned for the door and called out, 'I'll look forward to hearing you play in *The Feathers*. Bye.'

On arrival back at the farm, John asked Polly to prepare him a packed lunch before enquiring where he might find his father.

'He's still working in the bottom field,' Polly informed him. Are you planning on being away for the day? I can delay dinner if need be.'

I think you should assume I won't be back, at least until tomorrow afternoon. I'm going up for a bath and a shave. I'll pick up the lunch on my way out. Nothing fancy, bread and cheese will do, oh, and put in some cider if we have any.' Without another word, he left Polly alone in the kitchen, feeling even more that she was no longer welcome in the house.

Half an hour later, John was dressed in his civilian clothing, all of which now looked several sizes too large for him. He collected the packed lunch from Polly, stuffing it into his knapsack. With a curt nod in her direction, he let himself out into the yard and headed for the shed in which the wagon was kept. After dropping his gear on the wagon bed, he examined the wheels, brake and seat before walking down the lower field where he could see the two men hard at work with picks and shovels.

'Morning John,' called Phil, having seen his son's approach. He had stopped work and had lifted his cap to scratch the top of his head. He wisely refrained from enquiring where his son had spent the night.

'Morning Dad. Can I borrow Graham for a while, to help me hitch up the wagon?'

'Sure. Where are you taking it?' He had already guessed the answer before asking the question.

'You said yesterday that Jo's currently at a place called Dapdune Wharf in Guildford. I'm going there to see her and find out for myself what's going on.'

'I see. Want me to come with you?'

'No Dad. I think it would be best for me to talk to her on my own.'

'As you wish.' Turning to Graham who had been leaning on his shovel, listening to the conversation, he said gruffly, 'Go and do as he asked, Graham. I'll wait here.'

John had not driven more than three miles before he realised that this was to be a hard, painful day for him. Already the pain in his chest was becoming apparent each time the wagon hit a rut, or a stone in the lanes. However, once he had reached, and passed through Farnham, the roads were metalled and became easier. With the change in motion, he found that he was actually enjoying the ride. The regular clip-clop of the horses' feet combined with the rumble of the wheels, as well as the creaking of springs, all had a soothing effect on his troubled mind. He stopped for lunch after leaving Farnham. Graham had stowed plenty of feed and water in the wagon for the horses after which, John allowed them time to rest before tackling the long haul to the ridge which would eventually take him into Guildford.

~~~

With the sand unloaded, the task of hauling *Red Rose* up the ramp and out of the water, was started. It took several men, on each of the windlasses, a total of two hours to complete the task. The family had little they could contribute to the manual labour, so, at Ed's suggestion, the morning was spent visiting the cathedral which overlooked the city. This was a real treat for the hard-
~~~

working boaters who rarely had time for such frivolities as sight-seeing. The ladies were resplendent in their new clothes, and Ed was chuffed to be wearing his new waistcoat. For once, they were not shunned, as gypsies, by the folk they encountered. They were particularly pleased when a member of the clergy took time to show them, and explain, some of the main features.

It was mid-afternoon when the exhausted but happy family walked back through the open wharf gates. In their excitement, they failed to notice one of the labourers staring at them as they walked past the steaming boiler of tar.

That girl looks so much like the bitch at Meadow Farm, Patrick thought to himself. *Could be a twin sister if I didn't know better. That hoity-toity bitch wouldn't even look at the likes of that sort.*

It was with that bitter thought in his mind that he heard Jo calling to Beth who had left the group to run to the stable to check on her beloved Skippy. *That's her voice! Blimey. It* is *her! It has to be! That's the girl who pitchforked me! What the hell is she doing here? I can't imagine how, but luck has brought her to me.* For the first time in weeks, Patrick had a broad smile on his face. A smile which failed to reach his slitted venomous eyes.

~~~

The happy band of boaters, one at a time, climbed the ladder to reach the counter of the beached narrowboat. Marge had gone first, amidst much laughter at her efforts, while Ed inspected the work that had so far been done on the hull. Oddy displayed his pleasure at the return of his pack as he licked the faces of each of them upon drawing level with the counter. By the time Ed had swung himself onto the counter Marge had the kettle singing on the stove.

There was much chattering and laughter on *Red Rose* at the moment the horse-drawn wagon stopped just inside the wharf gates. The driver leaned down to speak to the foreman who had walked over to investigate the unexpected arrival. The driver looked in the direction pointed out by the foreman before tipping his cap and flicking the reins.

Approaching the boat, John could hear laughter amidst loud excited conversation, also the barking of a dog. Drawing the wagon alongside the boat, he noticed how restless Blacky had
~~~

become as the horse nodded her head within the constraints of the tack. Not comfortable with the thought of stepping across the gap uninvited, he called, *'Hello?'* The laughter continued although the dog's playful barking changed to a more challenging tone. It was Ed who poked his head through the hatch.

'Can I help you, Mister?' he enquired of the stranger who had, in his opinion, drawn up the wagon far too close to his boat.

'I'm looking for Jo,' answered John.

'Oh? And who might you be, may I ask?'

'I'm her brother. The name's John.'

With that startling revelation, Ed grinned before lowering his head through the hatch and calling, 'Jo, someone up here to see you.'

The laughter stopped abruptly. Jo who had been setting out cups and saucers ready for tea was puzzled as to who could possibly be asking for her in this place, she instantly climbed the steps alongside Ed's legs.

'Hello, Jo.'

'John? … *Oh, my god! It's really you!'*

'Yep. As far as I can tell, it's really me, Sis.'

With a squeal of delight, Jo squeezed past Ed and stepped across the gap straight into her brother's outstretched arms. They were still clutched together when Beth and Marge made it to the counter. Knowing that she would need it, Ed removed his neck-erchief and passed it to Marge who immediately dabbed it to her eyes as the three of them stood and watched the happy reunion.

It was some minutes before Jo was able to lift her streaming face from her brother's chest to say, 'John, you're so thin, you're all bones. Are you okay? Oh, I'm so happy. What are you doing here? It's our farm wagon and there's my beautiful horses! This is the best day of my life. Are you hungry? Are you in any pain? Oh, John, I can't believe you're really here.'

'Steady on, Sis, give us a chance. I'm pleased to see you, as well.'

'Can you stay? Oh, please say you can,' pleaded Jo. 'Blacky and Champ can be stabled here, and you could get a room in one of the Inns.'

'Well, I was hoping to take you back with me, Jo. Dad would love to have us both there together, just like the old times.'

As Jo thought about his suggestion, Ed called across, 'You must go with your brother, Jo. We'll be here for at least another six days, I imagine. You can decide whether, or not, you want to re-join us by then, but don't feel you have to. Family is the most important thing, after all.' Having said that, Ed stepped across the gap and took John's hand, saying, 'Pleased to meet you, John. Jo's told us a lot about you. Assuming you're staying for the night, we can get your horses stabled here and you're welcome to join us for a meal, although it'll be a bit cramped.'

John took the proffered hand and gave it a firm shake. 'Thanks, I must confess to feeling a bit rough after that journey. Not fully recovered, you see. I would be interested to hear how my sister fits into all of this, and what she means to you. You can imagine, this has all been a bit of a surprise to me, coming home and finding out that Jo has taken on a new life.'

Having walked into town, accompanied by Jo, John booked a room for himself in a nearby Inn and together they returned to the tantalising aroma of one of Marge's stews. It had been agreed that

Jo would return to Meadow Farm with John, in the morning. Although nothing was said about whether she would eventually return to *Red Rose.* The atmosphere between John and the family warmed significantly once he realised how much they had helped his sister in her time of need. There was a great deal of talking as John learned about life on the canals. He was particularly interested when Ed proudly talked about his son having signed up.

'We didn't want him to go, but he was determined,' said Ed. 'He was sent across in no time, because of his experience. They apparently wanted more trained soldiers to work on the boats, transporting weapons and men.'

'Strange you should say that,' mused John. I met a lad working on the hospital barge that brought us to the coast. He told me that it was his first time, having just arrived in France. He came from this area, as it happens. He was apparently working with his family on the Basingstoke Canal before he signed up. Unfortunately, he was killed while attempting to rescue a crashed British pilot.'

There was a moment of stunned silence in the cabin, until Ed looked into John's eyes and asked, 'Did he tell you his name?'

'Yes, he told me his name was … Oh, my god!'

"Ben", breathed Ed.

'I'm afraid so,' said John. 'I'm so sorry, how stupid of me not to have put two and two together.'

With no warning, Jo suddenly jumped up from the stool upon which she had been silently listening. Without a word, she had pushed passed Beth who was sitting on the steps, and was through the hatchway before anyone had time to realise what was happening. Out in the darkness of the unlit wharf, Jo instinctively ran toward the stable to find the comfort and warmth of her Blacky. She was not to find that comfort, however, as a hand suddenly came out of the darkness and covered her mouth.

'Well, if it's not my little lady come out of the boat to find me, well, well, well.' Before she had time to struggle, Jo was quickly dragged into the greater darkness of undergrowth which surrounded the wharf.

Chapter 28

The occupants of the cabin were still sitting in stunned silence as the enormity of John's news infiltrated their minds. Beth was the first to speak into the silence. 'Is Ben killed, Mummy?'

'We can't be sure, sweetheart. It may not 'ave been our Ben that John was talkin' about. I expect there are lots of soldiers called "Ben" in the army, ain't that right, John?'

'Yes, I suppose so,' replied John doubtfully.

'Killed while trying to save another man's life,' muttered Ed quietly. 'That's the sort of thing he *would* do.'

'That's enough, Ed!' snapped Marge. 'We don't know. It's most likely a coincidence, if you asks me.'

'Yea, you're likely right, we'll just have to hope for the best, won't we?'

Looking at the closed door and becoming concerned, John commented, 'Jo's been gone for a while, is it far to the lavvy?'

Marge, who had been reassuring Beth with a hug, suddenly exclaimed, 'Oh my gawd! That girl's in love with our Ben. Quick! Go and find 'er!'

Ed was the first out onto the counter, closely followed by John. After taking a quick scan into the darkness surrounding the boat, he called loudly, *'Jo! ... Jo? ... Can you hear me, Jo?'* Both men stood for a moment, listening for an answer. 'Right, John,' commanded Ed as he pointed. 'You go that way and check all the boats and buildings. I'll go this way and do the same. Keep calling.' By this time, Marge had heaved herself through the hatchway. 'Marge, you stay here with Beth in case Jo comes back while we're gone.'

Walking away from the boat, and into the shadows of buildings and other boats in various stages of repair, John became aware of the movement of the dog which was scampering amongst the many obstacles on the wharf. *'Find her, boy! where is she?'* he called. Not being familiar with the place, John found himself stumbling around and tripping over various objects in the inky darkness. Oddy, on the other hand, was scampering from one place to another, constantly sniffing at the ground as he flipped through the shadows. John could hear Ed calling in the distance, as he himself continued yelling Jo's name. He was fast becoming desperate, and sick with worry. Jo had not mentioned anything about her feelings for Ben, he thought, although it might explain her determination to stay with this family, apart from her debt of gratitude. He had now reached the boundary of the wharf where he encountered a wooden fence with trees and bushes beyond. It was then that he realised he had not seen, or heard, the dog for a while.

Not knowing where to go next, John paused to listen for anything that would give him a clue. He was peering into the darkness of the woods when he caught the sound of barking coming from that direction. In a flash, regardless of the increasing pain in his chest, John climbed over the fence and blindly stumbled through the bushes in the direction of the distant barking and what he could now hear, growling and someone yelling. As fast as he ran through the thorny maze, suffering a multitude of scratches as he did so, he didn't seem to be getting any closer to the sounds. *'Jo! ... Jo, it's me, I'm coming! Hold on!'* His own voice sounded desperate and feeble in his panic. Jo was in serious trouble, of that, there was no doubt. *'Ed! Over here, Ed! This way!'* Although he continued calling, he had no real hope of Ed hearing his plaintive cry.

Running blindly in the direction of the barking, John suddenly fell headlong into a ditch. Thick mud slightly softened his fall, although the sickening sound of his collarbone breaking was clear to hear. In sickening pain, he managed to climb out of the ditch whilst doing his best to hold his arm across his wheezing chest. The shouting and growling seemed a little closer as he stumbled forward, his eyes now becoming more accustomed to the darkness. *'Jo! I'm coming!'* he called. Suddenly there came a high-pitched yelp followed by nothing more than the sound of rustling leaves and branches as John pushed through the tangle of bushes. Almost without realising, he found himself in a clearer area where he could make out the form of a man leaning over the still body of the dog. In his hand was a short log. At the same moment, he saw Jo lying on the ground, her dress pushed up above her waist, exposing her under-garments. She was lying still, just a few yards away from Oddy. An uncontrollable rage took over any other thought as John shot across the gap. Regardless of any rational thought, John slammed into the man who was in the process of lifting the log above Oddy for a further blow. Together, both men fell amongst the bushes. Pain coursed through John's body as he tried to regain his feet. He was still struggling on one knee when a blow to the side of his head sent him sprawling to the ground, where he remained still.

Turning back to the prone figure of the unconscious girl, with single-minded determination, Patrick removed his coat and unbuttoned his trousers as he stepped over the dog. *Shame I hit her hard enough to knock her out. It would have been nicer to look into her frightened eyes as I took my pleasure.* So intent was he to free his stiffened member and satisfy his uncontrollable lust he failed to hear the hurried approach of another person pushing through the bushes.

Ed quickly took in the scene as he entered the clearing. Like an enraged unstoppable charging bull, he crossed the gap before Patrick had time to turn and face him. Grabbing the man's shirt collar, Ed swung him round and smashed his fist into the attacker's nose. The blow was hard enough to send the man sprawling into the bushes. Wasting no time, Ed knelt down to check on Jo, covering her bare legs as he did so. With relief he could see that she was starting to come round.

'Wh .. what happened?' she asked weakly as she lifted her hand to the side of her head. 'Where's …'

'You're safe now, sweetheart. We're here,' replied Ed as he took Jo into his arms while listening to the sound of the fleeing man. Still holding the trembling girl, Ed became aware of John's movement as he tried to sit up while nursing his injured shoulder. 'Are you alright, John?' he called.

'I've broken my collarbone and my head's spinning,' he replied through gritted teeth as he staggered over to join them. 'Don't worry about me. It's Jo I'm concerned about.' With his good arm, John stooped to hold his sister who gratefully leaned into him.

'I know who it was, John,' Jo was able to say through her sobbing. 'It was Pat, the labourer who tried to rape me at the farm.'

'Shhh, don't worry about him, he's gone now,' replied John as he looked at Ed who was still kneeling on the other side of Jo. 'The important thing now is to get you back into the warm, and check you're alright.'

'I didn't let him do anything,' said Jo through her tears. I was fighting him and scratching his face, then Oddy appeared from nowhere and started biting his legs. Then he hit me and I can't remember any more. Oh my god! Where *is* Oddy? Is he alright?'

At the mention of the dog, Ed got to his feet and stepped over to the animal who was lying still. Carefully, he lifted his brave dog and held him to his chest. 'He's still breathing, we'll check him over back at the boat. Are you two able to walk?'

Slowly, John helped Jo to her feet, using only his good arm. 'John! You're hurt!' exclaimed Jo.

'It's nothing that won't mend,' replied John.

'It's your collar bone, I can see it is. Wait!' Before either of the men had time to realise what she was doing, Jo had lifted her skirt and removed her underskirt which she then used as a sling for her brother's arm.

As they slowly started to move away, Ed noticed the discarded coat lying on the ground. 'We'll take that with us, might be evidence in identifying your attacker, Jo.'

Meanwhile, back in the wharf, Marge was engaged in berating the night-watchman for earlier having left his post. 'Where was you when our girl went missing? She could be anywhere by this time. I've a mind to tell your wharfinger you ain't up to the job.'

'I've already told you, I just slipped over to the pub to get some fags. I was only gone ten minutes,' wailed the worried man.

'Ten minutes, my arse!' snorted Marge. 'I can smell ya beery breff from up 'ere. Now, you go an' 'elp the others find that girl, or I won't be 'eld responsible fer where I poke this 'ere windlass.' After watching the old man scurrying away into the darkness, with a heavy heart Marge returned to the warmth of the cabin to console Beth who hadn't stopped crying since hearing the news of Ben's death. 'There, there, my luv. It might not 'ave been our Ben 'e was talkin' about. If Ben were dead, I'd know it, cos I'm 'is mum, and mums know when their children are in trouble.' As she said those words, Marge wished they were true, and now there was the worry of Jo taking off so suddenly. *That poor girl. She must love Ben so much to 'ave run off like that.*

It was just a few minutes later that Marge heard Ed's voice approaching. *'Get the kettle on, Marge,'* he was calling. *'We've got her, and she's okay, apart from a sore head.'* Soon, Ed was helping both Jo and John up the ladder while still holding his dog which was feebly licking his face.

'Right then, which one of you needs my attention first?' asked Marge who was set to take control. 'Jo, you've got a nasty bruise comin' out. 'Ow ya feelin'?'

'Don't worry about me, Mum. It's John who needs attention. Looks like a broken collarbone to me, as well as a large lump on his head.'

Soon, Marge was at work with her ointments and bandages, tut-tutting as she listened to the account of what had taken place in the woods. Nothing more was said about Ben as her work continued. 'I'm afraid it's 'ospital fer you, John. Ed can walk you down in the mornin'. No knowin' what damage 'as been done to yer war wound, apart from ya shoulder. I fink it best if Jo goes to the Inn wiv ya to keep an eye on ya till mornin'. Ed'll come and collect ya both first thing. They can check you're okay as well, Jo.' Marge had noticed that Jo was shaking, as though in shock, as indeed she was, following the news of her Ben as well as the second rape attempt by Patrick.

It was as Ed was helping brother and sister down the ladder that the night-watchman appeared out of the darkness. ‘You’ve found her then,’ he called up to Marge who was standing on the counter.

‘No fanks to you,’ she replied disdainfully.

‘I noticed this coat by the ladder,’ said the old man while holding it out to Ed. ‘Did you find it somewhere?’

‘It belongs to the man who has just tried to rape our girl,’ replied Ed.

‘Well, I know who owns that coat,’ responded the old man, while trying to redeem himself, ‘He’s a traveller living in a caravan on the edge of town. He works here.’

‘Would you be willing to tell that to the police?’ asked John, hopefully.

‘I owe it to you,’ replied the man.

‘What time do you finish in the morning?’ enquired John.

‘Seven-thirty.’

‘Okay,’ said John. We’ll come in at that time and you can come with us to the nearest police station.’

‘What about your injuries?’ demanded Marge.

‘That can wait, thanks to your treatment, Marge. The important thing is to get that monster behind bars before he gets away, or tries it on with any other females.’

‘Well, you look out for our Jo, she’s ‘ad a shock, lord knows what it’s gone and done to ‘er ‘ead.’

‘I’ll be okay, Mum,’ said Jo. ‘I’m still shaking but I think it’s more from the cold now. I’m stronger than you think, and I’m safe with John. You can stop worrying now.’

As brother and sister walked toward the gate, watched by a concerned Marge who was still standing on the counter, John asked, ‘Did I hear you call that woman “Mum” just then?’

‘Yes,’ replied Jo. ‘It’s a long story but we’ve sort of adopted each other. You may remember having had a mother, but I never knew her. Marge has become the mother I never had and when I most needed one. I hope you can understand, John?’

‘After what I’ve been through, Sis, nothing can surprise me ever again. There were times when many of us were calling out for our mothers, me included. I reckon Marge would have been a great comfort. If nothing else, she would have put the fear of God up those Hun soldiers,' he laughed. 'You want a mum? Seems like Marge would fit the bill nicely. The world's gone mad.'

The world had indeed gone mad in Jo's mind. The streets which had been filled with such happiness just hours ago, was now filled with menace. Ben dead, and was that man still there, watching them, she wondered? Would she ever be free of his evil intent?

It was shortly after two in the morning when a loud crash, accompanied by frenzied barking from Oddy, brought Ed instantly awake to become aware of the smell of burning kerosine and the flickering of flames beyond the bed curtains.

'Marge, Beth, wake up! Fire!' Pulling the bed curtain aside, Ed was shocked to see flames already licking across the floor and onto the side-bed where Jo would have been lying had she been there. The curtains were alight and flames were reaching the wooden ceiling. Ed knew then that there was nothing he could do apart from to get all three of them, and the dog, off the boat before it was too late. *'Come on Beth! Run for the steps and get out,'* he shouted above the roar of the flames. *'Come on, Marge. No time*

to save anything, get out!' Ensuring that they had reached the steps without catching their nightclothes alight, Ed quickly grabbed a tin box from beneath the cross-bed before jumping through the flames which were now covering most of the floor. Smoke had quickly filled the small space, so much so that it had become impossible to breath any air still remaining in what had once been his home, soon to become a blazing inferno. Stepping from the foot of the ladder onto solid ground, Ed quickly moved Marge and Beth away from the blazing boat and into the relatively warm stable where he left them, in order to see what could be done. The night-watchman, seeing Ed emerging from the stable, hobbled over to inform him that he had phoned for the fire-brigade from the call-box just beyond the gate. The darkness of the cold November night was transformed into flickering light as the cabin, and everything the family possessed, was consumed by the hungry flames. There was little to be done when the fire-engine finally turned through the wharf gates which had been opened wide by the old man. The hull and fore-cabin of Ed's beloved *Red Rose* were still partly intact but the main cabin was gone. As he stood in his nightclothes with tears in his eyes, Marge, with a horse blanket wrapped around her shoulders, came out of the stable to stand alongside him.

'In one night, we've lost our son and our home, Marge. And we might have lost our Jo. What did we ever do to deserve this? That's what I want to know.'

'I don't understand 'ow it could of 'appened,' replied Marge. 'We was always so careful with the lamps and stove.'

'I'll tell you how it happened, Marge. The night-watchman told me that he saw that traveller running from the boat just before the fire. That bleeder did this to us! Well, he ain't going to get away with it! How's Beth? Is she okay?'

'She's 'ad a good cry, now she's lyin' down in Skippy's stall. She'll be alright. What we gonna do, Ed?'

Placing his arm around her shoulder and staring into the flames, Ed sadly replied, 'Right now, at this minute, I don't know, luv. I at least managed to save the insurance and banking stuff, so we'll get through this in the long term, but, for now, I just can't get our Ben out of my mind.'

~~~
~~~

The traveller, now in his caravan, was lamenting the loss of his coat and cursing the unknown man, and the one from that boat, who had not only spoiled his fun but had also most likely broken his nose. *Just so they could have the girl to themselves where I left off.* He allowed his crooked lustful thoughts free range as he relished the memory of slipping past that stupid old man sitting and smoking by his brazier, and of creeping up to that boat and mounting the ladder, being careful not to spill the oil. That moment of lighting the lamp before quietly easing the door open had been almost as good as the pleasure he had been denied with the girl. *Think they can set their dog on me, do they? Well, that's shown them they can't mess with me.* The mirthless laughter coming from the wharf that night was the sound one expects to hear in a horror film in the Roxy. Inhuman and haunting.

~~~

The sight that met John and Jo's eyes early the next morning as they walked through the wharf gate was indeed something like a scene out of a film. Ed with Marge and Beth standing either side
~~~

of him, was standing statue-like gazing at the remains of his beloved *Red Rose,* now a heap of wet fire-blackened ribs and beams, with whisps of smoke still curling up from one or two places, to be snatched away by the gentle breeze. The three figures were still in their nightclothes, each wrapped in well-used horse blankets. The dog was sitting at Ed's feet. John could see that he would not need to accompany the night-watchman to the police station, for the old man was talking to a constable, who was taking notes, close to the stable.

'Oh my god!' breathed Jo as she quickened her pace. 'Are you all okay?' she called out as they came closer to the devastating scene.

'Yea, we're all okay, luv,' responded Ed. 'Can't say the same for our dear old *Red Rose* though. What about you two? How's the shoulder, John?'

'Still painful. What happened here?'

'It would seem that madman did it, according to the night-watchman who saw him running away just after the fire started. He's already told the police sergeant where to find him. We've all been asked a few questions but they want us all to go to the police station this morning to make formal statements. First thing though, is to get you two to the hospital.' As Ed was talking, Beth left his side and threw her arms around Jo, pressing her face into her "sister's" breasts as she folded her arms around the distraught girl.

'You must all come back to the farm with us,' Jo suddenly said. 'We can buy you all something warm clothes to wear when the shops open, then, when we've finished at the hospital and police station, we can all fit into the wagon. You must stay with us until things get sorted out.'

'But we can't expect to dump ourselves on your family, just like that,' objected Marge.

'It's not a problem, Marge,' said John. 'It's the least we can do and, if you will forgive me for stating the obvious, you don't seem to have any choice. From what I've heard, you've done so much for Jo. Without you, we might have lost her.'

'Please, Mummy! Can we go with Jo, like she says?' This was the first words the little girl had spoken that morning.

Without answering Beth, Marge looked at Jo for a brief moment before saying, 'Give us an 'ug, Jo. Course we'll come wiv ya. Just till we get things sorted, mind.'

Chapter 29

'Phil, you haven't touched your dinner. You should eat to keep up your strength. You barely ate anything last night, or this morning, you're going to make yourself ill if this goes on.'

'I'm sorry, Polly,' Phil replied as he pushed his plate away. 'I just can't stop worrying about them. John's been gone two days now. What do you suppose has happened? He just took off with no explanation, presumably to fetch Jo, and not a word since. What if he's become ill again? After all he's only just come out of hospital. Or maybe something's happened to Jo.'

Placing his knife and fork down onto his cleared plate, Graham spoke up for the first time, 'You're allowing your imagination to run away, Phil. It would have taken John a full day to get to Guildford. As you say, this is only the second day. They could be on their way back right now, although I imagine tomorrow is more likely.'

'I suppose you're right, perhaps I could eat some of this,' replied Phil as he looked at his dinner without enthusiasm.

'Good,' said Polly. 'That's more like it. I'll warm it up over a boiling saucepan if you can wait a while. Why don't you two go and finish that domino game you started before dinner, while you're waiting.'

~~~

By the time John had been free to leave the hospital that morning he never again wanted to see the inside of such a place. The pain of re-setting his clavicle, as the doctor had called it, was as bad, if not worse, than anything he had experienced in France. After a brief examination, Jo was declared fit, with a warning to visit their local doctor should she experience any dizziness.

Upon walking through the exit door together they were pleased to see that Ed, Marge and Beth were now dressed in new clothing, including coats and scarves. It was fortunate that Ed had managed to save the box containing his banking and insurance papers and was therefore able to obtain the necessary cash for the purchases.
~~~

With a smile, he recounted the looks of shock they had received as they had walked into, first the bank, then the store, still wrapped in their less than fresh, horse-blankets.

'I see they've got you well plastered John,' said Marge approvingly. 'They're expectin' you at the police station for you to make statements.'

'You'll be pleased to know they've got that man safely locked up,' added Ed. 'The sergeant reckons they'll throw the book at him. Arson, attempted rape, assault and battery, oh and theft. They apparently found lots of gear stolen from the wharf, in his caravan. He's going to be behind bars for a long time.'

'That's a relief,' said John. 'Now, I suggest you all go back to the wharf while Jo and I make our statements, then, if your business is done there, we can make a start for Warningford. I'm afraid we won't get there till well after dark this evening. It would save some time if you could hitch-up the wagon and tie your mule to the back.'

It was with relief that John saw the lights of Warningford ahead. Travelling the lanes in the dark had been extremely difficult and it was only the fact that the night was pierced by a near full moon that enabled them to do so. His arm and chest had become painful within the first few miles, although he denied it when Jo enquired. The reins were first in the capable hands of his sister but, as the light began to fade, Ed had insisted upon taking over. They were all physically and emotionally exhausted, so-much-so that conversation had stopped over two hours ago. Thankfully, Beth had immediately fallen asleep in Jo's arms once she had given up the reins to Ed.

Passing *The Feathers*, John could hear the cheerful sound of the accordion and allowed himself a weary smile as he remembered fondly the softness and warmth of June's bare breasts.

At last, the Meadow Farm appeared in the gloom. Ed carefully negotiated the horses and wagon through the gateway and pulled up in the centre of the cobbled yard. Applying the brake with his foot he said to no-one in particular, 'Okay, safe to get off everyone.' John was already climbing down while using his good arm to hold on. Jo was gently waking Beth from her long sleep in her stiff arms as Marge groaned with her attempt to shift her numb backside from the wagon floor. It was a strange site that met

Phil's eyes in the yard, having heard the rumble of wagon wheels and quickly stepping to the front door. Before he had time to take in the unexpected site of so many people appearing in the darkness, Jo had approached him with a child in her arms to give him a one-armed hug while kissing him on both cheeks.

'Oh Dad, it's so good to be here. We've brought some guests with us; I hope you don't mind?' It's a long story and we're all very tired and hungry.'

'Of course, I don't mind my love,' replied her confused and mystified father. 'I'm so happy and relieved to see you home safe. Bring your friends in out of the cold, Graham will see to the horses.' Peering over the heads of the strangers, he asked, 'Is that a pony, or perhaps a mule I see out there?'

'As I said, It's a long story, Dad.'

'At that moment, John, with a huge grin on his face, came and stood beside Jo. 'Sorry I left so abruptly, Dad. As things turned out, it's a good job I did.'

'Okay,' said Phil. Come in everyone, I can see this is going to turn out to be an interesting evening. John, why are you wearing that plaster and sling?'

While Polly cooked up a meal of fried sausages, eggs and beans, introductions were made and slowly the whole story was told, although not necessarily in the correct order, as each of the new arrivals had their own version to share. The welcome meal was consumed long before the full account of events was completed.

'I don't know what to say,' sighed Phil while shaking his head. 'You've all been through so much. And now, Ed and Marge, you've lost your home as well as your living. Well, you're more than welcome to stay here. I think we'll find that Polly is already preparing a room for you upstairs. It's late, and you're all tired. I suggest we all go to bed and work it all out in the morning.'

'You awake, Ed?'

'Yea, what time is it?'

'Dunno, but it must be gettin' on. I 'eard someone movin' about a while ago and it's gettin' light.'

‘Beth’s stirring,’ said Ed who felt the movement between them in the bed.

‘I didn’t notice her climbing into our bed during the night,’ sighed Marge. ‘Poor little mite must ‘ave been afraid, finding ‘er-self in a strange bed, specially after all the goings on yesterday.’

‘Think we should get up?’ asked Ed. ‘I need a pee anyway.’

As they were both pondering that question, there came a gentle knock on the bedroom door.

‘Come in,’ called Marge. ‘We’re all decent.’

‘Good morning, thought you might like a nice cup of tea.’ It was Polly who had entered the room carrying a tray which she placed on the dresser. ‘Tea for you two and milk for the little one.’

‘Thank you,’ said Ed who was feeling embarrassed having been caught in bed by the lady he barely knew. Not being able to meet her eyes he asked Polly, ‘What time is it?’

‘It’s gone seven. Milking’s done, but I’ve left the eggs, as I thought Beth might like to help me gather them. The bathroom is free at the moment and breakfast will be ready in half an hour, although you can take longer if you need to.’

As Polly closed the door behind her, Marge said, 'That's nice. Can't remember the last time I 'ad tea in bed. Mornin' Beth, you're awake then? Did you sleep alright?'

The girl was lifting herself onto her elbows as she said, 'I had a bad dream about being on fire and you weren't there to save me. And Skippy had taken a look and I couldn't get him out, cos I was trying to get my burning frock off. Then a bad man laughed at me and didn't try to help, even though I was screaming.'

Taking the troubled child into her arms, Marge soothed her, saying, 'It was just a dream, luvvy. We'll always be 'ere to look after you. You're safe now.'

Meanwhile, Ed had slipped out of bed and had pulled his trousers on over the pyjama bottoms Phil had lent him the previous night. 'Just going for a pee over the side.'

'Don't you dare!' exclaimed Marge. 'Use the lavatory like a civilised man.'

'Just joking. Back in a mo, then I'll enjoy that nice cuppa.' Before leaving the room, Ed handed Marge her tea and Beth the glass of milk.

Down below, in the kitchen, Polly and Jo were sitting at the table together, each nursing a mug of tea in their cold hands. 'John's still asleep, I didn't want to disturb him,' said Polly. 'Your dad's still in the cow shed, happy as a lark. He's so pleased to have you both back. I imagine you'll be staying here now the boat's gone?'

'I suppose so,' replied Jo. 'I haven't really thought about it. It's all such a mess, and goodness knows what's to happen to my friends. Oh! I've just realised, I'm sorry, you're wondering about your own situation. Well, you mustn't worry. You and Graham have been brilliant and this is your home for as long as you want it.'

'Thank you, but this is your kitchen, Jo. You'll naturally be wanting to take over again. I just can't see how it'll work.'

'Don't you worry about that, Polly. I've not really thought about it yet, but if I'm to stay here, I will be insisting upon Dad retiring and I will do what I've always wanted to do, and that'll be to work the land alongside John, and your Graham. There's plenty of room for expansion, and food crops are badly needed while this war continues, and a long time after, I would imagine.'

After sipping her tea, Polly asked, ‘What’s to become of that poor family, they’ve lost everything, including their son … Jo? Are you alright?’ Polly had noticed the tears forming in Jo’s eyes. ‘Oh! You were sweet on him, weren’t you? I’m sorry, Jo. I hadn’t realised.’

‘I loved him, Polly. Still do. I just wish I had told him, but I didn’t realise it myself until he was gone. I can only hope that the Ben my John was talking about was a different Ben to mine, but I’m not building my hopes up too much.’ Dabbing her eyes with her hanky, Jo asked, ‘Can I help with breakfast? Just say “No” if you prefer me to keep out of your way.’

‘I would love you to help, Jo. I think we could be a good team, don’t you?’

It was an hour later when all eight of them were sitting at the table. Polly and Jo had indeed worked well together, serving a cooked breakfast to each individual, over a period of time, as he or she entered the kitchen, with John being the last to appear.

Having cleared away the last of the dirty plates, Polly addressed herself to Beth who had been sitting unusually quiet between her parents. 'Would you like to come with me to find out what the hens have left for us, Beth? Let's see which one of us can find the most eggs.' Beth looked at her mother with raised eyebrows without answering.

'Of course, you can go, luvvy,' said Marge who had found it strange and uncomfortable not being the one working in the kitchen. 'You go with Polly and mind you do as she tells you.'

'Okay,' said the subdued girl as she got down from the table. She was suddenly keen to be outside exploring this new place in which she had found herself, and to be away from the strained atmosphere around the table.

'Put your coat on!' called Marge to the retreating figure.

'Yes, Mummy.' She was gone.

For a moment, there was silence around the table, none wanting to be the first to ask the question, "What next?" It was Marge who broke the awkward silence. Turning to her husband, she said, 'Tell them what you told me, Ed.'

'Well,' responded Ed. 'The boat was insured, but having read through the documents, it would appear that the cover doesn't include acts of vandalism or arson. We've got a fair amount of money in the bank, enough to get us by for a while, but not enough to buy another boat. With luck, we might be able to take on a company boat somewhere, but that might take a long time. I'm intending to go to Odiham Wharf today to put the word out, and also to see if there's any mail for us, that's where it will be if there is anything.'

Seeing that Ed was clearly thinking of Ben, Jo quickly responded by offering to go with him, saying that she knew the way and that they could take the wagon. 'It's an idea, Jo,' interrupted Phil, 'but are you up to another day on the wagon?'

'Yes, Dad. I'll be alright.'

'That's settled then, as long as you're sure,' replied Phil. 'Now, to more practical matters.' Addressing himself to Ed and Marge who were sitting together at the table, he continued, 'You are welcome to stay here on the farm for as long as it takes to get yourselves sorted. It's the least we can do, and no arguments.' He had noticed the objection which was about to be uttered by Marge. 'I realise the difficulties that will raise with three women wanting to work in the kitchen,' he said with a grin, 'but I'm sure you will be able to come to some understanding.' He then went on to ask, 'Ed, have you ever worked on the land?'

'As a matter of fact,' replied Ed, 'I was raised on a farm, before my father decided to give it up as the land was poor. That's when he bought *Red Rose.'*

'Good! In that case, while you are with us you can be of use working with myself and Graham. John won't be up to much for a while, so it will be a great help to us. Are you up for that?'

'Suits me,' responded Ed. 'Is there a school nearby that could temporarily take Beth, by any chance?'

'Yes, there is one in Warningford. That's where John and Jo were educated. I believe it's still going, is that right, Jo?'

'Yes, it is,' replied Jo. 'I loved it there, though things may have changed. Marge, it's Monday tomorrow, would you like me to come with you and Beth, to find out if they can take her? I might even meet some of my old teachers.'

'Blimey, is it Sunday?' asked Marge. 'I've lost track of the days with all the goings on. Yes please, Jo, that would be nice of you. On me own I'd get all flustergarsted in a school, cos they makes me nervous about not bein' able to write anyfing but me own name.'

'You can't write?' asked Jo in amazement. 'Well, if you'll let me, I'll teach you. Looks like we'll have plenty of time now.'

'If it's alright with you, Phil, and you're ready, Jo, we'll set off straight away.' said Ed who never wasted time once he had decided on any course of action. Although not wanting to reveal his emotions to these kind people added to his haste to be out of the room.

'Okay with me,' beamed the discerning Phil. 'Jo can make some lunch to take with you while Graham gets the wagon ready.'

A moment later, Polly and a transformed and excited little girl returned to the kitchen. Beth was carefully holding a large wicker basket in front of her, using both hands. *'I won, I won,'* she shouted. 'I found three more than Polly did. Some of them have even got feathers stuck on them and I was careful not to get pecked, or to drop any of them.'

'Clever girl!' exclaimed Marge. 'Praps you'll be married to a farmer one day if you're that clever with chickens.'

'Don't be a silly-billy, Mummy, I told you I'm going to marry a prince, don't you remember?'

'Oh yes, sorry, I forgot, but I'm sure Mister Prince would like some eggs for his breakfast.'

'That's alright, princesses can gather eggs, I expect.'

Noticing how much the basket had started swinging rather alarmingly during the conversation between mother and daughter, Polly quickly took it from Beth's hands and placed it on the draining board.

Still chuckling over the delightful girl's serious prediction of her future, Phil asked Polly, 'I assume you're intending to go to church this morning, Polly?'

'Yes, that was our intention,' replied Polly. 'Is that okay?'

'Certainly! In fact, I would like to come with you, if that's alright. This morning, I feel that I have a lot to be grateful for.'

'You can count me in on that,' said John, who had remained silent throughout the preceding conversation. Looking at Polly who was still standing by the sink, he said, 'I was rude and abrupt with you and Graham when I came home the other day. I'm sorry. It was all a bit of a shock. I'd like to get to know you both better and we can have a nice chat as we walk along together.'

'I'd like that,' replied Polly. 'Thank you. And there's really no need to apologise, John. I could see how difficult it was for you. Okay everyone, the service starts at ten-thirty, we'll just about make it if we hurry.'

Chapter 30

'Tell us all again about how ye managed to survive that explosion three weeks ago, Ben'

'I keep telling you, Jock. I had nearly got to the plane but I didn't see the tree trunk because of the brightness of the flames in my eyes, I fell flat on my face, hit my head on something hard, and the next I knew, you'd all gone off and left me there. Fine lot of mates you are. I could have *died* out there.'

'Well, that's the point, laddie. That's exactly what we all thought. Anyhow, that tin-kettle skipper wasn't about to hang about looking for your body bits lying around, so off we went like ducklings following their mother-duck. Just as well you decided to walk back to the CCS, instead of trying to catch us up. That mother-fucker skipper just kept going right through the night, like he had a haggis snapping at his bum. Well, laddie, at least you've managed to do two round trips with us since then before you decided you'd had enough. Have another beer.'

'It's not my fault, Jock. I didn't ask for the transfer. It's orders.'

'Oh aye, some people have all the luck,' laughed Jock as he reached for another bottle. 'We'll miss your ugly mug, but orders are orders I suppose. What ye going to do over there anyways, and why you of all people?'

'Apparently, I was noticed by the Colonel in Aldershot. He was impressed with my experience and decided I would be of more use as an instructor rather than as a corpse. So, he pulled the appropriate strings and bob's your uncle.' At that moment, a gust of wind lifted the door of the mess tent, causing the candles to flicker and the listeners to sink deeper into their turned-up greatcoat collars.

'Well, with a bit of luck ye'll be home for Christmas, you jammy sassenach. I just hope you manage to find that girl of yours somewhere on that canal.'

'Oh, I'll find her alright, Jock. Even if I have to walk the whole length from London to Odiham, and I've done that more than a few times let me tell you.'

'Well, all I can say is, best of luck to you, boy, it's been my pleasure to have you on my team, even though it's been for such a short time. Kiss that girl for me. Now, ye'd best shift yoursel, that train isna going to wait for ye, even if you are a hero.'

It was with mixed feelings that Ben walked away from the camp at Saint-Valery-sur-Somme. He had enjoyed his short time working with Jock on the hospital barge. He had felt useful and appreciated by the medical staff and the patients he had listened to in his spare moments. He would have liked to continue working with Jock and the team but now he was on his way back to the safety of the Basingstoke Canal, and the possibility of seeing his family, and Jo, much sooner than he had ever expected. Later, sitting on the train that would take him to Calais, Ben's thoughts turned to the pilot of that doomed aircraft. What were his last thoughts just before hitting the ground, he wondered? Was he thinking of his mother? His girl back home? The thrill of the dog-fight? Had he ever considered that he had no hope of surviving beyond a few weeks over the lines? If so, why did he volunteer to join the Flying Corps? He remembered the long yellow scarf worn by the flyer. Dashing and brave, but surely a tempting target for the Hun to go after. None of it made any sense. He was sent to France to do a job and in less than a month he was being sent back. None of it made any sense. Thousands upon thousands of men killed, not knowing why. None of it made any sense…None of it made any sense …None of it made any sense … None of it made any sense … The repetitive sound of the train wheels, clickety-clacking along the track, slowly lulled him into a troubled sleep, until the train finally pulled into the busy port of Calais with its grinding of breaks and hissing of released steam.

***

'Thank you, vicar an interesting sermon,' said Polly while taking Reverend Perkins' outstretched hand. May I introduce Mister Simons and his son John? Both from Meadow Farm'

'I'm very pleased to meet you both at last.' responded the vicar while holding out his hand in Phil's direction. 'You are welcome here at any time. I understand Polly and Graham are now staying with you? How is that working out?'

'Fine, thank you,' replied Phil. 'They are a great help on the farm.'

'And you, John? I see you have an injury. Are you serving in the army?'

'I've been discharged injured,' replied John. 'Now, it's back to farming, once I'm fit enough.'

'Well, don't be strangers. If there's ever anything I can do to help, don't hesitate to let me know.' Turning away from them he greeted an elderly couple exiting the porch. 'Good morning Mabel, glad to see Francis up and about again.'

Walking down the gravel path, Phil muttered, 'He was fishing.'

Polly responded with a laugh, saying, 'I suppose that's a part of his job. Why don't you three pop into *The Feathers* for a drink. I need to go and have a chat with my landlady, then I'll go back and see how Marge is getting on with lunch.'

'A good idea,' said John. 'I could do with a beer after all that singing.'

~~~
~~~

For Ed, arrival at Odiham Wharf on the driving seat of a farm wagon was a novel experience when he considered how often he had arrived there as Number One in his brightly decorated narrowboat. At first, the wharfinger didn't recognise the familiar figure out of context as the wagon was pulled up in front of his office.

'Well, I'll be damned. Look who's just arrived on a grand carriage,' exclaimed the overworked man. 'Don't tell me you've mislaid your boat, Ed. Well, it ain't here,' he finished with a laugh.

'Hello, Charlie, as a matter of fact, I *have* lost *Red Rose.* At Dapdune Wharf in Guildford. Fire, a total loss.'

'Hell's teeth. How the heck did that happen?'

'Arson. A crazy man who had a grudge against our Jo, here. He tried to rape her but got his nose broke for his efforts. It's a long story, Charlie. If you've got time to spare, I can tell you about it in *The Swan* over a pint.'

'Sounds good to me. Take the horses over to the stable, I'll meet you both in the bar in fifteen minutes.'

In stunned silence, the wharfinger listened to the tale, the likes of which he had never heard before. Wiping the froth from his upper lip with the back of his calloused hand he asked, 'Glad Marge, and the nipper are okay, although I imagine she's distraught?'

'She'll get over it. As a matter of fact, we've landed on our feet in a way. We've been offered to stay on Jo's father's farm till we find another boat, that's one of the reasons I'm here. I want you to put the word out that we're looking to crew a company boat anywhere if one becomes available.'

'You'd hate that, Ed. After being your own man,' replied the wharfinger, shaking his head. 'Still, if that's what you want.' Turning his attention to Jo who had been sitting quietly sipping her glass of port, he asked, 'How about you, young lady? What will you do now?'

'I'm staying on the farm to work the land with my father,' she replied while trying not to show her feelings of guilt for having brought this misfortune onto the family she had grown to love.

After a moment of silence, apart from the sudden fall of a half-burned log in the large fire place and the low murmur of conversation by some of the older locals on the other side of the room, Ed cleared his throat before saying, 'We have cause to believe our son Ben has been killed in France. Nothing certain yet but it looks that way.'

Placing his tankard down on the beer-stained table, the wharfinger looked down for a moment before muttering, 'I don't know what to say, Ed, apart from how sorry I am. I liked that kid. Had his head screwed on right. Blimey, you have been through it! Have another beer?'

'No, we'll be making our way back. Do me a favour, Charlie.' Ed fumbled in his coat pocket and brought out an envelope bearing the address of Meadow Farm. 'Can you forward any mail … or telegrams … to me at this address at the farm? As you know, this wharf is the address I've always used when needed. Any news will come here.'

'Yea, the least I can do, mate. Hope it all turns out right for you … and for you, Jo.' Thus saying, he pushed his wooden stool back and rose to his feet. 'I'll get the lad to hitch-up for you while Jo finishes her drink.' He was clearly upset and not wanting to display any weakness or emotion. After all, he was a tough wharfinger with a reputation to maintain.

~~~

Heaving his kit-bag over his shoulder, Ben left the crowded railway station after asking for directions to the despatching office. There, he produced his transfer orders and identity papers to a harassed naval lieutenant. 'If you're quick, you might just make it to HMS Tiger on C Quay. She's a corvette bound for Portsmouth. Captain Trent. Take this.' The Lieutenant was already scrawling something on a buff-coloured form.

'Thank you, Sir,' Ben responded as he took the form and gave a clumsy salute while trying not to drop his bag. Emerging from the office, Ben was relieved to see the corvette in question, which was displaying a large amount of black smoke above its open bridge. A sailor was already lifting the loop of thick rope from the bollard to which the bows had been attached. Running through the jumble of the busy quay, as best he was able, with the kit-bag
~~~

constantly bouncing on his shoulder, he was just in time to dash across the short gangplank before it was drawn back from the ship's waist.

'Who the hell are you?' demanded a powerful looking Chief Petti-Officer who had been standing rigidly by the gangplank. Do you think this is the Gosport ferry, or something? Well? Explain yourself before I chuck your miserable hide in the drink!'

'Sorry, Sir. I was told to report on board, to Captain Trant.'

'It's "Chief" to the likes of you, not "Sir". CPO Waller. And the man you are to report to is Captain Trent, with an "E", not Trant, understood?'

'Yes S .. Chief.'

'And before you smartly salute me, don't. Keep that for the officers. Now, get yourself below out of the way, sonny, and wait till you're called for. The captain has more to think about than entertaining kid soldiers out on a joy ride. Cor blimey, what's the army coming to?'

Amidst the frenetic activity of getting the ship under way Ben managed to find his way below where he appreciated the warmth of a mess room in which he dropped his kit-bag and, through a salt-encrusted porthole, watched the ships progress out of the harbour. Ben never did meet the captain, or any other officers for that matter, during the relatively short crossing of the Channel. By the time HMS Tiger slipped into the narrow entrance of Portsmouth Harbour, Ben had found his way back on deck where he could watch the process of berthing alongside the quay. To his astonishment there were dozens of naval ships of all types and sizes, moored either against the quays or to large buoys in mid channel. They included a converted cargo ship boasting a flight deck and little else above the hull. There were also smaller boats including tugs, dashing hither and thither on their respective business between Portsmouth dockyard and the submarine base in Gosport on the other side of the narrow harbour entrance.

Watching all the activity, Ben was unaware of the approach of the previously short-tempered CPO. 'On your way lad. Get your body off my nice clean ship. Turn right after passing Signal Tower then out through the gate. You can't miss the train station. Where are you making for, anyway?'

'Aldershot, Chief,' replied Ben, remembering the correct form of address.

‘You’ll be wanting the Waterloo train but you’ll need to change, most likely at Woking. They’ll put you right at the ticket office. Run along, and the best of luck for whatever’s in store for you. I’ve got a son about your age in the army. I live in hope.’

After his long weary journey, Ben finally arrived at the Aldershot barracks in time for dinner in the canteen. He was tired, cold, and hungry, and ready for the stodge he had grown to expect from previous experience in that place. He sat alone, but not alone, as khaki-clad men jostled for places at the long tables which were spread throughout the room. Peering around the tables in the increasingly noisy room he was slightly disappointed not to see any familiar faces. He was once again on familiar territory and as he ate, he thought back to recount his short but interesting experiences since last, he had eaten in this place. He was curious to know what tomorrow would bring for him. His orders were to report to the same adjutant he had met not many weeks ago. He had hopes that he might be allowed a short period of leave before taking up his new duties, whatever they might entail. As he considered that possibility, his thoughts inevitably took him to his family as he speculated where, along the cut, they might be at that moment, and how he would go about finding them. He concluded that, when the time came, his best chance would be to walk the towpath in the direction of Odiham until he came across someone who last remembered seeing *Red Rose.* Inevitably, images of Jo began to dominate his mind; Jo listening intently as he explained something about their work; Jo enthusiastically inspecting a creature he had spotted amongst the long grass; Jo helping in the tiny kitchen; Jo simply walking quietly alongside him. Her frown, her laughter, her smile which always started with her eyes, then twinkled her nose before moving to those kissable, but un-kissed lips. Several of the young soldiers sitting opposite him were nudging each other as they watched this stranger's broad smile as he idly forked his mashed potatoes.

~~~

'More mash, John?' Jo smiled as she passed the bowl across the crowded table. 'What about you, Graham? Have you got enough carrots? No need to hold back, plenty more coming.' As she was speaking, she took a glance at Polly who was standing at
~~~

the sink draining the peas. *She's got something on her mind, judging by the way she's humming and smiling to herself. I wish she would come out with it.* 'How are the peas coming along, Polly?'

'Coming now,' Polly replied, cheerfully.

'Pass your plate, Jo,' said Phil above the general buzz of conversation. He had been carefully carving the brisket into thin slices which he was managing to share around the table. As he watched the animated faces of his new friends, and his own grown-up children, he could hardly think of a time when he had been so happy. He was, of course, concerned for Marge and Ed, in their grief, but right now, they appeared happy enough as they both joined in with the general conversation and laughter.

'What are you smiling about, Polly?' whispered Jo as the older woman finally came and sat beside her. 'You're up to something, I can tell.'

'You'll see, after we've all eaten,' was the best Jo received in reply.

'How did things go at the canal?' Polly asked. 'Did Ed manage to do what was needed?'

'I think he was hoping for news of Ben, however unlikely that was,' she answered sadly. 'He talked about getting another boat, working for one of the big companies, but his heart isn't in it. He barely spoke on our way back.'

'Poor man,' sighed Polly. 'I feel so sorry for them, they've lost so much, and yet here they are, not allowing their feelings to spoil the meal.'

For a brief moment Jo watched the couple they were quietly discussing. 'If there's one thing, I've learned about canal folk, they are resilient in the face of anything that's thrown at them, and in some cases I mean that literally. I've grown to love them as though they are my own family, and I hope they'll never have to move far away from here.'

The meal continued with the constant easy flow of conversation and the scraping of cutlery on plates. Jo noticed the contented smile on her father's face as he animatedly talked to Ed about life on a farm. She also noticed that although John was having little trouble eating his vegetables with one arm, he had so far not touched the brisket. Without a word, or any of the others noticing, she reached across and took his plate before cutting the meat into smaller pieces. It was done, and John gave his sister a smile of appreciation.

Soon, the plates were empty, and thoughts were turning to the apple pie they all knew would be following. Polly arose from her chair and received all the cleared plates as they were passed along the table These she took to the sink, however, rather than lifting the anticipated pie from the range, she stepped back to the table and clapped her hands for silence.

'I have something I would like to tell you all.' As she spoke, she glanced at Graham who gave her an encouraging smile and a knowing nod. 'This morning, after church, I visited the landlady of our cottage which, as you know, we have temporarily continued leasing for any eventualities in our circumstances. She has agreed to my proposal that our lease be terminated at the end of the year, at which time, should they agree, Ed and Marge can take it over for as long a term as they wish. The rent will be the same as that which I have been paying. The cottage has four bedrooms and is large enough for the family. Ed, Marge, you have time to think about it, and Graham and I are happy to continue paying the rent until you are able to take it on, or until you find another boat somewhere.'

For a moment the Frasers, including Jo, were stunned, until Marge burst into tears and managed to sob, 'Oh, Ed. Our own 'ouse on the bank. It's been my dream for so long.' Ed was momentarily speechless as he placed his arm around her shoulder.

'I also have an announcement to make,' said Phil arising from his chair at the head of the table. I have a relatively large amount of land that's been under-used for many years. We have not farmed it as it would be too much for us to handle without expansion of staff, not to mention equipment. It's long been our plan to sell it off. It's good fertile land and John and Jo have agreed with me that we would like to offer it to you, Ed, as a partnership. We realise there would be a large outlay as you stock it with whatever beasts you prefer, though cattle and pigs would be my advice, and we would be happy to loan you whatever money is necessary till it starts paying you back. What do you think?'

'Please say you'll agree,' pleaded Jo. In that way I can still have my two families.'

'I don't know quite what to say,' said Ed with tears in his eyes. It's all like a dream and I'm about to wake up and find we've sunk and we've got water lapping under the bed.'

'Does that mean I can have my own chickens and collect my own eggs?' asked Beth. 'And can I take a baby pig to bed with me?'

'Well, what do you say to both offers, man?' enquired Phil. 'You would be doing us a favour taking that land and putting it to good use.'

All eyes were on Ed as he momentarily sat in silence shaking his head. 'What do you think Ma?' he asked as he looked at Marge.

'I think we would be daft not to accept. You're an 'ard worker, Ed. And I knows you can do it.'

'If it helps to make up your mind, Ed,' said Jo. 'I'd like to work the land with you. Dad's got John and Graham, Polly's doing a brilliant job looking after the house, I'm free to do what I've always wanted. We make a good team, you know that, don't you?'

'Marge, if it's what you want, it's okay with me, said Ed. 'In fact, I'm over the moon. Thank you, Phil, and you, Polly. We accept and we'll pay our way in time, see if we don't.'

'How about some apple pie and your thick creamy custard, Polly,' said Phil with a huge grin on his face. 'What does a man have to do to get his deserts around here? That's what I want to know.'

Chapter 31

Although rain had fallen all night, the early morning sun filtering through the trees promised a fine day. Ed had taken to the milking as though he had been born to it. With a grin he remembered that he had indeed been born to it. This, to him, was as natural as flooding a lock. Perhaps that explained his sense of homecoming. Standing alone in the puddled yard he gazed around, taking in the stable, the barn, the machine shed, the livestock barn which would be home to the cattle throughout winter, the large farmhouse in which he and his family had spent their first comfortable night, and in which they would be staying until Polly's cottage became their home after Christmas. The tranquil peace he was enjoying at that moment told nothing of the stress and anguish he had been going through, from the departure of his brave son, to the fire which had ended his long hard life on the cut. Thinking of Ben, his mind returned to the day Ruby had died just eighteen months ago, after falling into the lock at the age of fifteen. Two children, now gone. He was glad Beth would grow up to have a better life, a home, made of bricks and mortar, an education, warmth, better clothing and food. He would see to it that she would grow up to be a fine woman who could hold her own in a world in which she would have more choices and opportunities.

At that moment, the subject of his thoughts came racing around the corner of the house, Oddy barking at her heels.

'Daddy, Aunt Polly sent me to tell you your breakfast is nearly ready,' Beth was saying as she approached her father. 'What are you doing?'

'Oh, just thinking poppet.'

'What are you thinking?'

'How much I love you, and how exciting it's going to be to see our new home this morning.'

'I can't wait, Daddy. Why can't we live there straight away?'

'Well, we first have to give Polly time to decide what she's leaving there, then there might be extra things we need to buy when we've had a chance to see what's left, then I'm going to get a room ready for a princess.'

'Will I have a proper bed, with springs?'

'Yes.'

'And will we have a proper toilet, and a bathroom?'

'I imagine so.'

'Will it be near the school that I'm going to?'

'So I'm told. Come on, too many questions before breakfast. You'll soon see for yourself.'

'Daddy?'

'What now?'

'I love you.'

Stooping down, Ed reached for his daughter and, without effort, swung her up into his arms where she nestled into his neck. With a lump in his throat, and a dog at his heels, he marched in the direction of the breakfast he was certainly intending to enjoy.

Beth didn't know whether to be excited or nervous as, holding her mother's hand, she walked through the Warningford School gate. She could see other children through the classroom windows, some seemed to be looking out at her. Together, she, her mother, and Jo walked across the empty playground and on into the cloakroom where she noticed rows of pegs with coats hanging above pairs of boots and shoes.

‘Nothing seems to have changed,’ observed Jo. ‘It’s just as though I was here yesterday, although it all looks so much smaller now.’ Following a sign in the corridor beyond the cloakroom the trio walked in the direction of the secretary’s office, all aware of children’s voices singing behind the first door, and a female teacher’s voice calling for attention behind the next door. Arriving at the open door of the secretary’s office, Marge felt as though she was looking at a senior girl who was sitting behind the desk as she stepped over the threshold, still holding Beth’s hand.

‘How may I help you?’ enquired the young attractive secretary, with a smile.

Unconsciously, Marge addressed the young woman in her “poshest” voice ‘We wants … would like to know if my daughter can start school ‘ere ..here? We’ve just moved into a farm down the road.’

‘Hello, little girl,’ said the secretary, smiling as she arose from her chair. She walked around the tidy desk and dropped to one knee. ‘What’s your name?’

'Elizabeth,' replied Beth who immediately felt at ease with the kind lady. 'But everyone calls me "Beth", cos I prefer that.'

'Then that's what I'll call you. How old are you, Beth?'

'I'm five and a half, and I like cutting-out.'

'Well, that's good, because there's a lot of cutting-out going on at the moment,' replied the secretary. 'The other children are all helping to make Christmas decorations. Would you like to do that?'

'Yes, I'm good at cutting out decorations, I helped Mummy last Christmas when we decorated the cabin.'

'I'll tell you what, Beth. I'll take you along to Miss Hudson's class where you can stay for a bit, while I have a chat with your mummy. Is that alright?'

Beth nodded her head but didn't speak. She had suddenly become nervous with the thought of being separated from her mother. 'Come along then Beth. This way,' the secretary said as she pointed out two chairs for Marge and Jo to use whilst they waited. Releasing her mother's hand for the first time, Beth followed the lady back into the corridor and along to the second door they had passed on their way in. With a brief knock the secretary opened the door and ushered her charge into the classroom where together they approached the teacher. As the secretary was explaining the situation to the teacher, Beth shyly glanced around the room. The noise level was rising following the teacher's distraction and several girls were grinning at Beth.

Soon, the secretary left the room and Beth was addressed by the teacher. 'Hello, Beth. My name is Miss Hudson and I understand you will be starting school here. You will be in my class, so this morning you will be able to meet some of the children while you are here. Now, let me see,' Miss Hudson looked around the room before saying to one of the girls, 'Maisy, come and meet Beth and show her what you are doing. Let her have a go if she wants to.'

The selected girl gave a huge grin and left her place to come to the front to meet Beth and take her by the hand to her desk. 'Are you starting here?' she asked as they sat down together.

'Yes, my mummy's talking to the lady in her room. What are you doing?'

‘Making paper chains, I’ll show you.’ With that, Maisy picked up two different coloured strips of paper, licked the end of one of them and looped it through the end of a chain she was already making. ‘It’s easy. Do you want a go?’

‘Yes please,’ replied Beth who had no difficulty in grasping the principle. Soon, the two girls were chatting together as they lengthened the colourful chain.

‘Do you want to be my friend?’ asked Maisy. ‘I haven’t got any friends of my own cos I haven’t got a mummy.’

‘Yes please. I’ve only got two friends. One’s my mule, called Skippy. The other’s my dog, called Oddy, because he’s got odd ears. Oh, and there’s Jo, but she’s very old and more like my sister.’

‘Is your mule a real one, or a toy?’

‘He’s real. He used to pull our boat along, but now we’re living on a farm, although we’re going to move to our own house after Christmas. That’s where we’re going next, to meet Aunt Polly who’s waiting for us there.’

'I want a pony,' replied Maisy wistfully. 'But Daddy says we can't afford one and we wouldn't have a place to keep it anyhow. What's the difference between a mule and a pony?'

'A pony is for a princess to ride on and a mule is for pulling her carriage when it's too wet, or cold, to ride on the pony, or when she's going to a Ball in a posh dress.'

'I would like to come and see your mule one day,' said Maisy. 'Will you let me?'

'Yes, we can share him and you can even ride him if you want, and play with Oddy.'

All too soon the secretary returned to fetch Beth to re-unite her with her mother and Jo.

'You can start 'ere tomorrer Beth,' said Marge who had reverted to her normal voice. Passing the door of Miss Hudson's classroom, Jo asked 'Did you like it in the class, Beth?'

'Yes, we were making Christmas decorations and I've got a new friend called Maisy,' replied the excited girl.

'A friend already? Well, that's good,' said Marge as she winked at Jo, 'Now we're going to walk to our new 'ome, what an exciting day you're 'avin' luvvy.'

The walk from the school to Polly's cottage took no more than twenty minutes. Beth, who was part walking and part skipping between her mother and Jo, while holding each of their hands, talked animatedly the whole way about her experience in the classroom. 'Some of the children were painting pictures of Christmas trees, some were blowing up balloons, some were cutting out stars and colouring them in with crayons and the rest of us were making paper chains. I like Miss Hudson, she's pretty and has long hair. I like my new friend Maisy as well; she lives in the village and her daddy's a blacksmith. She lives upstairs where he works. Maisy says he makes horseshoes, and pokers, and gates and things. She thinks he's ever so clever. I told her she can come to the farm to share Skippy with me.'

'I think this must be it,' sighed Marge with relief, as much due to the ear-bashing as the walk. Together, they stopped to look at the pretty cottage nestled in front of the woods alongside the lane. A whisp of smoke was slowly lifting from the chimney and climbing straight up into the still air. The farm wagon was parked by the gate with Blacky and Champ contentedly nibbling on the grass along the verge. Marge stood looking at her new home, with tears brimming down her chubby cheeks. The front door was suddenly opened by Ed who then stepped out backwards while holding one end of a writing bureau in two hands, followed by John who was holding the other end as best he could with one hand. Noticing the new arrivals upon reaching the gate, he said, 'This is it, Marge, our own home to be. Just clearing out a few things Polly wants at the farm, this, the sewing machine, all her clothing of course and a few smaller keepsakes. All the bedding and furniture are remaining.'

Jo had stepped around Marge to help John as Ed was speaking, 'Don't overdo it John,' she cautioned. 'I know how you want to help, and how frustrated you must feel, but the sooner your body can mend, the sooner you'll be working on the farm.'

Beth could contain herself no longer. She quietly stepped through the door and began her exploration of the cottage. Having spent her life in the restricted space of *Red Rose* this place seemed palatial in her eyes. Lots of rooms to look into; an entrance hall with a place for coats; a nice warm parlour with a sofa and chairs as well as a posh sideboard, and a cheerful fire in the stone fireplace. Having flung herself onto the soft sofa with its array of cushions she looked around at the pictures of country scenes hanging on the walls. Next, the kitchen which was large enough for the well-used table with four chairs tucked under, as well as a large dresser with plates and cups arranged in a pretty way. In addition to the butler-sink there was also a dolly-tub and a mangle, items Beth had never seen before. She couldn’t resist reaching up and turning the handle of the mangle to see what would happen. Best of all, a hidden staircase behind a door in the kitchen. Quickly, she climbed the creaking wooden stairs to find herself in a narrow corridor with a sloping wooden floor. There were four open doors. Entering the first room, she found herself in a bedroom overlooking the front garden. There she discovered Aunt Polly who was busily packing clothes and books into bags and wooden boxes.

‘Hello, sweety. I wondered if you would be the first one up here. Do you like your new school?’ Polly was seated on a large bed which was covered with a colourful patchwork quilt, as she folded more clothes.

‘Yes, Aunt Polly, I’m starting tomorrow and I’m going to be in Miss Hudson’s class. She’s pretty and I’ve got a new friend called Maisy, only she doesn’t have a mummy.’

‘And what do you think about your new home?’ Polly asked with a smile.

‘I think it’s the best home in the whole wide world,’ replied Beth as she swung her arms to embrace the whole cottage.

‘Wow, that’s nice to know,’ replied Polly. Rising to her feet, she continued, ‘Come with me and I’ll show you the other bedrooms, one of them will be yours.’

‘You mean, I’ll have my own bedroom?’ Beth asked with wonder in her eyes.

‘Oh yes, and I bet I can guess which one you’ll choose.’

Looking through the sash window, out into the rear garden and the woods beyond, Beth said, ‘I like this room best of all and I like the lovely springy bed. Can this really be all mine?’

‘Well, you’ll have to see what Mummy says, but I don’t see why not. This used to be Uncle Graham’s room.’

‘I like Uncle Graham and his funny eye, but I didn’t before, cos he came and took my sister away. Are you really going to get married?’

‘Yes, maybe next year, we haven’t decided yet’

'Can I come and be a bridesmaid, I've always wanted to be a bridesmaid, just like a princess.'

'Of course, you can, sweety, I would like that very much. Now, shall we go and look at the garden? Did you know, there's a swing in one of the trees?' Looking down at Beth who had suddenly gone quiet, Polly exclaimed, Sweety, you look as though you're about to cry. What's wrong?'

'I'm so happy, but I'm sad at the same time. I want Ben to be here with us. It's not fair, why did he have to go away and be killed?'

Lost for an adequate answer, Polly knelt down and took Beth in her arms. 'There, there, sweety. You've had a busy exciting morning and you're all mixed up. Let's go down and see what the others are doing, shall we?' Opening the door at the foot of the stair and entering the kitchen, they found Jo preparing a light lunch for everyone. 'Beth, why don't you go out into the garden, while I help Jo?' suggested Polly. 'Take Oddy with you. See if you can find that swing, I told you about.'

In spite of the cold, Beth enjoyed exploring outdoors, she had found the swing the moment she had gone down the back path which meandered between a variety of trees; apple, pear and cherry mostly. Oddy had a great time retrieving small logs which Beth had found scattered amongst the long grass.

Above the sound of birds singing in the woods alongside the lane, Ben slowly became aware of excited barking and a child's laughter. He remembered this lane from his visit all those weeks ago when he had accompanied Jo on her aborted visit to the farm. He could even remember having seen a woman hanging out a lot of washing in the garden of the cottage he was now approaching. It was clear that the child and dog he was hearing were somewhere in the garden behind some shrubs. Coming closer, Ben noticed a half-filled wagon with its two heavy horses standing alongside the open gate. *Looks like someone's moving in, or out,* he mused. The front door was open and he could hear voices from within.

This had been a long day for him. Yesterday, he had been informed by the Adjutant who was busily looking through his papers, that he had not been expected back for at least three weeks. He had then surprised Ben by saying that he was to be an appointed instructor on the canal in the new year and, as such, was to be accepted onto an officer training course with the rank of Subaltern, starting on the first of January. The best news was that, until then, he was not required and therefore he was to have leave for the whole of December. Determined to find his family as soon as possible he had set out with his kit, soon after five on this frosty morning, to walk the canal in the hope of obtaining some information. He had reached Odiham Wharf by ten-o-clock. The Wharfinger’s deputy, on hearing Ben’s enquiry about *Red Rose*, had remembered that a note had been left by his boss the previous day to the affect that enquiries, or mail for that boat should be directed to Meadow Farm in Warningford.

Puzzled by this news, Ben had thanked the man before leaving the wharf to retrace the walk he had made with Jo back in the middle of October, remembering their disagreement about him joining up. Now, as he approached the village of Warninford, he was close to finding answers to his questions, if not his family.

Suddenly his thoughts were interrupted as a log fell at his feet, shortly to be followed by a brown dog with one white ear.

Epilogue

So, dear reader. This is the end of my story. It's a story of love, violence, fortitude, loyalty, bravery and hope. It's a story of ordinary people who suddenly found themselves caught up in a series of extraordinary events over a period of less than two months.

All of this was four years ago. Four years that witnessed three weddings and one death.

John and June surprised us all when, just six months after his return from France, they announced their intention to be married in the spring of the following year. That would be 1918 at the tail end of the war. He had regained full health by the time he slipped the wedding band onto June's finger, although he was often seen resting at odd moments as he worked through the first winter. June had insisted that she be allowed to retain her job in the Post Office, otherwise how else was she to keep in touch with all the gossip and goings-on in the village. She also continued playing her accordion in *The Feathers* on Friday and Saturday evenings.

Her performances were regularly appreciated by John's extended family, although the excellent ale served by the pub had much to do with that, I suspect.

Ed and Phil became great friends. They liked nothing better than to spend many hours together, at the farm kitchen table, planning for each coming season, for both the existing farm and also for the newly leased land. With Jo's significant input, it wasn't long before Ed's land was generating a healthy income. He had decided to concentrate on cereal crops which, he was forced to agree, should be carried to London by train rather than by the slower method of using the canal. This went against the grain (no pun intended) but his business sense was greater than his nostalgic inclination. Meanwhile, Marge took a great deal of pride in her home and garden and it was she who often supplied and arranged the flowers in church, ready for the following Sunday service, which she never attended.

Beth, who is now nine years old, going on fourteen, settled down in school extremely quickly. It wasn't long before she had a large following of friends who loved spending time on the farm. Maisy became her best friend, and I imagine they will maintain a loyal friendship for the rest of their lives. Beth thrives on learning, she tells me that every subject is her favourite, although judging by the amount of time she spends with me as I'm writing, I think English Literature and Grammar will remain top of her list. Who knows, maybe one day she'll write her own novel, for she has an excellent imagination. What stories she could tell about family life on a narrowboat.

As promised by Polly, Beth was our sole bridesmaid when we married back in June last year. She looked beautiful, just like a princess, and she was so proud. She loves the cottage but still spends much of her free time here on the farm, mainly helping Jo who she still, and will always, regard as her older sister.

I must put this transcript to bed soon, for at three-o-clock this afternoon Polly and I will be sitting in church eagerly awaiting Jo's entrance. I imagine Ben down the front with his best man, both looking extremely smart in their Lieutenant uniforms, I'm particularly impressed by the swords. I gather there's to be a guard of honour outside as he and Jo leave the church as husband and wife. My mind goes back to that wonderful moment when excited screaming announced the entrance of Beth as she dragged her big brother into the kitchen that day. I don't know who was more amazed, us seeing a young soldier presumed to be dead, or Ben finding his family in the cottage. Everyone was talking at the same time, until Jo quietly stepped across the kitchen and slipped into her sweetheart’s arms. There they stood, oblivious to the rest of us, gentle swaying together in the longest kiss I have ever seen. Come to think of it, Polly and I don’t do so badly, even after all this time. Where was I? Oh yes, Ed and Marge were standing together, hand in hand while watching the young couple who were always meant to be together. Jo had watched three young men walk away to war. One didn’t return, one came back injured, and the other came back into her arms, whole, never again to return to that madness over there.

Ben and John have become close friends. Strange to think they met on that hospital barge during the war. What a coincidence that turned out to be.

I often think back to those dark days of poaching. What luck that I happened to be out, in that spot, on the night Jo ran away from home. That was a life changer for all of us in our circle of family and friends. Perhaps it wasn’t luck, who knows how these things happen? What I do know, is that we need to follow our dreams in the pursuit of happiness and fulfilment.

I mentioned there was a death during these four years. Somewhere in a thicket just outside of Guildford, is all that remains of a traveller's caravan. It's covered by overgrown bushes and weeds and is tipped over to one side. The wheels are long gone, as are the fittings. The once decorative paintwork is faded and covered in years of dust and grime. There's evidence of someone having used it for shelter, most likely a tramp, although there would be little enough shelter with no door or glass in the windows. A beautiful vehicle, probably owned by a number of mobile families during its lifetime, died of shame and neglect, never again to be seen on the road. How do I know it's there? you might ask. I don't, but I do have an active imagination, as every writer should.

Maybe, one day I'll go there and "Take a look".

The End

If you have enjoyed reading this book you may like to read other books written by Paul Ludford. He can be contacted by emailing paul.ludford45@gmail.com